STONES OF
THE
MADONNA

Jan Mazzoni

STONES OF THE MADONNA

THORN WOOD BOOKS
• WILTSHIRE •

STONES OF THE MADONNA

First published in 2008 by
THORN WOOD BOOKS
Wildings, Hazelbury Hill, Box
Wiltshire SN13 8LB

ISBN 978-0-9556167-0-9

Produced and printed by members of
THE GUILD OF MASTER CRAFTSMEN

Cover Design: Marcus Martell
Cover Photograph: J. R. Ong. www.artemisworks.plus.com
Book Design and Typesetting by Cecil Smith
Typeset in Minion

Printed and bound in Great Britain by
RPM PRINT & DESIGN
2-3 Spur Road, Quarry Lane, Chichester, West Sussex PO19 8PR

THE AMALFI COAST
ITALY
1939

Eleven thirty.

He'd gone into the surgery early, before eight, shutting the door behind him quietly, the faintest click, though Lily had heard it of course. She was already awake, had felt the bed dip as he got up, heard the gentle slap of bare feet crossing the tiled floor, shortly afterwards the sound of a spoon scraping against the side of a cup.

Three and a half hours he'd been hidden away. There had been no movement for some time now, his surgery could have been empty, but Lily knew he was still there, sitting hunched with his elbows on his knees, fob watch in hand. Just as she was, he'd be aware that the funeral was due to begin right now. Like her he'd be picturing it: the sombre little chapel up on the hill, the nose-tickling smells of incense, the white robed priest with his bowed head and voice that made Lily think of thick green olive oil. Rays of dusty sunlight would spotlight the coffin. The mourners – oh, and it would be packed to the door – would be hushed, sniffling, their lips moving in silent prayer.

Or instead of praying would it be his name on their lips, James, il dottore? Would they be cursing him?

Lily longed to go to him, put her arms around him, say it wasn't his fault, how could it be, he hadn't killed the woman.

Not that he would let her comfort him. He would push her away, tell her not to be so stupid, that of course he had, not by what he did but by what he hadn't done. He'd known the woman was critically ill, had promised he would return that night, and yet he'd gone away, no-one knew where, he just disappeared. Gone away and left her to die.

But then, wasn't it Lily's fault he'd gone? And if so, shouldn't she take a share of the blame for the woman's death?

It was stifling in the drawing room. She wished she could open the shutters but didn't dare. There had been a rock thrown through the open window last night, voices shouting, a torrent of angry words she didn't understand though there was no need. James had marched across to the window, his face stern and composed. Would they have seen his expression? If so they'd have assumed he didn't care about what had happened, felt nothing. How wrong they'd have been. He'd closed the shutters calmly, returned to the book he was reading, flicked the pages with a steady hand. It had been left to her to remove the rock from where it had landed by the fireplace, to brush the pale grey dust that remained behind.

She was frightened.

The stones lay on a lace doily on top of the tallboy, three of them, no bigger than grapes, each one pierced as though it had been run through with a spear. Stones of the Madonna, that was what the locals called them. Lucky stones. When she'd found them she'd been as excited as a child, caught up in everyone's enthusiasm, wrapping them in a silk hand-kerchief before pocketing them. That same night she'd washed them carefully in spring water, then polished them until they gleamed like pearls. They'd had a smell about them of deep oceans and green fronds.

Now she picked them up, moved them around in her hand. They felt warm, smooth, she could almost feel them pulsating, as though they were alive. No wonder she'd been tempted to believe they really did have powers.

How could she know that everything was about to go so horribly wrong?

They'd come here to start a new life together; to put aside the problems of the past, the cross words and silences that said even more, the hurts he'd inflicted on her, intentional or not. Such high hopes, they'd had. James knew Italy well; he'd spent two years in Rome before they were married, he and another doctor had set up a small but busy surgery in Trastevere. He'd loved it. She would be happy in Italy, he'd promised. No-one could be otherwise, not when the sun is always shining and everyone sings, and there are flowers as big as your hand, and wine smooth as honey.

She'd believed him, had left her home, family, friends without a second thought. On the steamer that had pulled away across the still grey waters leaving the coast of England to fade, become a single line, then to disappear altogether, she hadn't even looked, had turned her back. She wanted only to look forward. Despite everything, she loved him, this husband of hers, was determined that their marriage would not fail. On her head she'd worn a new hat, a red cloche with a brim that came low over her eyes. She'd worn her confidence in much the same way, head held high.

And now, this.

She walked over to the shutters, pushed them open just far enough to be able to peep out. The only movement came from the ginger cat who was sitting on the steps licking methodically at a leg that stuck straight up into the air. The sky, what she could see of it between the houses, looked to be cloudless. It was too beautiful a day for a funeral; funerals should take place on grey, wet days, when death seems somehow more acceptable, not on days like this. The contrast was too shocking.

There had been a funeral on the day they'd arrived. But how different she'd felt about that one.

PART ONE

One

$\mathcal{S}$idney had arranged for them to be met from the boat in his Pontiac, a low slung panther of a car but surprisingly comfortable, which was just as well as Lily was exhausted. James had suggested she try to sleep, but she couldn't possibly, not when the steep road out of Sorrento began to twist and turn, its terrifying hairpin curves cut into towering cliffs, below it a sheer drop down to a shimmering sea. She'd hardly dared breathe. As they'd entered the village it had felt like they'd reached the end of the world.

Then the car suddenly halted, the engine went silent.

A funeral crossed in front of them. First came two high stepping horses, black and shiny as tar, with ostrich feathered plumes swaying above their heads; next, a carriage out of a fairy tale, ornate, spangled so that it glittered, a black-draped coffin just visible inside; and behind that, a shuffling cluster of men and women, not speaking, their eyes lowered. With the dazzling whiteness of the air, the artificial blue of the sea and sky making a backdrop, the whole scene looked unreal, like something out of a Hollywood film.

And then there was a sound, gentle, like a fountain, and for a moment Lily thought it was raining, though knew it couldn't be. Looking around she realised that the sound came from the villagers who were lining the road. They were applauding.

James said something in his clipped, precise Italian to the driver. The young man half turned, politely directing his reply at both James and Lily though he must have realised she didn't speak Italian.

"He said it's the funeral of the owner of the mill. He was a popular man, businesslike and certainly no fool, but kind. When anyone in the village was in trouble they'd go to him. He knew about poverty."

"And the applause?"

"For having lived a good life, I guess."

Lily had understood some of it. When she tried, really concentrated, she could get individual words, but there was something hypnotic about the language that put her into a trance so that she listened to it as though it was music, it flowed over her, the words becoming notes. How could anyone say hateful things in Italian?

The road was empty now except for some stragglers: an old woman with a barefooted toddler clinging to her hand, a gang of boys shoving each other playfully. As the car wheeled slowly right, two men in suits stopped what looked to be an argument, stared briefly before lifting their hats, and then turned back to each other. A small, grubby face topped with a scrunch of black curls appeared at the car window, bobbing up and down as a young girl tried hard to see inside. Someone called and she scampered away.

"They must wonder who we are," James said in Italian.

"They know," said the driver. "Everyone is happy that at last we have a doctor coming to live in the village. We need a doctor badly."

Lily reached for James' hand. Even though her skin was damp and sticky, she felt the need to touch him, to share the moment with him. He let her hand lie loosely in the circle of his fingers.

"We're happy to be here," she said in English.

"*É contenta?*" The driver met her eyes in the mirror above his head.

"*Si, molto,*" she said.

Over a thousand miles they'd travelled to be there. It was no wonder she was weary. From the boat they'd taken a train to Paris, another down to Rome where they'd stayed a week with friends. James had said she absolutely must see the sights and they'd all gone together; to churches, museums and galleries, vast echoing buildings full of gold-leafed frescos, and sculptures and paintings, many of which she found depressing though she didn't dare say so. She preferred the cobbled back streets with their little bakeries, women perched on wooden stools in patches of sunlight shelling peas, dogs curled up in the shade. She'd liked the Spanish Steps too. And the parks with their tall stiff pine trees, little brown birds pecking in the dust. And the fountains shaped like shells, dolphins, horses, fish; she'd never seen so many fountains.

It was as they'd emerged from a park near the zoo that she'd noticed a sign written on a wall in red paint. She understood the words *gli Inglesi*: The English. When she'd asked their friends what the rest of it meant the wife had shrugged, said not to take any notice and changed the subject. Not to take any notice of what? Lily had wondered, but had soon forgotten about it.

Then there had been the night train down to Naples, the

boat across to Sorrento. They could have come on by another boat – most people did the journey that way – but Sidney had insisted about the car. He'd said they should arrive in style.

And now they were here and it was all so overwhelming, so beautiful, so strange that Lily found herself on the verge of tears. Tears of joy, that was. She wondered if James felt the same – not about crying of course, she'd never seen him cry – but about being there. She'd have liked to ask. But he was in conversation again with the driver, so instead she sat back and looked out of the window, and thought what she really could do with right now was a nice cup of tea with fresh milk and one spoonful of sugar. She hadn't had one for weeks, not proper tea like she was used to. Tea wasn't popular in Italy, James thought they might not be able to buy it at all. It was alright for him, he was American, he preferred coffee anyway. But she was going to miss it, she knew, which was why she'd tucked some packets of PG Tips in with their luggage. She'd also sneaked in a supply of Quaker Oats, some Bird's Jellies in her favourite lime flavour, and even a few tins of Spam.

That should keep her going for a while at least, until she got used to Italian food. James said she was going to love it. James said she was going to love everything about their new life, and he was usually right.

Two

*S*he'd become aware of the Madonna, of the power she wielded, almost at once. The Madonna, who the villagers turned to when they needed something: a listening ear, the money for a new coat, a miracle. When she disappointed them, they forgave her. When they disappointed her they would be punished, sent off to say a string of Hail Marys, to drop coins they couldn't afford into the polished wooden box at the back of the church. Though it was not secured, no-one ever stole from the box.

Lily remembered the one visit she'd made to a Catholic church, years ago, to attend the wedding of a friend of the family. She'd been both fascinated and a little intimidated by the strangeness of the place, the feeling of being not just in a theatre but part of the drama, the way the congregation had to keep standing and sitting, chanting, kneeling, praying, standing again. Beside her, in a niche on the wall, there had been a statue of a woman holding the limp body of a man wearing a crown of thorns and a loin cloth. Lily had averted her eyes.

Here, though, the Madonna wasn't just to be found in church.

It had been one of the first things she'd noticed in the house they were to rent: a dome made of glass underneath which stood a delicately carved figure of the Madonna. Her robes were painted in faded blues and crimson; on her cheeks was a dab of what looked like Woolworth's rouge; her thin white hands were pressed together in prayer. Also under the dome, propped against the statue, was a faded photograph of a young man in uniform.

Then there was the picture on the wall in the entrance hall. The Madonna and baby Jesus floated on cotton wool clouds over a village by the sea – it was this one, Lily decided, many years ago – with, in the foreground, a galleon with sails plump as cushions.

"Madonnas wherever you look!" Lily said.

"Of course. This is Italy. These people don't go to church once a week then forget it, religion is part of their everyday lives. And it's a matriarchal society, too, here in the south. Mothers are the most important members of the family. I guess you could say the Madonna is the ultimate mother."

James had been brought up Catholic, had discarded his faith along with his striped college scarf, his spots, his passion for nights spent drinking bourbon and discussing politics. So he'd told her when they first met and he was more talkative, more open, wanting to tell her everything, every little detail, this quiet young English woman with whom he seemed to be falling in love.

"Ultimate mother or not, couldn't we please put just this one somewhere else?"

It hung above their bed, a painting depicting the

Madonna crouched on the ground cradling the dead body of her son. Though it was not well painted, Lily thought it the saddest thing she'd ever seen; there was something about the expression on the mother's face, the young man's body, cold and lifeless as marble. She didn't want it to be the last thing she saw at night, the first thing every morning.

"Don't forget we're only renting this house, Lilian."

He was standing in front of the mirror doing up his bow tie, his face contorted with the effort. She went to him, turned him towards her, pleased to be able to help.

"How would you feel if someone came and took down one of your pictures because they didn't like it?"

"Tell you what," she said. "We'll hang it in your surgery."

She gave the tie a final tug before turning for him to fasten the hook at the back of her dress. Sky blue shot taffeta, her favourite. And to think, they'd nearly not brought such clothes with them, never imagining that they would be going anywhere grand enough to need bow ties, strapless dresses, earrings. Fancy dress, as James called it. They'd worn it often enough in London. They'd been part of the social scene even though James spent a lot of time working with the poor; he was forgiven, being American and from a wealthy family, and so tall and good looking. They'd been invited to dinner parties and weekends at country houses, and though they often made excuses, they did sometimes accept. James felt they ought to. He understood the importance of keeping up appearances, of being accepted, of belonging. Lily enjoyed the socialising even though she didn't much like the kind of people they were socialising with. They might be wealthy but most of them were dull, unadventurous, set in their far too comfortable ways.

She didn't want to be like them. They weren't like them. Dull people didn't up and away to foreign parts for no other

15

reason than that they wanted to. She and James were not dull. Foolhardy, friends insisted when they told them of their plans. Heartless, her tearful mother had complained, nearly making Lily change her mind. But dull, no, never.

James bent and kissed the back of her neck.

"Are you ready, dear? We mustn't be late."

There was to be a party. *Una festa*, as Sidney called it. To welcome them to the village, give them an opportunity to meet some of the local people. The mayor. Don Federico, the priest. The owner of one of the few hotels, the biggest and best; it had chandeliers, a marble tiled terrace with palm trees in pots, and a band wearing tuxedos playing Ivor Novello favourites on summer weekends. Useful people to know, Sidney said.

He'd sent the car again, though the house he'd found for them was above the main road and they would need to first make their way down three flights of steps. He had warned them. He'd told them how the first time he saw the village he'd thought of a cluster of limpets clinging to a sheer rock face. To go anywhere you need to first go up or down steps, there is no avoiding them.

Outside the air was cooler now, but still warm considering that when they'd left London the gutters had been full of grey, gritty snow. As they made their way down to where the car waited – passing half open doors, peeling walls that led into tiny courtyards, the steps themselves crumbling so that Lily had to take extra care, her high heels far from ideal for such a descent – they could hear a man singing, an aria she seemed to recognise, his voice strong and melodic. James had been right; the villagers were poor and lived simple lives, yet they sang all day long.

To think she'd had doubts about coming to Italy. Not at

first, but as their plans had become a reality, they'd booked tickets, sold their furniture, then the niggling had begun. What if they hated it? Or if James couldn't make enough money for them to live on? What about his career, would the medical world forget about him altogether once he was no longer seen around town? Only once had she tried to talk to him about her doubts, asked him to at least think carefully.

As if James could be talked out of anything he'd made up his mind to do.

"Careful!"

He caught her arm as she tripped, tucked it under his, safe within the folds of his shiny black jacket.

"I want you to look gorgeous tonight," he said.

She saw herself through his eyes: a plump woman though fine boned beneath her soft flesh, her skin white and freckled. Not classically pretty but she endeavoured to do the best with what she had. Kept her hair long because it was heavy and a rich chestnut colour, though usually she pinned it up off her neck. Chose pretty shoes to draw attention to her dainty feet. Sometimes she applied mascara to highlight eyes that she thought of as grey, though more than once she'd been told that they weren't a true grey. One man had said they reminded him of lilac blossom, just before it opens; he'd sworn to love her forever, though when he'd been posted to Singapore, he hadn't asked Lily to go with him, nor even said goodbye.

Still, if she'd married him she'd never have known James.

She too wanted James to be proud of her, as she was proud to be with him. People liked him, she knew. Trusted him. Sidney considered him to be not only a good doctor, but one of the best. And entirely wasted in London dealing with hysterical women who had nothing else to do with their time but worry about the ailments they might have, though mostly didn't. One had given James a canary in a cage, to thank him for saving her life, though he told Lily all he'd done was give her sedatives. Another had taken to writing him poems on pink paper perfumed with Lily of the Valley. He'd kept the first two or three, flattered, but then she'd begun to irritate him. Lily had lied on his behalf, said he wasn't available and that she should seek advice from another doctor, had even suggested some names. The poems had stopped abruptly.

Not that Sidney knew much about doctors. He was a writer, not a medical man. But he was successful and intelligent, and he was also very persuasive.

"I'm virtually living there myself these days," he'd said that cold afternoon. Afterwards they'd agreed he'd picked that day to make his proposal on purpose. "It's an exquisite setting, superb climate. The locals are mostly fishermen, peasants, people who work with their hands. They cut terraces into the rock and somehow manage to grow vegetables, keep a pig and some chickens."

He'd tipped his cup to get the last drop of tea and Lily had reached for the pot.

"Then there are the foreigners – artists, writers, dancers, bohemians of one kind or another. Always has attracted them, the village, so I'm told. You get some Italians coming down too, city people who can afford to spend their summers by the sea."

"It sounds lovely," Lily had said. "I'd like very much to see it one day."

"Ah. That was what I wanted to talk to you about."

Sidney had settled back in his chair, crossed his legs, fixed them both with eyes that through his wire-rimmed spectacles always looked slightly startled.

"Why don't you come and live out there for a bit? The place badly needs a doctor. There was one old fellow, but he died a year or so ago. Since then, it's either herbal concoctions made up by somebody's grandmother, or going to Sorrento or Salerno, both of which are long, long journeys. Especially by horse and cart."

"No-one has cars?"

"There are four in the village." Sidney had smiled, a little embarrassed. "Two of those are mine. There's nowhere to buy them, people have no money, and besides, the roads are atrocious."

He'd tucked his pipe into the corner of his mouth, flicked his lighter and held it over the bowl. James too had gone very quiet. Lily listened to the wind in the trees, the grandfather clock marking each second, and realised with a shock that James was interested, was giving the idea serious consideration.

When he started talking again it was to ask questions. How many inhabitants were there? Enough for him to be busy most of the time, Sidney said. But would he be able to earn a living? The foreigners could pay, certainly; the villagers would either pay in cash or in produce, but that wouldn't be so bad, would it? Where would he go for the pharmaceuticals he needed? Sidney wasn't sure but he could check that. It wouldn't be a problem.

Looking at James's face, Lily had seen a range of emotions flicker across it: excitement, doubt, longing. It was as though he was a mirror, was reflecting what was going through her own mind. She'd felt her blood racing. To visit, that was one thing. But to live there, to leave behind the life they knew, the people, their own language, everything? That was frightening.

Now, though, she felt ashamed of her timidity. Settling back in the car for the second time in a week, she tried to imagine what would be outside the window if they were

19

driving down Bond Street, or crossing Trafalgar Square. She couldn't. London seemed unreal, grey and shadowy by comparison with this Mediterranean world where everything was so vibrant: the colours brighter; the air somehow tingly on the tongue, like champagne; fruit trees laden with fragrant blossom. On one she'd seen lemons growing, and on the same tree new flowers. Nature followed a different set of rules here.

Their host hurried across the tiled floor to meet them, a short man with a paunch of which – from the way he thrust it before him – Lily assumed he was proud. He shook James's hand, holding it in both of his. To Lily he gave a small bow.

"*Dottor* Hogan. I am *Signor* Andrea Motta. You must please call me Andrea."

Then began the introductions, unfamiliar names that Lily knew there was no chance she would remember, however hard she tried. She nodded, smiled. A pink aperitif had been handed to her; she sipped it partly for something to do, liked its bitter and yet sweet taste, its fizz. She hardly noticed that she'd finished it and that her glass had been replaced with a full one.

Sidney arrived late. He'd been making a telephone call, he said. There was only one telephone in the village, at the post office, and half the time that wasn't working.

"Bloody nuisance sometimes. But that, of course, is why people come here," he said, shrugging. "To cut themselves off from the nasty world out there."

He shook his head at the aperitif, said he'd prefer whisky.

"Trouble is, that nasty world out there is where the publishers are. Not to mention those foolish but delightful people who actually pay money for the privilege of reading the rubbish I write."

He swigged the whisky in one go. They were standing by a tall window, the three of them, Lily watching as a small flock of birds crossed the vast pink sky, circled, then dipped towards the sea. She was used to sky being a patch of grey between chimneys. The room was crowded now, a sudden screech of laughter causing eyebrows to be raised, but still the conversation flowed, glasses were emptied, refilled, emptied, cigarette cases flicked open and extended.

Lily leant closer to Sidney.

"And where are all these other escapees from the real world?"

"They don't mix in much with the locals," he said. "Not socially anyway. Have no fear, they'll find you. You'll be sitting on a wall and up one will pop, or you'll be almost run over by one on a bike, or eating out and a party of them will be at the table next to yours. Did I tell you about the restaurants, by the way? There are only a couple, pretty basic of course, but…"

As though on cue, Andrea announced that food was to be served, food prepared by his wife and daughter, he said with no attempt to hide his pride. They had been working in the kitchen all day, and would everyone please come and help themselves.

"*Buon appetito*," he said.

Then, with another small bow, he took Lily onto his arm and the crowd parted as he led her through to the adjoining room and the groaning table.

Three

$\mathcal{S}$o much sun, sun every day. And then just as she was getting used to it, the weather changed. Lily remembered the shock she'd had that morning, opening the shutters to find the sky heavy with clouds. As she stood there the rain began, beads streaming down the window, bringing to mind city streets, umbrellas, taxis shushing up sprays of water that soaked your feet and the hem of your coat.

Their neighbour – a woman who wore an apron tied with string around her sagging body, had countless children around her legs, Lily couldn't believe they were all hers – had told her just yesterday that at morning mass they'd offered up prayers for rain. It was early in the year and already the ground was so hard it was impossible to dig. When Lily looked blank the woman pretended to dig, and Lily nodded. Already they had worked out a way of communicating. The woman sighed. Without rain there would be nothing to eat, everyone would have to live on lupin seeds as they did once before to protest about taxes. At least, it had sounded like lupin seeds, though Lily couldn't imagine eating them and decided she'd misunderstood. She would check her dictionary later.

"*Non vogliamo una siccità,*" the woman had said, shaking her head.

Lily had looked up *una siccità* too. It meant a drought.

Well, she thought, their prayers had worked. Meanwhile, she felt cold and fed up. And – for the first time since they'd arrived – just a little bit homesick.

James put his head around the door.

"I'm expecting someone, a girl. Gina. I want to go through some notes so will you let her in?"

Lily said of course. She wished he'd let her do more than just answer doors. During the war her mother had helped at a hospital for soldiers, had told her probably more than she should have about the young men sent home from the front, not only with horrible injuries but emotionally shattered too, who'd seen things no-one should see. Lily had asked if she could go with her, had insisted. Time and again it was Lily sitting on the edge of a bed swinging her skinny legs, socks bunched around her ankles, who'd managed to bring a smile to the frozen face of a boy only a few years older than her. She'd decided then and there that when she grew up she'd be a nurse, dispensing medicines, taking temperatures, changing bandages with gentle hands and kind words.

It was how she'd come to meet James. She'd applied to work for him as a receptionist in his small east London surgery. She'd sat straight backed, gripping her handbag tightly.

"What I need is someone who can not only type, but who's had enough experience of nursing to be able to sort the serious cases from the trivial, possibly even to help out sometimes. Like in emergencies for example."

"I've had experience," she'd said. "Well, quite a lot."

Unused to lying, she'd felt herself blush.

The job went to a woman twice her age with tightly permed grey hair and flat shoes. When James told her he'd said he understood her disappointment and was truly sorry, and would like to ask her to accompany him to the theatre by way of apology.

It will change now, she'd thought, a year later when they'd stood side by side outside the church in Surrey, a beech tree rustling in the breeze, her three bridesmaids giggling, her parents smiling proudly as the photographer's camera flashed. He'll let me work alongside him now. That's what doctor's wives do.

She'd been wrong. At first he'd wanted only to pamper her, as though to prove his love. He'd even employed a kitchen help and had provisions delivered, though that had stopped when he discovered how much it all cost. He sat her down, took her hands in his and explained: though some of his patients did pay him, his desire was to help the poor, they had the most need, but sadly it meant he and she would have to manage without life's little luxuries, for now at least. She'd said she didn't mind, as long as they had each other.

Then she'd become pregnant, could remember still the nausea and low dull backache that she'd accepted with such joy, her breasts full and tender so that when he'd crushed her to him, his eyes tightly shut, saying her name over and over again, she'd almost cried out. She was going to have a baby, his baby. The world was a wonderful, wonderful place.

Was that someone at the front door? Lily thought she heard a scratching, so faint it could have been her imagination. No, there it was again.

The girl on the step was wet through, her blouse sticking

24

to thin shoulders, her sandals leaving puddles as she followed Lily across the tiled hallway. She didn't look up. Lily knocked on the door to James's surgery as she knew he liked her to. When he replied she ushered the girl in, watched as she moved forward hesitantly, staying close to the wall. She reminded Lily of the stray dogs she'd seen on the streets in Rome, skinny, pathetic creatures waiting to be kicked.

The door clunked shut.

Alone again, Lily hesitated. Now what? She could clean the kitchen, which was something she'd intended to do from her very first sight of it with its curtained off shelves in the corner of which lurked pieces of dry bread, dead spiders, the curtains themselves in need of a good scrub too. So, come to that, was the large square sink, its once-white porcelain now cracked and stained. And the stove, its blue and white tiles filmed with dust, the protective iron rail with its brass knobs dull and greasy to touch. A boy would bring wood, Sidney had said. Or charcoal if they preferred, which was better for cooking but cost more. Cooking hadn't been a problem so far, but then they'd follow the local custom of eating in the evenings. Lily imagined having to stand in the small cramped kitchen when the weather was really hot – as it would be soon, Sidney had warned them – the stove throwing off even more heat. They would eat salads, she decided. Lettuce, cucumber, tomatoes. She would grow them in pots out on the terrace that ran along the back of the house. She would lose weight which would be a good thing, would be able to count her ribs again.

It was unnaturally dark now, a deluge of rain obliterating everything, sea, sky, even the houses below. She put on the light. Not a day for tackling the kitchen, she decided.

Instead, she would write to her mother. She missed her parents and Cissy, already she'd written more times than she usually did in a year. At the back of the huge dark wood desk in the room she'd decided to call the drawing room – though one room led into another, a maze of them, all with terracotta floors, white walls and sparse furnishings so it was hard to know what was the intended function of each – she searched for paper.

Before she could start she heard the girl leaving. James came into the room, crossed and knelt down by a tea chest full of books.

"We should get these unpacked and sorted," he said, taking them out in handfuls, glancing at them before piling them on the floor. He meant arranged on the shelves that lined a wall of his surgery, and which were the reason he'd picked that room. She made a note to do it next time he was out. She'd enjoy it, putting them into a logical order. Like a librarian.

"How did it go with the girl?"

James fanned the pages, couldn't find what he wanted, tried another one.

"Usual thing. She's pregnant and wanted me to arrange an abortion. The boy she went with is the son of a sworn enemy, the two families haven't spoken for three generations. They cross the street to avoid each other."

"A real life Romeo and Juliet then."

"She's convinced her father will kill her if he finds out."

"I can't believe that. What did you say?"

"What could I say? It's not just against my principles, it's against the law."

Poor girl, Lily thought. It must have taken such courage to come and ask. James was right, of course. James always did what was right. He was an honest, law abiding man. He had standards. You could tell it from the way he dressed, the precise centre parting in his pale and silky hair, from the neatness of his desk and his insistence that it was dusted daily. It was what had attracted her to him in the first place, his solidness, his quiet confidence. That and his soft Bostonian accent that was so subtle it was hardly there; he could almost have been taken for an Englishman.

"Boston is a very British city," he'd said by way of explanation.

He'd gone to medical school there, had left with honours. Lily often wondered if it was at this red brick building in a leafy suburb that he'd also acquired the skill of being able to tell people the truth, no matter how unpleasant, his tone gentle but firm. I'm afraid I have to say that your chances of surviving longer than a few weeks more are small. Or, I'm sorry but I cannot help you abort your baby. Go home, talk to your father, he will understand I promise you.

Or, no I don't think you should try again to conceive. We, that is. He'd said it to Lily, his hands cupped around hers, his skin cool, not like flesh and blood. Hers had been damp from wiping away tears. It's too dangerous, he'd added.

"Once more, let's try one more time," she'd said, pleaded.

"Lilian, you've had three miscarriages. Each time you've lost a lot of blood. Each time it's taken you longer to regain your health. My dear, you must know that each time the risks increase."

"It will be alright, James, I promise it will."

"I don't want to lose you, you're precious to me." He'd run the back of one finger down her cheek and along her collar bone. Sighed.

"Very precious."

He'd stood and walked away, their conversation finished. He would not give in. He said he loved her, so why couldn't he understand how much she wanted to have a baby? She was bursting with love, with a need to be needed. She would make

27

a good mother, she knew she would. He wouldn't let her help with his patients, he wouldn't let her have a baby. She didn't want to be treated like an invalid, or royalty, why couldn't he understand?

"Have you seen that new book on haematology?" he said now. "The green one, I bought it a few days before we left."

She went to help him search, found it almost at once. He checked the index, nodded, took it with him back to the surgery. At least a decision had been made: she would unpack the remaining books.

The rain was letting up. Far out over the sea the sky was lighter, slashed with streaks of yellow, as though someone had been busy with scissors. She loved the smell of the outdoors after rain. Maybe later she would go down to the bar where they also sold things, bread, cakes, fresh ground coffee. It would give her a chance to practise her Italian. It would also get her away from the house for a while.

Four

ily had a dream.

She was walking through the village streets, and everywhere there were babies, babies scrabbling in the white dust, clambering up steps, tumbling down them, babies chuckling and gurgling. She had to be careful where she put her feet, there were so many of them. They were all wearing white nappies and she thought of cherubs with their podgy fingers and dimpled knees. It seemed she was the only adult in this nursery world and she felt privileged.

The desire to hold one came over her suddenly. It was as though she had an itch that had to be scratched or she would go mad. She bent, reached for one that was sitting quietly plucking at its toes, tucked her hands under its hot little arms, lifted. As she pulled it towards her it started to struggle, fingers clenching and unclenching, feet kicking, its face scrunched up. Then the wailing began.

Lily jigged it, hummed a few notes of some long forgotten

nursery rhyme. The baby seemed stronger now and she thought of a cat that doesn't want to be held, how it squiggles and squirms. Like a cat the baby suddenly arched backwards and she lost her grip. It fell to the ground with a thud, lay there, still now, silent. She noticed its black eyelashes, a fringe of silk against plump pink cheeks.

I've killed it, I've killed a baby Lily thought, her heart banging. Knowing she had to do something, she had no choice, she slid one hand under its neck, the other under its splayed legs. This time, surprisingly, it was light, seemed almost to float up. With a faint click the eyelids flipped back. Inside, nothing. Black emptiness.

It was a doll.

As she screamed Lily heard someone say her name.

"Lilian? Are you alright?"

She'd woken James.

"I was dreaming. It was... horrid."

"Poor you. You were sobbing."

"I'm sorry I woke you."

Though the room was still dark she could just make out his face on the pillow beside her. He reached and pushed damp hair back from her forehead.

"You're sure there's nothing I can get you? Some water?"

"Nothing. Go back to sleep."

He hesitated, then turned away from her and within minutes was breathing steadily again. Lily lay there staring at the ceiling.

What was it, this obsession about babies?

It wasn't her fault; everyone here seemed to share it. Young mothers tossing long black hair, trailing their off-spring like the wealthy back home trail fur stoles, showing off their femininity. Middle aged women pregnant for the third or fourth time, patting their swollen tummies fondly, looking exhausted but proud. Grandmothers even. Lily saw one old lady with a toddler on her shoulders, his little fingers entwined with her sparse grey hair, still managing a toothless grin as she stumbled along.

And it wasn't only the women. Just a few days before Lily had watched a young man – barefooted, covered in soil and dust so that she assumed he'd just returned from working – pick up a baby, dangling it above his head until it drooled with a mixture of fear and delight. Satisfied he then changed to hugging it, smothering it with kisses. Catching Lily's eye he'd smiled, wished her *buongiorno*, not at all embarrassed.

She thought of men back home, most of them having next to nothing to do with their children. They patted heads, admonished, caned bottoms when warnings were ignored. They had discreet conversations with sons about the facts of life, daughters of course being their mother's responsibility. Those who could afford it paid to ensure a good education for their sons, very occasionally for their daughters too. They paid for weddings. That was it, their duty done.

She tried to imagine an Englishman kissing and cuddling a baby out on the street, in full view of the neighbours.

Or an American, how would an American behave?

It was because of the girl, of course, that Lily had had the dream. The girl who wanted to kill her baby. Lily couldn't get her out of her mind. In her rational moments she sympathised; the girl was in a dilemma, trapped, frightened, she couldn't win whatever she did. To kill a baby though, your own baby. That Lily couldn't understand.

Five

$\mathcal{L}$ike many of the local houses, the one they were renting was situated right on a flight of steps. Lily was used to going down them when she left the house. But what if she turned the other way and followed them upwards? They must eventually meet one of the paths that led up into the hills and beyond, to the foot of the mountains that nestled behind the village – as Lily had written in a letter home – like slumbering elephants.

She would do it one day, go up into the hills and explore.

Already she was becoming familiar with the village, its few shops, bars, even knew some of the people by name. Antonio, the son of their landlord, who had his own boat, went fishing most nights and always bought her something, cold silvery fish, or slimy creatures she usually didn't recognise, though she steeled herself to accept them with grace. Maria who said could her daughter please come and clean house for *il dottore*, do the cooking, not for money, she wouldn't take a single lire, but because he was a good man. When Maria's husband had collapsed with appendicitis, James had arranged for him to be transported at once to the hospital at Sorrento. Maria was in his debt, she said. Wasn't there something they could do?

There were the children, too, who – whenever she appeared – had stopped playing and stared at this pale skinned woman in her tweed skirt, neat blouses and sensible walking shoes. She'd won them over with toffees. Now they seemed delighted to see her, even when her pockets were empty. One of the girls had clutched her hand, pulled her behind a shed to show her a mother cat with a litter of new kittens, blind and helpless, and together they'd gazed in awe.

But up into the hills, that was different altogether: that was an adventure. In a way she felt nervous, especially about going alone. She'd mentioned it to James, asked him if he'd join her and he'd said of course, good idea, as soon as he had a free hour or two. He'd never make time though, he didn't want to enough, whereas Lily found herself increasingly drawn to the idea.

Then one afternoon she made up her mind. The steps were steeper than the lower ones, and by the time she emerged onto the rough gravel path she was already breathless. She would stay in the centre, keep a lookout for snakes, scorpions, and tarantulas, too, those black spiders big as a hand that would – if the myth was to be believed – send you into a whirling, dancing frenzy before you dropped like a stone, dead.

Down below her, the village lay like a pile of scattered pastel coloured bricks.

Above, the top of the mountains were lost in mist.

She took some deep breaths. Gradually she relaxed. Clouds of insects hovered like gold dust in the sunlight. Birds twittered, unseen as they hopped about in the scrubby bushes, and she remembered how back home she'd put out crumbs and pork crackling for the birds in winter. There were cacti, too, some so tall they towered above her head. One had buds like plums that she assumed would open into brilliantly coloured flowers, its thick, rubbery leaves covered in lethally sharp needles. On the leaves of another something had been carved with a knife. She moved closer.

Claudio e Rosa, 9 luglio, 1935, it said.

So young lovers did that kind of thing here too.

She and James had never carved their names on a tree.

It was shortly afterwards that she suddenly heard voices. She stopped, unsure what to do. Three men were coming towards her. At first she couldn't decide what they were carrying on their shoulders, then she realised. Large earthenware pots. Of course. She'd heard about a spring that emerged from underground somewhere in the mountains, and that the water was like wine, sparkly and intoxicating. They were collecting water; a lot of people were prepared to make the climb, she'd been told. It was that good.

She would brave it out.

As she came face to face with them, the men stopped talking, slowed, then stood there shoulder to shoulder, barring her way on the narrow path. Her legs felt weak. But before she could decide whether to demand that they move, or turn and run, they'd burst into laughter, stepping aside, bowing low and waving her past.

She said *grazie*, edged between them, aware that they'd left only a small space so that it was difficult not to brush against them. Their eyes were on her, black eyes, soft and teasing. They spoke to her, or to each other, she wasn't sure, didn't understand what they said. *Bella*, didn't that mean beautiful?

Blushing, she hurried on up the hill. Only when they were out of earshot did she allow herself to slow down. A thread of perspiration trickled between her shoulder blades and not for the first time she wished she had on a light dress, and sandals like the locals wore. When she saw the green leafy cleft in the rocks, heard water running, she almost ran towards it. Using her cupped hands to scoop up the crystal clear liquid, she drank thirstily. Then, taking a handkerchief from where she'd tucked it into the waistband of her skirt, she soaked that in water, ran it around the back of her neck, over her face.

What a mess I must look, she thought. And, what on earth would my mother say. Wrapping her skirt tight around her legs – to keep out insects and crawlies as much as for modesty – she collapsed onto a rock in the shade, closed her eyes. The silence was smooth and thick. She felt sleepy, almost nodded off. Then, realising she also felt hungry she became aware of the time: it was late, she must be getting back

On the way back down she passed a patch of open ground where spots of blue and yellow at first brought to mind wild flowers. These, though, were not flowers, but feathers from a bird that had been killed, torn apart, an explosion of feathers going everywhere then drifting down again. There was no sign of the carcass.

Lily picked up a tail feather, long and soft, tucked it into the buttonhole on her blouse.

It was getting dark when finally she reached the house, worried now that James would be waiting, wanting his evening meal, maybe worrying about her too.

She ran up the steps to the heavy wooden door, hurried inside.

"James? Where are you?"

Silence.

She went from room to room, sure that he would be in one of them, but the house was empty. On the kitchen table was a note.

There has been an emergency. Please go ahead and eat without me. I have no idea how long I shall be.

He'd signed it J, as usual. Not love, no crosses that she could interpret as small dry kisses. Just J.

Though she felt she should wait, she was too hungry. She boiled a couple of eggs, sliced tomatoes, finished with biscuits that she dipped into a cup of tea. She washed dishes left over from midday, dried them, put them back in their right places, and still James wasn't home.

A young boy came to the front door. Silently, he handed her another note.

> *Sorry, Lilian. Things not going at all well here.*
> *Probably best if you don't wait up for me.*

She thanked the boy, then beckoned him inside whilst she found her purse, dug for some coins. He stood just inside the door, feet together, unmoving.

As he turned to go she changed her mind.

"Wait," she said. "Can you take me to my husband?"

He stared at her. She tried again.

"*Mio marito… il dottore…*"

Lily resorted to sign language, pointing to the boy, then to herself, then to somewhere beyond. He blinked, then nodded. She snatched up a cardigan.

The house he took her to was off a small piazza. There was a light on downstairs, the flickering light that came from an oil lamp. Lily was surprised; she'd assumed that like them everyone had electricity, even though it had only recently arrived in the village. She thanked the boy, went up to the door, but when she was sure he'd gone she moved back down without knocking. Instead she sat on the stone steps opposite the house, steps still warm from the heat of the sun. Figures passed the window, back and forth. Voices murmured, then were silent.

How often had she waited for James, the table set for two: silver cutlery that was a wedding gift purchased at Harrods, glasses for the water that James liked to drink with his food, plates gleaming. The quiet clunking of a pendulum seemed to emphasise his absence; he'd brought the grandfather clock with him from Boston, it was a family heirloom, exquisite to look at, an impeccable time keeper. How often had she longed to be with him, to be saving lives, doing something worthwhile. Not polishing silver and dusting heirlooms. Not sitting waiting.

The scream was sharp as a knife. In a distant house a baby started to cry; a cat streaked by.

Lily felt it slash through her, doubled forwards, and in a moment was back on a London street on a freezing cold morning, hardly light yet and fog making it impossible to see so that the taxi driver had grumbled, said what did they expect him to do, the impossible? James had said never mind, they'd walk. It was one of the few times she'd accompanied him. She'd insisted, and he'd been in too much of a hurry to argue.

She'd regretted it, of course.

There had been two bombs, both in underground stations. Hidden in attaché cases and placed in the Left Luggage offices on a threepenny deposit ticket, the newspapers said next day. The IRA claimed responsibility. The force of the explosions had turned pieces of glass, metal, wood into bullets. Most of the injured were too stunned to speak or even cry; they lay there covered in blankets, waiting to be whisked away to hospitals that were already on alert. The IRA had posted warnings. Just the day before, other bombs had maimed and killed.

It was as James bent down over a young, dark haired woman, his voice soft, gently encouraging her to tell him where she hurt, that she suddenly arched away from him, her eyes wide and terrified. Her scream too had seemed to make the air vibrate. She'd been hit in the stomach; as she'd moved a tear had become a hole and Lily could see inside her, could see organs moving about like creatures that were escaping, spilling out over the woman's lap, sliding down onto the ground. Never before had Lily seen so much blood. James turned and said something to her but she didn't hear. Already she was backing away, going up the steps and out of the exit into the street where, beyond the cordon, buses were passing taking people to work, ordinary people just like those who were lying down there injured, bleeding, dying. She'd been sick against the wall, was furious with herself. She couldn't stop shaking.

They'd walked home afterwards.

"So pointless, so bloody pointless," James had kept muttering. Lily had taken his arm, wanting him to know that she understood.

It was the same now. If only she could have taken those few steps across the road.

Eventually the door opened; against the pale light she saw a man emerging, another man stepping out behind him. They stood talking, a brief conversation, Lily couldn't catch what was said. Then the first man put his hand briefly on the other one's shoulder before turning, moving away. The second man went back inside.

"James?"

He was collecting his bike from where it was propped against the wall. He'd taken to using a bike, it was the best way of getting around. Startled, he paused for a moment, then walked on, one hand pushing the bike, the other holding his jacket looped over his shoulder. Lily fell into step beside him. For a bit neither of them spoke.

"She died," James said. "There was nothing I could do."

"It was Gina, wasn't it?"

Lily had known she wouldn't take no for an answer. She'd seen it in the girl's face.

"She went to someone else?"

"A woman who lives along the coast, in a hovel by all accounts. A witch, they call her. I'd call her a butcher. She didn't use witchcraft, she used some kind of metal implement, God knows what."

Their footsteps were the only sound until a dog chained up in a garden they passed started barking, was answered by another on the far side of the village. There were no street lights here, but a full moon lit the road; below them the sea shivered, each ripple touched with silver.

Lily couldn't remember James being so angry, not for a long time. As though it was all his fault. Don't get involved; hadn't that always been one of his rules? Do all you can, but never get involved.

It was this place, something about it that made you feel everything with heightened intensity. As though all your nerves were on edge.

In the house she turned to him. There was blood on his shirt, his jacket, even a splash on his face that she wiped at with her fingers.

"You must be hungry," she said.

"No."

"But James, you ought to have something. If you don't eat you'll…"

"I said no!"

He walked towards the bedroom, stopped in the doorway, ran his hand across his face.

"I'm sorry, Lilian. I… I guess I'm over tired."

"I know," she said. "I'll get you some water."

She took a jug of tap water in to him, a glass and a small

carafe of wine, a sample to try from a neighbour who made his own. Picking up the shirt from where James had dropped it on the floor, she watched the muscles of his back move beneath his pale skin as he splashed water onto his face, his chest, under his arms. She handed him a towel. She poured wine, sipped just a little of it herself before passing him the glass. He downed it in one quick gulp and when she poured more, he drank that straight off too.

"Lie down," she said. "Try to get some sleep."

He did as she instructed, his eyes closing at once. Watching him, imagining the softness of the lace bedspread beneath him, she felt suddenly weary too, took off her skirt and blouse and stretched out beside him.

Upside down she found herself looking into the eyes of one of the fat cherubs someone had painted on the polished headboard of the bed, cherubs like those she'd seen on clouds in museums in Rome. Cherubs like the ones in her dream. Though presumably they were meant to personify innocence, she thought there was something lascivious about them, with their coy smiles and nakedness.

She switched off the light, closed her eyes.

When she awoke she'd no idea how much time had passed. James was still sleeping soundly. She bent and touched his bare shoulder with her lips. His skin was cool, tasted of Pears soap. She leant across him and kissed his chest, the small patch of fine hair, then touched it with her fingertips, circling.

He sighed.

"James," she said. "Put your arms round me, will you?"

He opened his eyes, and even in the dark she could tell that for a moment he was still far away, hardly recognised her. Embarrassed suddenly, she moved away from him, muttered about being cold, that they needed another cover. Now though he was awake, wrapped his arms around her from behind, pressed his face against the side of her neck, and for a moment she felt safe and loved. He cupped one breast in his warm hand, and that too felt good. He slid his hand down across her tummy. But when suddenly he twisted so that he was above her, tugging at her slip, struggling with his trousers, in a frenzy and unable to control himself, she nearly hit out at him. What was the matter with him? Why was he acting this way? Had he gone mad?

Instead she lay absolutely still beneath him, let him do what he wanted, and in a matter of minutes he suddenly pulled away from her, shuddered as though in pain, and it was over.

Still he hadn't spoken.

He fell asleep again almost at once, facing away from her. It was death, of course. Coming face to face with death seemed to stir up some inner urge to create new life, it was a known fact. If only, Lily thought. If only.

She got out of bed, felt her way across to a chest of drawers and found a blanket. As she lay there, warmer now, calmer, she remembered the eyes of the men she'd met up in the hills.

It was a few days later that the girl's father came to the house with two chickens, string tying together their knobbly legs that reminded Lily of wax, the way it goes into blobs down the side of a burning candle. She said she was sorry but the doctor wasn't there. He indicated he would wait. She led him into the drawing room where he balanced awkwardly on the edge of the faded chintz sofa, his unblinking eyes staring at the ground between his sandaled feet.

He'd lowered the chickens to the floor where they shuffled about muttering to themselves and plucking at the rug.

Would he accept a cold drink? Lily said. Or coffee, a

biscuit? He shook his head.

When James returned the man stood, said slowly and clearly what sounded like a prepared speech. He must pay for the doctor's help, for trying to save the life of his daughter. He understood that the doctor had done all he possibly could. With an almost imperceptible shrug, he handed James the strings.

Lily could see James was moved. He shook the father's hand.

"And what are we meant to do with them?" she said when they were alone again. There were a couple of small green mounds on the floor beside the sofa. Lily went to the kitchen, found some rag.

"Eat them?"

"Oh dear."

Lily's life had been spent in the city. She couldn't bear the thought of wringing their necks, plucking feathers that would go everywhere, cutting off their heads. It had to be done, of course. But by someone else, not her.

"Let me know when you want to cook one," James said. "I'll do it."

He passed her the strings.

"And meanwhile?"

There was no garden to go with the house.

"We can keep them out on the terrace," James said. "Lots of people do. They even give them the run of the house."

It was true; she'd seen it. Chickens peering out from upstairs windows, glimpsed through open doors as they picked crumbs from under the table. Not just chickens either, but rabbits and pigeons too. A man down the bottom of their steps kept his pig in the house. *Mia moglie*, he'd said, laughing, slapping the pale rump of the creature who'd turned to give him a reproachful look. My wife. He was a widower; it was rumoured he'd murdered his wife, but that she deserved it. She was a hussy, much younger than him and after the fortune he'd been promised by an uncle who'd emigrated to America and now owned three pizzerias in Chicago. Everyone knew it. She was continually complaining, nagging him, making his life a misery. Then she refused to cook, do his washing, even to make love. When he came home late from playing poker he'd find himself locked out.

"Right, you two. Come with me."

Lily led them out through the door that opened onto the terrace. She'd feed them vegetables peelings, bread, other scraps so they wouldn't cost much to keep. It would be like having a pet. She missed the dog she'd left with her mother and father, a black mongrel, silver muzzled now, stiff legged, but his tail never stopped wagging which was the important thing.

The chickens were not so friendly. Of course, they were frightened, had no idea where they were or who she was, she understood that. But having been pecked mercilessly as she tried to hold the struggling bundles of feathers still in order to cut the strings and free them, Lily wasn't so sure she liked them. They were silly creatures, spiteful too. After fluffing up their feathers and depositing some more droppings on the tiles, they retreated to a corner and settled down behind a pot that contained what Lily had decided was a grape vine. One of them could just reach inside over the rim, started pecking optimistically at the dusty soil.

"It's up to you," Lily told them. "Your choice. You can either be my friends, but you're going to have to behave yourselves. Or you can be dinner."

They really were pretty, though, with their soft creamy white feathers. She made a vow that she would not allow herself to grow fond of them.

Six

And Natalia, how much of what had happened was her fault?

Lily had seen her around. She was the kind of woman it would have been hard to overlook in Knightsbridge at midday on Saturday, so how could you miss her in this dusty, sleepy village with its half empty streets? Though she certainly wasn't beautiful – her black hair was short, shaved at the back, her nose slightly curved and sharp, like a bird's beak – there was a grace about her, a fluidity in her movement. Lily guessed at once that she was a dancer.

Was being the key word, according to Sidney. He said her name was Natalia Yakovskaya.

"Russian, of course. Used to dance with the Kirov ballet until she discovered there was more to life than pirouettes and pas de deuxs. She's got through a couple of husbands already, and she's still young, same sort of age as you I would say, mid thirties?" He pulled a face.

"God help the rest of us."

Lily was intrigued. It was worrying the way she'd already got into the habit of enjoying the gossip. Poking her nose into other people's business, as her mother would say. Then again, there wasn't much else to do to pass the time here. No Derry and Toms to trail around, no theatre, cinema only once a week in a room below a restaurant down by the beach where – she'd been warned – the sound rarely matched up with the pictures, and in any case, the films were so ancient she'd almost certainly have seen them. Years ago.

"So what does she live on, this Russian ballerina?"

Sidney shrugged. They were sitting outside a bar, close to the wall for shade. From a small cage above their heads came an occasional trill of clear, rich notes which – Lily noted with dismay – were sung by a solitary blackbird. The woman was at another table with two young men, one of whom was yellow haired and delicate looking, the other olive skinned, wearing black top to toe. The yellow haired one had a Kodak camera which he kept picking up with long white fingers, pointing at things and then putting down again without taking a shot.

"Allowances from her ex husbands probably. Also, when she first came to Western Europe she carried on dancing for a while. Paris, Vienna, London. Everyone wanted to see this wonderful new Russian ballet. She must have made a few pennies then."

Lily didn't think she looked like the kind of woman who would save money, no matter how well she was being paid. Thrift was for the cautious. Natalia looked more like someone who considered life a fast flowing river into which to throw yourself without a thought about the current, the rocks, how far away the other side might be.

As she got up, gathered her things together, she caught Sidney's eye and waved. They could hear her silver bangles clinking.

Sidney beckoned.

"I'll introduce you," he said, lowering his voice. "Then you can ask her yourself."

The two women shook hands. Natalia's was amazingly cold, her fingernails so long they made Lily think of claws. Close to, she could see the heavy make up: green eye shadow, crimson lipstick shaped in a perfect cupid's bow. She caught a whiff of a perfume so musty that it tickled the back of her throat. Not so long ago Lily would have considered Natalia cheap, lacking in taste. Certainly not someone she'd want to socialise with. Now she found her fascinating.

"I must go, we're already late."

She indicated that the two young men – who were waiting patiently – were included in her lateness, but didn't introduce them. Her eyes met Lily's then looked her up and down, taking in everything. When Natalia gave a small nod Lily felt she'd passed some kind of test.

"But we'll meet again soon, I'm sure. This place is so small, it's inevitable. Everyone spends all their time bumping into everyone, isn't that so, Sidney?"

"Speak for yourself," he said. "I spend most of my time trying not to."

Though he seemed to pull back as Natalia bent to kiss him lightly on both cheeks, Lily noticed him watching her every step as she moved away, a young man on either side, her arms linked through theirs.

"She seems nice," Lily said.

"Seems, true. But she's not." Sidney dug in his pockets for change, dropped some coins onto the table.

"Didn't you say she was a friend of yours?"

"A friend, yes. Nice, no. In fact, she'd probably be insulted to be called nice."

Lily still couldn't decide whether he approved of her or not.

"Think of her as a cat. One moment it's lying there all soft and warm, purring as you tickle its tummy, and the next – and for no reason at all – it's a bundle of spitting fury that wants only to scratch your eyes out. It's the way cats are."

Was he talking from experience? Had he and Natalia…?

"Next thing you know it's rubbing itself around your ankles." He gave a small shrug. "And you forgive it everything."

Lily wouldn't have thought he had it in him. Set in his ways, dressing well but not ostentatiously; his china tea and rhubarb marmalade at breakfast; the pipe with which he was forever fiddling, digging at it, banging it against his pale hand. Everyone back in London thought of him as a little dull. A dear, of course, but not the kind of man to have a mistress, especially not a fiery Russian ballerina.

You old dark horse, Sidney, she thought. Good for you.

"And have you ever watched a cat playing with a mouse?" he said.

"I like cats," Lily said, defiantly. "There's a ginger tom on the steps outside our house, skin and bones so I suppose it's a stray. James says not to feed it or it'll never go away, but how can I ignore it?"

Sidney grunted, his thoughts elsewhere.

When, a few days later, the yellow haired young man turned up at the house asking for the doctor, saying Natalia needed him urgently, Lily ushered him inside. Whilst James went for his bag, she said she hoped it wasn't anything too awful, not wanting to ask straight out but anxious to know what was wrong. But he just paced back and forth, said please, could

47

she see what was keeping the doctor?

Lily hated not knowing. It was frustrating. She busied herself, dusted, shook out rugs, swept the house from top to bottom with the ancient broom she'd eventually found propping up a shelf in the wardrobe. So the last people to rent the house couldn't have been Italians; the local women were always sweeping.

When James returned he went straight to his surgery, shut the door. Best not to disturb him, she decided. It wasn't until they were about to eat that she broached the subject. James broke off some bread – they'd given up trying with the one blunt bread knife – as she ladled stew into his dish.

"There was nothing wrong with her. It was her monkey."

He dipped bread into the gravy.

"A nasty brute. There's a German woman, used to be in films though she's retired now, you've probably seen her about. She keeps a pack of yappy stunted little dogs."

"The dachshund lady?"

"That's her. One of the dogs bit the monkey, though I gather the monkey started it."

He sipped water.

"Next thing, I'll be getting an urgent call to treat the dog."

"Was it a bad bite?"

"Needed a couple of stitches but he'll live. As long as I don't have to treat him again. Look."

James rolled up his shirt sleeve, turned the under side of his arm to show her a clear circle of teeth marks just above his wrist. Around the marks the skin was red and swollen.

"He bit you? Oh James."

She'd noticed the stronger than usual smell of antiseptic, hadn't thought he might be using it on himself.

For some reason she felt it was her fault. As though she should have got it out of the young man that it was a monkey who needed treatment, should have explained that James treated people not animals. And what if the monkey had rabies? Just last week her neighbour had told her how, up in the mountains, a rabid dog had savaged three goats who'd all had to be shot, their bodies burnt. The dog was found dead a few days later.

Of course Natalia's pet monkey hadn't got rabies. And James would probably have gone even if he'd known why he was needed, he was like that. He would have felt it his duty to see what he could do.

"As I was leaving she said she's having a party with some friends on Friday night and that she'd be delighted if we'd join them."

"She said that? Delighted?"

James nodded.

"Can we, James? Just for an hour or so?"

His plate was empty and Lily jumped up and brought the saucepan across to the table, refilled it. She poured more water. He glanced up at her.

"Do you really want to?"

He didn't, she knew that. It was the chance to escape from parties that had particularly appealed to him about coming here. Besides, he didn't approve of bohemians, eccentrics. Self-centred show offs, he called them, and he was probably right. But though in many ways she admired his upright, moral approach to life, she worried that he was becoming too serious. A bit of a bore even. She couldn't recall when she'd last heard him laugh.

"I would have thought we should make an effort. It's a small village. If we don't mix socially now and again we'll never really belong, we'll always be outsiders."

"Which is another way of saying you want to go. Right. We'll go."

He pushed back his chair, went outside, and after piling the plates in the sink Lily followed him. Strange how it lured both of them, this narrow terrace with its black and white tiled floor that seemed to hang suspended over the village. Below they could see rooftops, the occasional patch of dusty ground with a few scrubby plants, then lower down still, the Moorish mosaics on the cupola of the big church. Beyond that, nothing but sea and sky. Now there were lights in some of the windows. Weary mothers shouted for children to come in. From some way off, a cockerel called.

Their two chickens were very quiet. It was as though they didn't want to make nuisances of themselves, were on their best behaviour. In a weak moment Lily had given them names: Laurel and Hardy because they were so funny. Silly thing to do. It would just make it harder to eat them.

Now she sat down on the bench beside James. She was glad he'd agreed to the party, it would do him good.

"Thank you," she said quietly.

But what on earth should she wear?

It became something of a preoccupation. She didn't want to look dowdy – not in such exotic company – but neither did she want to look ridiculous. And though she'd optimistically anticipated some kind of social life, still she'd left most of her dressier clothes in a trunk in her parent's attic. Opening the heavy doors of the wardrobe she could move the hangers along with ease, there were so few things inside.

She made her choice: a crushed velvet dress, sleeveless, the colour of milk chocolate. She would wear a wide silver bracelet, and do something different with her hair, loop it maybe, and fasten it low on her neck. And she would paint her fingernails.

It was fun, anticipating meeting new people. She was lonely. Hardly a day went by when she didn't speak to half a dozen or more people, yet she had no friends, not real friends like she'd had back in London. Friends who shared things with her: recipes, dress patterns; those fears that seem unbearable when you lie awake at night, yet when you talk them over, laugh about them, can soon be seen for what they really are, mere foolishness.

Natalia's crowd would be more like the people she used to know, at least in some ways. More sophisticated, more worldly. People who knew how to foxtrot. Who'd not only heard of Helen Wills Moody but knew how many times she'd won at Wimbledon. People who shared her admiration for film stars like Leslie Howard, who she thought was divine, especially in Pygmalion, which she'd seen three times. Though James didn't know, of course; he wouldn't have said anything but he'd have given her one of those looks that always made her feel like a spoilt child.

People who spoke her language. She was working hard at her Italian, spent time each day studying the grammar from a book. But it wasn't easy, what with all those endings, verbs changing for the most obscure reasons, adjectives having to agree with genders of nouns, not to mention direct and indirect object pronouns. And then there was that formidable list of irregular verbs.

Natalia, it seemed, spoke not only Italian, but excellent English too.

In the end, they nearly didn't go. James was called to see a child with suspected pneumonia. He was gone for what seemed like hours. When he came through the front door he found Lily sitting there in her crushed velvet, cologne behind her ears, waiting.

"God," he said. "The Russian woman's party. I'd forgotten."

"Natalia. Her name is Natalia."

He looked tired.

"We don't have to go." She smiled to cover her disappointment.

"Of course we do."

He put on a clean white shirt, his waistcoat and jacket. She couldn't understand how he could continue to wear so many clothes in such hot weather, but he did look handsome when he dressed up. She recalled when she'd first introduced him to her friends. What a catch, they'd said enviously. She'd been so proud.

"I'm ready if you are."

He was making a special effort for her, and she was grateful.

The party was taking place at a cafe right down near the beach. Lily had only been that far a couple of times. There was nothing much down there: fishing boats, nets spread across the sand like vast lengths of grubby curtaining. Seaweed, a smell of salt. And something she'd come across by accident and wished she hadn't: the slaughterhouse. She'd heard a pig squealing, couldn't think for a moment what a pig would be doing down by the beach. Then she'd realised.

That was the other end though, turning right at the bottom of the steps. The cafe was to the left.

Upstairs was where the local men went to escape from their wives and children. They sat at the tables playing cards, shirt sleeves rolled up, cups at their elbows. Coffee, Lily supposed. Or the coffee substitute people drank here much of the time, real coffee being hard to get. She didn't much like its bland taste, though once her tea supply ran out she was going to have to get used to it. The men spoke little, the only sounds being the quiet clip of cards being dropped onto other cards, cups being replaced in saucers, someone having a coughing fit. When a player did something especially daring or stupid there were grunts, exclamations, a clap on the back.

They were directed downstairs by a man in a white apron. The cellar into which they emerged made Lily think momentarily of hell, the smoke that hung motionless like a fog, the faint glow of red lighting that could have come from flames, so many bodies crushed close. Everyone seemed to be talking at once.

"*Ecco, il dottore!*"

It was Natalia who pushed her way through to them, dressed in a purple sheath, very Twenties really, except that on her it looked somehow the height of fashion. Around her neck, like a necklace, she'd looped a skinny strip of bright red fur.

She caught one of their hands in each of hers.

"Darlings, I'm over the moon that you came."

She managed to sound genuine, even though she hardly knew them.

Still holding on she drew them towards a table where a number of people were sitting, some of whom smiled, or nodded, one man standing to bow. A girl was whispering with a man old enough to be her father; their heads were almost touching, the feathers in her hat like a veil around them. They didn't notice the new arrivals.

Drinks were poured. Lily asked what it was but no-one seemed to hear, so she sipped it anyway, decided the sweet, thick liquid reminded her of aniseed balls.

James tried it too, then pulled a face.

A hand waving above heads turned out to belong to Sidney. Lily waved back, mouthed was he enjoying himself, and he mouthed back you bet. Someone shouted for music, and the cry was taken up. Music, music. Hands were banged on tables making glasses jump, feet thumped up and down.

There was some fussing in a corner, and suddenly it began, a little scratchy but still recognisable as Benny Goodman. At once a man in wide trousers with slicked back hair pushed through the crowd, shouted for everyone to clear a space, beckoned for a girl to join him.

"OK, folks. Watch and learn."

His accent was American. Lily glanced at James, but he was listening intently to a woman with a long grey plait who was smoking a black cigarette as she talked. Lily hoped she wasn't telling him about her health problems. It happened all the time. Poor James.

Now all eyes were on the dancers who were circling each other as they kept time with the music, eyes locked, moving lightly on the balls of their feet. Suddenly the man reached out to catch the girl around the waist, lifted her and swung her to one side, then to the other. Then she was back on her feet, spinning, before he picked her up and swung her overhead. Lily thought of acrobats rather than dancers, loved it whatever it was. Her own feet wouldn't keep still.

"What dance is that?" she said to the man next to her who was also sitting twisted around in order to watch.

"The jitterbug. You don't know it? It's all the rage in America. Daniel's just come back, he keeps us up to date with what's in fashion and what's out."

Of course she'd heard of the jitterbug. Who hadn't? Men and women behaving no better than savages in the jungle, that's what the newspapers said. Disgusting. It should be banned. Lily had to admit she thought it looked fun.

"You're English then?"

The man lit a cigar, watched her as he drew on it.

"I am, yes. My husband…"

"Unpopular, we English. Had any trouble, have you?"

"Here, do you mean? No."

She wondered if he was drunk. His eyes were red rimmed, his words a little slurred, she thought, though it was hard to be sure with all the noise.

"Not here. The locals don't care what nationality you are, what you do. As long as you pay your bills, keep your hands off their daughters. Or sons, depending on your preference in such matters."

He reached for a bottle, slopped some of its contents into his glass then, as an after-thought, into hers. A small bubble of colourless liquid lay on the wooden table. Without thinking, Lily dabbed at it with her fingertips.

"It's different up north though. Very unpopular, we are. Hitler's fault, him and Mussolini. I don't imagine they much like the Americans either, but then they have money. With money you can buy friends wherever you are."

The music had stopped.

"Seen them spitting on union jacks, setting fire to them out on the street. Crowds of thugs."

He leant closer.

"I was spat at too."

He watched for her reaction.

"In Florence. I was drinking in a bar, minding my own business, and someone walked up and spat in my face."

Perspiration was making his skin gleam. He was drunk, Lily was sure of it.

A cool hand rested lightly on her shoulder.

"Don't listen to his stories. I should have warned you. This is the most depressing man in the village."

Natalia smiled at him.

"Come, Lily, I'd like you to help me choose some music, something romantic and sensual, not this terrible swing. I hate trumpets, don't you? They're so aggressive."

Relieved, Lily excused herself, followed Natalia to where

on a table stood a wind up gramophone, beside it an assortment of records in brown paper cases. Natalia picked one, glanced at it, passed it to Lily. She reached for another.

"September In The Rain? No, too early in the year. It's A Sin To Tell A Lie? What do you think?"

Lily had started on another pile.

"Here," she said. "I love this, it makes me cry."

"You like to cry? Me, no. Life is too short. But for you..."

Natalia placed the record on the turntable, reached for the handle and turned it until it stiffened, lowered the needle. A man's voice, soft and warm, sang about red sails in the sunset.

"So." Natalia said. "So now you go and dance cheek to cheek with your husband."

"James? Oh, James won't dance."

They used to go to dances when they were first married; Friday nights at the local town hall, tea and biscuits included in the entrance fee. Had enjoyed them too, or at least, she had. She'd thought he had, he'd seemed to, but gradually they'd gone less often, then not at all. It had just happened.

She had a feeling he'd say no tonight, and she didn't want the embarrassment.

"He won't? Then you must dance with me."

In an instant Lily was a girl again, learning to dance with her sister, mother standing to one side giving them instructions. It had felt odd to be face to face and so close; there was the warmth of Cissy's back under her hand, her hair tickling Lily's face. They'd kept their arms stiff so that their bodies didn't touch, their eyes averted. They were no longer children, their mother insisted. They were young ladies and must learn to comport themselves as such. Which had only made matters worse, comport being such a pompous, old-fashioned word. Cissy had been unable to keep a straight face, and her giggling had set Lily off so that soon both of them were in danger of becoming hysterical. Though their mother had acted exasperated, they could see that she wasn't, not really.

Dancing with Natalia, though, Lily forgot the awkwardness of partnering a woman. Probably because Natalia moved so well, she too seemed to be gliding across the floor, as though she was skating on ice. It was good too being part of a group, everyone moving in unison, smiling or teasing other couples; Natalia spoke to someone over Lily's shoulder, and when she eventually faced that way she saw that it was the two young men who'd been with Natalia at the bar. They had their arms around each others' necks.

The record finished. Someone put it on again.

Lily's head was swimming. Natalia's body close to hers felt as though it was all bone.

When James came to say it was time they left, Lily managed to control the urge to plead with him, to say not yet, can't we stay a little longer? How could he do this to her? Just when she was having such a good time. He was a spoil sport. She realised that he was probably bored, but that was his own fault. Anyone would think he was an old man and he wasn't even forty yet, not old at all. What would he be like when he really was old?

They walked up the road in silence, the air moist and perfumed after the smoky café. Overhead the stars looked like splinters of glass. Everything about this place is magical, she thought. Of course, she was being unfair to James; he'd come with her even though he was tired, he'd made an effort. She linked her arm through his, and he squeezed her hand.

Seven

As usual James had his head in a book. Lily didn't like to interrupt him, but she had to know.

"So what did you think of her? Natalia, I mean."

"In what way?"

Lily couldn't stopped thinking about her. She was so unlike anyone else Lily knew. What did she eat? Did she in fact eat at all, or was her lithe body the result of living on olives and sticks of celery? Did she spend hours each morning at a *barre* in front of a wall of mirrors, wearing leotards, stretching her muscles like elastic bands? Or did she not care any more? How did she fill her days? Like Lily she must have lots of free time, more because she lived on her own and so didn't have to look after anyone else's needs. Was she lonely? Even people who were always surrounded by friends could be lonely, behind the façade.

Lily shrugged.

"Well, I guess she's typical of that artistic type. Highly

strung. Friendly but almost too much so, considering we've only just met her. Generous, which obviously she can afford to be. No doubt she regrets the fact that she's thrown away any chance she had of being a great dancer, which is why she drinks too much."

"You think she drinks too much?"

"You didn't notice? But then so, it seems, does everyone in set."

He returned to his reading.

Lily realised she'd been hoping to meet the monkey at the party. Maybe he didn't like crowds, smoke, loud music. Not so long ago she would have agreed with him.

A telegram came. It was from a doctor they'd met up with one evening in Rome, an older man, German. He was en route for Salerno, wondered if he could visit them, possibly even stay for a night.

Delighted, James went at once to the post office to send back a message. Lily was pleased too. He'd enjoy the company of another doctor, someone with whom he could discuss serums and the latest discoveries about anaesthetics and immunology. She knew the terms, had heard them used often enough, seen them in books, reports, but they meant little to her.

In some ways, James must be lonely too, she thought with surprise.

Had she known, at that stage, that she and Natalia would become close? She couldn't remember, though even now she could recall the pleasure she'd felt that morning when she heard her name, recognised the voice.

"I'm up here!"

Natalia was hanging over the edge of a bourgainvillea

draped balcony, way up above the street, waving.

It was the day their visitor was due to arrive and Lily had gone down into the village to shop for what she wanted to be a special meal. James had said why didn't they have chicken; reluctantly she'd agreed and then, that same morning, Antonio had brought them a fish he'd caught during the night, a huge thing with bright, sad eyes. He'd caught two and wanted the doctor to share his good fortune.

Lucky for the chickens, too. Despite resolving not to, she was growing fond of them. And there had been some eggs, small but delicious; she'd boiled them lightly and the yolks had been smooth as cream. Lily hoped for more eggs to justify their stay of execution. It occurred to her that she ought to re-name them.

She'd bought broad beans from a man selling his surplus crops from a wheelbarrow beside the road, also some tiny potatoes. There was a vegetable she didn't recognise, not unlike a small cucumber. *Zucchini*, the man said. At the tip of each was a wilted yellow flower.

"How do I cook them?"

He held one up, speaking slowly so she could follow his Italian.

"You slice like this." He chopped at the courgette with a stubby finger.

"Then fry in oil, turn, fry the other side."

He made his hand into a spatula, flipped it. She said yes, she'd take some.

"But the best, you know what it is? *I fiori.*"

"The flowers?" She must have misunderstood. *Si*, he said, the flowers. Dipped in batter, fried. He bunched his fingers together, kissed the tips, something she'd seen others do to denote excellence. And *aglio*? He held out the small white bulbs she'd discovered everyone used all the time, but that she found too strong. Garlic, that was it. She still preferred onion.

A young boy, tousle haired and barefooted, tugged at her skirt. Thinking he wanted a toffee, she dug in her pocket, but then saw he was holding a bundle of folded leaves. Lifting the top one he showed her what was inside. Wild strawberries; he must have collected them up in the hills. They smelled like icing sugar.

"You want me to buy them?"

He watched her with round eyes as she got out her purse, dropped some coins into his small hand. He grinned. As he turned to go she called, gave him some toffees too.

"*Grazie, signora*," he said. He scampered away.

Their soles must be made of rubber, these children, she thought; already she could feel the heat of the gravel road coming up through her sandals. She'd taken to wearing sandals now, at least during the day when she was pottering around. Her feet felt liberated. She'd bought a hat too, straw, with a ribbon that trailed.

It was as she was heading back up the road towards home that Natalia had called to her.

"Wait. I'll be right down."

A door opened, slammed shut. Natalia emerged.

"I was visiting a friend," she said. "I saw you passing."

"I'm glad you did. I've been wanting to thank you for inviting us to your party."

Natalia fell into step; Lily noticed she too was wearing sandals, her toe nails silver.

"You enjoyed it?"

"I loved it. Especially meeting all those new people. You have some very interesting friends."

"They're interesting, yes. Disreputable, though, most of them. Here in this village they are tolerated, but in more conventional society they'd be... well, ostracised at least. If

61

not thrown into prison, or burned at the stake."

Lily had the impression that Natalia thoroughly approved of them. She wasn't so sure how she herself felt. She'd been brought up to believe in the importance of such things as good manners, doing the right thing, taking responsibility. And being concerned about what other people thought of you, that too was important.

It was all very drear, really.

"Well, I like them," she said, with determination. "And I don't believe that anyway, what you said about them being arrested or burned."

Natalia laughed, a liquid sound.

"Darling," she said. "You're so sweet."

About to object – Lily wasn't sure she liked being thought of as sweet – she came to a halt as Natalia caught her arm and pointed out to sea. It was so dazzling she had to screw up her eyes.

"Look. You see those islands?"

Lily had noticed them before; one large island, and was it one or two smaller ones? It was hard to tell, they were a long way off.

"Let's go there, shall we? We could take a picnic, swim, tell each other secrets. You'll love it, I promise you."

A woman in black went by, bent over a stick, chewing at her gums. She muttered *buongiorno*. Lily waited until they were alone again.

She didn't like to admit that she couldn't swim. Nor that James probably wouldn't approve. Though he certainly didn't expect her to spend every moment running around him, he did expect her to behave like a doctor's wife. Doctors' wives didn't go off to distant islands for picnics with strange people they hardly knew.

"I'm not sure. And anyway, how can we get there?"

"By boat, silly. How else? I'll organise everything, don't worry, all you have to do is come. Maybe tomorrow, or the day after? You know where I live, you can send a message." Natalia's hand still rested on Lily's arm. She gripped a little tighter, then let go.

"Think about it, will you?"

Lily promised she would. That much was true. But she wouldn't go, of course.

The doctor arrived late afternoon on the boat from Sorrento. James went down to meet him at the beach. When the two men arrived back Lily watched them coming up the last few steps, James a little ahead, the older man stopping frequently, dabbing at his flushed face with what could have been a silk scarf. Even from a distance she could see that they were already deep in conversation.

In the hallway they left their jackets, hats, the small case James had obviously insisted on carrying for their guest.

"Dear, you remember Friedrich Karel?"

"Of course."

Friedrich rubbed his hands on the scarf before reaching to shake hers.

"I'd heard you have to be fit to get around this village. How many steps is it from the beach up to here, have you counted? I tell you, I feel like I've just climbed to the top of a mountain."

He collapsed into a chair, his large frame still heaving.

"There's another village higher up, and another one above that," James said. "Some two thousand steps, top to bottom, they say. I'm praying no-one up there ever calls me out on an emergency."

Lily went for the cold lemon squash she'd prepared.

The meal went well, Friedrich repeating more than once

how wonderful it was to have something besides pasta. He was sick and tired of pasta, he said. As a grand finale Lily had made a sponge pudding, topped it with a strawberry sauce, made custard using some of her precious supply of custard powder. Friedrich applauded as she carried it to the table. Nothing could have been less suitable for such a sultry evening, yet it was eaten, every last crumb.

Their guest had brought freshly ground coffee, a thank you gift. She served it black, in small cups, the Italian way. As she sipped she realised with amazement that she was beginning to prefer coffee to tea.

"Yes, but Fleming discovered penicillin over ten years ago, yet they still haven't found a way to manufacture it in a stable form. What's taking them so long? Don't they realise how many people are dying unnecessarily whilst they twiddle their thumbs?"

Already the two men had forgotten she was there.

"Every day we get reports of sightings of rabid dogs, foxes. A lot of it is hysteria, but even so, animals throughout Italy ARE dying of rabies. And so, unfortunately, are people."

Lily poured more coffee. They always talked about such depressing things. And yet – glancing from one to the other - she noted how animated they were, both sitting forward in their chairs. Now and again they even burst into laughter.

"…given intravenously makes all the difference. Think, James, of all the problems that are automatically eliminated."

She pushed back her chair.

"Friedrich, James, please will you excuse me? I'm feeling rather tired tonight, and all this medical talk…"

She gave an apologetic smile.

"Of course."

James pecked at her cheek.

The bedroom seemed airless. Without putting on the light

Lily slipped into her nightdress, then she opened another door that led onto the terrace – there were three altogether – and pulled across the net curtain she'd put up to keep out insects. She could see it billowing like smoke as she stretched out on the bed. The mens' voices were distant now, a mere mumbling. She fell asleep at once.

When she awoke she couldn't for a moment think what had disturbed her. She heard James's voice, louder now, and realised they'd moved out onto the terrace. It was no doubt cooler out there. She heard the clink of a glass being put down. They'd probably talk all night, she thought, smiling to herself. Turning over, she closed her eyes again, sure that in a moment sleep would return.

Why she started listening to what Friedrich was saying, she didn't know. The emotion in his voice may have had something to do with it. He was talking about an epidemic of some kind. Did he say Naples? The cholera epidemic then, back at the turn of the century. He must have been very young, newly qualified and keen. Wanting to help and oblivious to the dangers.

Lily drew her legs up, listened as he talked about the filth, the poverty, the fear, the smell of sulphur and carbolic acid. People dropping dead in the streets, being piled into carts and taken off at once to the cholera cemetery. Burials took place at night.

Friedrich's voice went even quieter. Worse still, he said, some victims of the disease went into a sort of death-like trance, their bodies went cold; you might pronounce someone dead when in fact he could still be alive, listening but unable to speak. Without doubt some people were buried alive. There was a pause, a match being struck, a flicker of light through the curtain. James said nothing. And the rats, Friedrich went on. Biggest you've ever seen. They were the only ones to do well out of the epidemic. You could hear them crunching as you passed alleyways, sometimes in the corner of a room. Not that they attacked the living, not at first anyway. There was no need. Though when the sanitary officials started working on the sewers, the half-crazed rats were forced up onto the streets in their thousands, and then...

Lily pressed her hands against her ears.

She didn't want to know any more. What was the fascination with such horrific stories when there were so many good things, beautiful things to talk about? Surely all anyone can do is get on with their lives, make the most of each moment, be happy?

In the morning she'd made up her mind.

"I'm going for a picnic tomorrow," she said when James returned from seeing Friedrich off. "With Natalia. If you don't mind, that is."

She waited for him to object, sensed him looking at her, though she kept her back to him, concentrated on folding the lace tablecloth she'd brought out specially for their guest. It was so fine and delicate, the colour of ivory; probably handmade by their landlord's mother, or wife. Whereas women back home knitted, here they made lace. She'd seen them sitting on stools outside their front door, bent over their work.

"Why should I? Do you good," James said.

Lily breathed out again. Obviously his visitor had put him in a mellow mood.

She was looking forward to it right up until the moment when she got to the beach, had tramped down over the burning pebbles to the boat, which looked tiny, like a child's toy. How could that fragile thing be expected to stay afloat with three adults in it? What if it didn't? The sea was deep and cruel; it would swallow you up and feed you to fish who'd pick your bones clean in no time.

"Lily, this is Ernesto."

Afterwards, Lily had often thought back to that first meeting. She'd hardly looked at him, her mind on the crossing they were about to undertake. There was an impression of a man not a lot taller than she was, stocky, dark, nothing more.

He'd nodded briefly, that she remembered. Indicated that they should step into the boat and they'd done as instructed, Natalia first, dropping into it with the grace of a cat, Lily following, bending forward so as to keep as close as possible to something solid, both hands holding onto whatever she could reach.

Ernesto pushed the boat away from the beach, kept pushing until the water was up past his knees, then jumped in behind Lily. For a moment they drifted, then she heard a soft splash as an oar slid into the water, then another, and slowly they began to pull away.

As the panic began she took deep breaths. She watched the oars, the circle of ripples left behind each time one of them entered the water. Growing bolder, she lifted her eyes, looked around. Never before had she seen such clear water, the colour one moment blue, the next green, then gold, like a kaleidoscope. And so smooth it could have been a pond. She released her grip with one hand, trailed her fingers over the edge of the boat; the water felt warm and velvety.

"OK?"

"OK."

Natalia was wearing a caftan, a turban hiding her hair, dark glasses. She brought to mind Greta Garbo in Mata Hari, it was the way she moved, her posture. Mata Hari had been a dancer too, of course. Lily could still remember the final scene, moments before the heroine went before the firing squad, when she and her lover were re-united. It still brought tears to her eyes. She understood why James called her a romantic, just wished it didn't sound so much like a criticism.

And if Natalia's outfit was unsuitable, what about Lily's? She had on her usual skirt and a blouse, long sleeved with pearl buttons at the wrist. She'd brought her straw hat with her too. James had said to watch out for the sun, that the water reflected it and she didn't want to burn. It was the only thing he'd said.

They were nearing the main island. The boat edged along parallel with the rocky coast for a bit, then suddenly there was a cove with dull beige sand, some stunted shrubs growing up from the rocks that had at some time fallen from the towering cliffs behind them. No sign of anyone. There was no other way onto the beach but from the sea.

Ernesto jumped again into the shallow water, tugged the boat up onto the sand with ease, as though it weighed next to nothing.

"*Paradiso*. Isn't this paradise?" Natalia said. She breathed out on the word as though it was a word that demanded to be said with hushed reverence. Like God and Death and Sacrifice.

She passed a basket to Ernesto, then her hand. Ernesto held out his hand to Lily but she ignored it, made it clear she could manage, though the drop was more than she anticipated and as she landed she stumbled, almost fell. He caught her arm.

"*Attenzione*," he said. It was the first time he'd spoken. His voice was so low it was almost a grunt.

Lily caught up with Natalia.

"But doesn't anyone own it, this island?" she said, feeling sure she'd heard that it belonged to a choreographer or an actor, someone anyway, in which case they would be trespassing.

"Yes, but he's never here. What a waste, don't you think? Anyway, how could he possibly object to us borrowing his little beach for a few hours?"

Lily wasn't so confident, trespassing was trespassing. But she would put it out of her mind.

Natalia, who'd disrobed instantly to reveal a simple black bathing costume, spread blankets over the sand. Next she rummaged around in the basket for glasses, a bottle; she'd thought of everything.

They touched glasses.

"To beautiful days," Natalia said. "And beautiful friendships."

Lily took a sip. The pale liquid tickled her tongue

"What is it?"

"Champagne, darling. What else?"

It was barely midday, far too early to be drinking anything alcoholic, let alone champagne. James was right about the drinking. And Lily didn't care.

"It tastes wonderful," she said, taking another sip.

Natalia glanced over towards Ernesto who was standing propped against the side of his boat, staring out to sea, smoking a cigarette.

"Ernesto, *vieni!*" she called.

"You don't mind, do you?" she whispered to Lily. "Seems awfully mean to leave him over there on his own. He's a nice young man, a bit moody sometimes, but then they all are, have you noticed?"

Before Lily could reply he was standing beside them.

"Come and sit with us," Natalia said in Italian.

Silently he did as he was told, crossed his legs, took the glass he was handed. His skin, Lily observed, was the colour of cinnamon, the hairs on his arms bleached almost white by the sun. He needed a shave, and even his stubble had pale streaks in it. In a way they made him look older, though she didn't think he could be much over thirty, his movements supple, his face hardly lined at all.

She had no idea what colour his eyes were; he kept them lowered. In respect or because he was shy, she wondered.

Finishing his drink in a few quick gulps, he thanked them, stood and moved away.

"Oh, well," Natalia said, topping up their glasses.

She stretched out on her back, said she was going to get a tan. Her hip bones stuck up like sharp ridges, her breasts had disappeared altogether. She's a stick of Blackpool rock, Lily thought, and I'm a bag of marshmallows.

"Everybody's doing it nowadays, did you know? All those years I spent dodging the sun, trying to keep my skin white, and suddenly it's chic to be brown."

She squinted up at Lily.

"What about you? You're not going to keep your things on all day, are you? Aren't you sweltering?"

"If I try to tan my skin will go red and blotchy. But you're right…"

She stood, turned her back and slipped off her blouse, undid her skirt. Like Natalia she was wearing her bathing costume underneath. The air on her skin was burning hot.

"I'm going to move over into the shade too."

Natalia waved a hand at her without opening her eyes.

Between the rocks further back the sand was cool. Lily sat there mesmerised by the glittering sea, by the silky feel of the sand, by a silence so complete it felt like they were the only people left in the world. Paradise, as Natalia put it.

There had been other beaches, of course.

One in Cornwall, many years ago, when she and her sister had spent a summer with some friends of their parents who had an old cottage, a chilly place with stone floors and windows like postage stamps. They'd had gooseberry pie every day, or so it had seemed, and she hated gooseberries, that bitter green mush, pips sticking between your teeth. And the man had smelt and was always scratching so that Cissy whispered he must have fleas, and they'd both feared they'd catch them, imagining them at night on the bed, tiny black specks that jumped. The beach had been just a few minutes away down a lane; you had to walk single file and even then your ankles got stung by nettles. She remembered the new buckets, shiny and so pretty; hers had been red, her sister's blue. She loved that bucket, had refused to put grubby sand in it, or baby crabs, or let anyone else use it. At night she'd slept with it beside her bed.

It was because of her red bucket that she'd had the fight. A bigger boy – she could see him now, fat with orange hair – had said give it to me and she'd said no, it's mine. He'd grabbed, she'd hung on. He'd pushed her hard. She'd fallen and gone face down in the sea water, and sheer panic had made her just lie there, unable to move until someone had caught her shoulders, yanked her up onto her feet. It hadn't been deep, a foot at most, yet she'd nearly drowned. She could taste it now, that water: salty, oily, fishy. After she'd been sick and they'd tried to wash her with the sea water, cupping handfuls of it to trickle down her arms and legs, but she'd screamed blue murder.

It had stayed with her, that hatred of the sea.

Though she'd enjoyed it with James. Their honeymoon, delayed because as usual James had been busy doing something or other he couldn't get out of. It had been winter, They'd gone to the coast and stayed at a boarding house where the landlady had said they were closed, but then seeing the look on Lily's face, had softened, said well, she'd see what she could do. She'd given them what she called her best room.

It had mauve flowered wallpaper and a chandelier and a four-poster bed with one post that was different from the rest, but they didn't care. Even though she lit a fire in the evenings, the room hardly warmed; in the morning there was a very fine film of ice on the inside of the window in which Lily scratched a hole with a penny piece.

They could see the beach from this window.

Mornings began with a huge breakfast. Then they would wrap up in scarves, set off to walk along to the pier and back. It was a pebble beach; the stones had crunched underfoot, slithered about, and to help steady her Lily had taken off one of her gloves, put her hand in James pocket, entwined her fingers with his. She hadn't minded, had hardly noticed the sharp wind, heavy grey clouds bowling along before it like sheep before a dog. The sea had been patterned with white frills; once or twice they'd got too close and had to jump back out of the way of a sudden thundering wave.

They'd pretended they could see France out there. I'll take you to France one day, James had said. To Spain, Tahiti, Paraguay, wherever you want to go I'll take you. And to America? she'd said. He didn't talk much about it, but she knew he missed it. She'd like to see where he grew up, to fill in the gaps. She wanted to know every little thing about him. And to America, he'd said, I promise.

At night they'd plaited themselves around each other, legs and arms entwined around legs and arms.

Natalia was getting to her feet, stretching.

"Coming for a swim?" she called.

"I can't swim."

Lily had said it before she remembered that she was going to make some excuse, keep her secret for a little while at least.

"No. it isn't true. Everyone can swim, it's like breathing, it's automatic."

"Not in London. Think of it, what chance do we get to learn? I'll paddle."

"Well, if you're happy…"

They went together to the water's edge, Natalia wading in quickly, then suddenly plunging forward and heading out to sea, arms whirling, going so fast that soon she was no more than a black dot on the horizon. What if she never came back? Lily walked up and down, the warm water lapping over her ankles, trying not to think about it.

Once she turned and Ernesto was watching her. She looked away quickly.

Afterwards, they ate. The salad was wilted in the heat, the cheese shiny with perspiration, and the bread dry and crumbly, yet it had tasted superb. They finished the champagne, opened a bottle of red wine. At some point Ernesto came across, crouched down again though he declined to sit with them, to take more than a glass of wine and a chunk of bread that he dunked into it. When he caught Lily's eye he held out a piece of the sopping bread.

"*Assaggia*," he said. Try.

She shook her head but he simply waited, and reluctantly she took it, surprised to find it tasted better than she expected. A bit like sherry trifle, she decided.

Natalia was chatting as she picked at the food: gossip about people at the party, stories of her past life that might have been true though were far more likely to be fantasies. Lily didn't mind. She could have sat there forever, lulled by the lilting tones of Natalia's voice, still not quite believing that all this was real. The realisation that Ernesto was still watching her grew slowly. When she caught his eye he looked straight back at her until she was the one to give in and turn away. She wished he'd stop.

When she laid back on the blanket it was to rest for a

minute. She awoke with a start, not sure where she was. The sun had moved around and she was in shade, but even so she felt as though she was burning up.

"You're awake, darling. Good." Natalia was sitting up now. "One last swim and we'd better be heading back."

"Oh, I don't think I want…"

"Come on. At least the water will cool you down."

This time Ernesto went in too, as at home in water as a fish, though he was gone from sight for so long that Lily thought he must be in trouble. When his head popped up it was far out.

Lily kicked at the timid waves, went in deeper, ducked down and felt the water revive her. She made a few pretend strokes with her arms.

He re-appeared suddenly at her side, shaking his head so that the water droplets flew around him.

"*Perché non nuotare?*" he said.

"Why what? Oh, I can't." She thought about it. "*Non posso nuotare.*"

He held out his hands and she hesitated, then took them. Slowly he backed out until the water was almost up to her shoulders.

"Your legs," he said. She understood, kicked out with her legs. Though she could feel the strength in them, sensed that they had the power to keep her afloat, even to move her forward, still she clung to his hands. What if he should suddenly let go? Or tripped and fell over backwards?

"*Bene,*" he said. He must have sensed her concern because he started moving back towards the shallows.

"*Con una mano sola,*" he said, gradually pulling one of his hands away from hers. She made wide sweeps with her free hand, but now the water was up to her chin, she kept dipping down into it, once it actually went over her clenched lips.

Suddenly desperate to stand up, she heard him laughing.

Her feet found the sea bed.

"*Grazie*," she said, pulling her hands away from him, dismissing him. Taking the hint he turned and waded back towards the beach.

About to follow, Lily felt a sudden determination. Everyone can swim, it's like breathing. Ducking down until the water came up to her neck she did a few slow strokes with her hands, feeling them pushing aside the water, then took a deep breath and lunged. For seconds – four, five, six – she stayed on top of the water, until gradually her legs grew heavy and began to sink, and she was standing again. But it was enough. She'd done it: she'd swum. And now she could hear him applauding from where he stood by the boat, and Natalia, wrapped in her towel, called out to him, he called back, and then she too started clapping.

"*Bravo, cara*," she called.

Looking back, Lily remembered that moment quite clearly.

It was then that it had come to her, the feeling that something was going to happen. She had no idea what it might be, just that it was the reason fate had brought her to this little village en route to nowhere. She knew it in the way that you know it's going to rain even when the sky is cloudless. There's a smell that tells you, a strange texture to the air as it touches your skin, a distant rumbling you can't hear but that some inner ear picks up, translates into a warning. Or a promise.

Changes. They could be good or bad, she didn't know, didn't care. All that mattered was that her life – her real life, the one she was destined for – was at long last going to begin.

Eight

$\mathcal{T}$he feeling stayed with her. It grew stronger.

In the sky, the sun expanded, throbbed, as black goats trailed up the dusty road, stopping to tear at clumps of yellow grass, sniffing under the wrought iron gates of villas where businessmen – down for the weekend from Naples – sat breakfasting beneath vine covered trellises.

Lily was patient. Maybe it was the heat, maybe she was adjusting to life here, learning to let things happen rather than trying to make them. *Piano, piano*, as the locals would say when she met them toiling up one of the many flights of steps. Slowly, slowly. She liked it when they spoke to her in Italian and she could understand, especially when they used dialect. It felt like she was a member of a select club. She never, of course, went out without her dictionary.

She discovered simple things.

Like picking nasturtiums on strolls above the village, digging in the back of cupboards for jars and filling the house with the moist green smell of them.

Like fussing the ginger cat who was always out on what she'd come to think of as their steps, sneaking him a saucer of milk, waiting as he licked it clean and then cleaned himself, every inch of fur carefully smoothed with his rough pink tongue.

Like watching the visitors. On her way down to the *latteria*, for the fresh mozzarella cheese they had for lunch most days, she'd perched on the wall to watch a man in a jazzy striped pullover who was strutting about with a cine camera. He was filming a peroxide blonde in high heels, slacks and a polka dot halter top who one moment gazed out towards the sea, a hand shading her eyes, the next turned, twirled and simpered at the camera.

The man caught Lily's eye, winked.

"Remember this moment, my dear. You are watching the birth of the next great movie star. She may be only a starlet today but look at her, have you ever seen such lips, such style, such oomph?"

He didn't wait for Lily to reply, moved on down the hill with the heavy camera over one shoulder, his other arm around his starlet's tiny waist. Lily exchanged a smile with a couple of local lads who'd joined her on the wall and were clapping the little performance.

She was surprised to realise she wasn't impressed, nor jealous. Nor even intrigued. Why should she be when she had so much?

One morning she watched another little drama, this one out on the terrace. A tiny jumping spider was clinging onto a dragonfly three or more times its size, not letting go, the dragonfly taking hours to stop struggling, to give up. Lily thought of trying to rescue it but it could be poisoned, might still die and the spider would go hungry. Later she saw what was left of its body being dragged across the tiles by ants. How horrid, she thought. And yet how impressive too. Nature has so much to teach us, she thought.

Standing in front of the bedroom mirror she noticed that – despite trying to stay out of the sun – her skin was beginning to colour. It suited her. She'd lost weight too, her skirts were definitely looser around the waist. She undid the top button of her blouse, took out her kirbigrips and shook her head. She smiled.

To think it was only a few months ago she'd imagined herself emerging from a cocoon, spreading her wings to dry, growing stronger every minute. She would discard it as she longed to discard the timid person she used to be, would stand there new-born and beautiful and ready. For what, she wasn't so sure. Whatever life offered. Whatever she could get.

One thing she knew: she wanted to try again for a baby. She had to make James see that she was willing to take the risks, more than willing, and that besides, it would be alright this time. How could it not be in this special place?

She'd wanted so much to belong here, to live the same simple life that the locals lived, not so very different from that of their parents, their grandparents even. Washing their clothes with ash, treading grapes to make wine, eating vegetables they'd grown themselves, singing, always singing. It was a hard life, true, and yet so rich in the things that mattered.

And now, instead, she was an outcast. She and James. Not just foreigners, but figures of hate.

Yesterday, in the street, an elderly woman stopped as Lily approached. Thinking they must have met, even though Lily didn't recognise her, she'd said good morning, muttered something about the weather. The woman hadn't replied but had continued staring, eyes like black olives. Then, as Lily passed, the woman had raised one tight fist, stretched her end fingers and pointed them at Lily as though putting a curse on her. Telling herself the woman was a lunatic, harmless but completely mad, still Lily's heart had pounded.

She hadn't told James. She'd wanted to, needed to share the way she felt with someone who would understand. She was not used to having people display such open hatred. But he would probably have shrugged, if he responded at all. Over the past few days it had become impossible to talk to him.

Surely they should be standing together right now?

If they faced the villagers hand in hand, that would be something. If all that had happened had at least drawn them close as adversity is said to, isn't it?

Together we stand...

The walls of the room seemed to be closing in on her. She felt a sudden yearning to be outdoors, to breath air filled with the smells of pine, of jasmine, of fish frying for someone's lunch. But even as she thought it there was a banging on the door – fists, something hard like a piece of wood – and voices calling.

"Assassino! Vai al tuo paese!"

Killer, go home.

The voices were of boys, children, they probably hadn't the faintest idea what they were shouting about, were joining in for the fun of it. For the fun of taunting the foreigners. She stared at the door for some minutes, transfixed even though the boys had gone, she'd heard them running off, jeering.

Come on, Lily. This won't do. Pull yourself together.

She would make coffee, take it in to James, make it clear that it was time to put all this behind them and get on with the day, with their lives.

He didn't reply to her knock.

She opened the door slowly. With the shutters drawn the room was dim, but still she could see him sitting at his desk, could tell from the curve of his neck that he had his eyes closed.. She placed the cup carefully on one side, avoided standing it on papers, knowing how that infuriated him.

"You've been in here for hours, James. I thought you might like a drink."

He didn't speak, didn't move.

"James?" She stretched out her fingers, touched his wrist. His skin was burning. She rested her arm across his shoulders,

lay her face against the top of his head. He pulled away.

"James, you mustn't let this ruin everything."

"I mustn't?" His voice was calm, too calm.

"It wasn't your fault, you know that. These things happen."

"For God's sake, Lily. Not another of your clichés, not now please."

Involuntarily she took a step back.

"It wasn't just one of those things. It could have been avoided. To start with, you could have stopped to think before you ..."

"Me? You're blaming all this on me?"

Lily couldn't help herself. Usually she could; it was something she was proud of, her ability to remain unruffled on occasions when others fell apart, said things they later regretted. This time, however, he'd gone too far.

"James, that's not fair. That's just not fair."

She heard herself sounding like a spoilt child, couldn't stop.

"You... I don't understand how you can... if you knew anything about being a proper husband, if you ever gave just five minutes of your precious time to talk to me, to listen to how I feel, but no..."

He was on his feet now, so much taller than her, his face distorted, a stranger's face. There was a clatter as the cup went flying, a brown stain spreading across the desk. He stood facing her.

"Don't," he said quietly.

"How dare you try to blame me for your mistakes!"

The pain as he hit her across her cheek was brief, not severe, more like a sting, but the shock of it stunned her. He'd never hit her before, hardly even raised his voice. Then as she tried to blink back the tears he'd wrapped his hands around her throat and was shaking her, muttering as he did so, his thumbs pressing hard against her windpipe.

"James, stop it," she managed to say. She could taste blood, must have bitten her lip, could feel it trickling from the corner of her mouth.

Abruptly he released her, turned to the desk and with one sweep of his arm knocked everything from it: books, files of notes, pens, the lamp they'd brought with them from London, its green glass shade smashing as it tumbled to the floor. In two steps he reached the bookcase, started taking down the books, hurling them across the room one at a time, pages fluttering like the wings of injured birds, the leather bound cover of an encyclopaedia splitting down the spine, the pile growing deeper, but still he didn't stop.

Lily stood with her back pressed against the door.

Somehow she managed not to scream.

PART TWO

Nine

God having his coal delivered that was what her mother used to say when there was a thunder storm. Lily could remember her sitting on the edge of the bed when she was very young, the two of them counting sacks: four, five, more sometimes. God was going to be snug as a bug in a rug next winter, her mother would say. Lily didn't find it much of a comfort. She'd hated the heart-stopping crashes and she still did.

Obviously this storm was stationary overhead.

The lightning – she could see through the wooden shutters that she always left ajar- didn't so much flash as flicker. Like a ribbon in a breeze.

Unable to sleep, she'd got up and gone into the kitchen to drink some water. James followed her, rubbing at his eyes. He said it sounded like water was gushing down onto the terrace, probably from a pipe somewhere, and he'd better go and see

85

that the chickens hadn't been swept away.

When the light went off, Lily thought for a moment he'd touched the switch as he passed. But of course he hadn't. It was the storm, storms affected power supplies. She wondered how long it would be before it came back on again, remembered seeing candles somewhere. In a drawer? On a shelf? She felt her way into the kitchen, reached inside the first drawer she came too and put her hand on one almost at once, then couldn't find matches. Damn, she muttered. James would know where they were. She'd ask him.

It was as she edged towards the terrace that she thought she heard knocking at the front door. She paused. Another crash of thunder shook the house, rolled away to silence, and then she heard it again. She wasn't imagining it. Why did she think at once of Ernesto? Suddenly she was convinced it was him; that he'd been hurt, or someone in his family, and had come for help. Hurrying towards the front door she collided with a chair, winced, moved more cautiously now, trying to remember which pieces of furniture stood where.

Rain bounced in as she opened the door, great beads of it. A figure stood there, half turned away and bent forward.

"Yes? Can I help?" she said, her voice drowned in the storm noises. Lightning flickered and in the sudden light she saw the man's face, an unfamiliar face, his lips moving but no sound emerging. As he took a step towards her, he reached for the doorway to steady himself. Then he crumpled at her feet.

For the briefest moment she hesitated, then pulled herself together. He was badly injured, or ill, or exhausted. She must get him inside. Bending, she caught his arm then dropped it. He was unconscious, a dead weight; she'd never be able to move him.

"James!" She shouted twice and still he didn't come. Starting to feel her way through the blackness, she heard him slamming shut the terrace door.

"Thank goodness. Quickly, there's a man. He's collapsed."

Between them they dragged him back into the hallway, James taking the bulk of the weight, Lily lifting his feet. She felt for a cushion, put it under the man's head.

"I've found a candle but no matches."

"Try my jacket pocket," James said.

Lily went for them at once, lit the candle and held it over the still motionless man. He was young, light skinned, his short hair neatly cut. She could see at once that his leg was broken; even though they'd laid him down as carefully as possible it was twisted to one side at an unnatural angle. There was blood on his shirt front, too, a great patch of it; more trickled down from inside a sleeve to edge between his fingers.

"Could you get my bag?" James said, gently feeling along the broken leg. "And some hot water and rags."

She lit a second candle, found the things he needed. As the water boiled she found cups. Might as well make a drink too; it was going to be a long night.

"What do you think?" she said, dabbing at James' face which was glistening with rain from the few minutes he'd been outside. He took the towel from her, ran it quickly over his head, dried his hands.

"He's been in some kind of accident. God knows how he got here in this state, it must have been agony to walk with that leg. He's got cuts, bruises. Might have cracked ribs too, I can't tell."

The man moaned briefly.

"You go to bed, Lily."

"But can't I do something? I'd like…"

"No." James began unbuttoning the man's shirt. "Go and get some sleep."

Go to bed, Lily. Do as you're told. It was always the same.

87

Longing to say she didn't want to, that she was quite capable of helping, might even surprise him if he gave her a chance, Lily knew it was wisest to say nothing. This wasn't the time.

She stood, left the room. The electricity was working again and she switched on the hallway light, blew out the candles. Once in bed she lay listening to the storm growing weaker, the thunder a distant grumbling now.

Why had she been so convinced it was Ernesto at the door? She thought of him as he'd sat looking out to sea, so still and self-contained; it was impossible to know what he'd been thinking. Maybe he was just sitting there looking out to sea. Who was it that had said these local people had no desires, ambitions, that they were content just to be? Someone at the party. It was meant, she suspected, as a criticism, but Lily wasn't so sure. She remembered Ernesto's hands holding the glass Natalia had given him, chunky hands, hands roughened by hard work. When he'd held onto her in the sea, pulled her along, they'd felt like hands you could rely on. The way, as a child, you know your father's hands will never fail you.

The man lying in their hallway didn't look strong. He looked like someone from the city.

Though she couldn't remember hearing James come to bed, he was curled up beside her when she awoke. Probably exhausted, she thought; even when she slid out of bed he didn't move.

The young man though was awake.

"I'm sorry," he said in Italian. James had somehow moved him into the drawing room, had piled cushions and blankets to make a temporary bed in the corner.

"What for?"

"For frightening you."

He attempted a smile.

"You didn't," Lily said. "Here."

She crouched down beside him, lifted his head and held the cup of milk to his lips. He wasn't from the area, that was for sure. His Italian was different, more precise, like the Italian spoken by the professor at the few classes she'd attended before leaving London. The local dialect was harsher, more guttural.

"Thank you," he said, in English this time. Well educated then. Or well travelled. As he closed his eyes, she tiptoed out.

James said he'd set the broken leg temporarily, but that he wanted to put a better splint on it. He still wasn't sure about internal injuries. Really he should get an X-ray done but that would mean taking the young man to a hospital and he wasn't in a fit state to travel. They'd just have to wait and hope. Certainly there were some nasty cuts, masses of bruising, but that should all heal, given time.

They'd finished their usual breakfast: *biscotti* with honey, a dark sweet variety from bees kept by the niece of the woman next door.

"Aren't you going to ask him what happened?" Lily said.

James shook his head. "He's in a state of shock, he needs rest. The questions can wait."

He stood, pushed his chair up against the table.

"When I undressed him last night I went through his pockets. There wasn't much, some money, a couple of photographs, one of an elderly couple, one of a girl. Across it was written To Paolo, with love."

"Paolo. It's a nice name."

James walked across to gaze out of the window. It was open and through it came a cool, damp smell that brought to mind green lawns dotted with daisies, deep leafy woods. He sighed, lowered his voice.

"Lily, I think we shouldn't let on that he's here. Not yet. The other thing I found in his jacket was a gun. I don't know what this is all about, but until we find out, it's best if he remains our secret."

"Of course," Lily said, her mouth suddenly dry.

And there she was thinking of him as the son of an upper class family, or at least a professional, a lawyer or something. He could be a thief, could have held up a bank, or broken into one of those villas on the outskirts of Naples, with wardrobes full of furs, ornately framed oil paintings on their walls. Did he panic and shoot someone, injure himself whilst making a desperate bid for freedom? They could be harbouring a dangerous murderer.

"I've hidden it," James said.

"Good." Lily resisted the temptation to ask where.

"So we tell no-one. Agreed?"

Lily nodded.

When he'd gone out she peered round the drawing room door. The young man was sleeping, head turned to one side, his mouth slightly open. Tiptoeing, she went and sat on a chair beside him, watching his chest rise and fall. She was tempted to push a strand of hair back from his forehead, but she might wake him. He didn't look like a criminal; he looked frail and vulnerable. Later she would go down into the village and get something special for him to eat.

With a start she realised she'd been sitting gazing at him for almost an hour.

She must get on, do something. She would check her plants. Out on the terrace she was growing things in pots: tomatoes, lettuces, some herbs. Because she missed her garden back home she'd also planted flowers, knowing it to be a foolish thing to do, that they would need constant watering and pampering, and would give nothing useful in return. She didn't care. Beautiful things always came expensive.

The rain, however had been heavy; there were leaves and petals all over the tiled floor, everything turned to brown papier mache. Beneath the jasmine that was growing up from somewhere below the terrace, entwining itself around the railings and drainpipes, whatever it could find, lay tiny white flowers, like snow flakes. Only the hibiscus with its tightly furled buds seemed unharmed.

Lily brought out the broom, started sweeping; found string and tied back sagging branches. As she worked she talked to the chickens who were clucking around picking at anything that caught their eye, just in case it was edible.

She'd written to her mother about the chickens. Her mother had replied saying – on the subject of pets – how much the dog missed her, at first he'd hardly eaten, had gone to skin and bones and they'd really worried about him, but that he was learning to live without her now. Lily had felt guilty. Then it occurred to her that her mother was, in her own way, saying she too missed Lily, wished she hadn't had to go off to live so far away. That made her feel twice as bad.

"*Signora?*" The voice came from inside the house.

Hurrying to him, it struck Lily that she was in charge, and that if he was worse, haemorrhaging or unable to breath, it would be up to her to do something.

With relief she saw that he'd managed to propped himself up on the cushions. If she had any to spare, he asked almost shyly, he'd very much like some more milk. She said of course, went to the tiny cupboard she called the pantry and brought out the almost empty jug. Whilst he sipped, she chatted on about it being goat's milk, fresh from the herd that made a round of the village, each goat taking it in turn to be milked. Back home, she said, milk was brought to the house by a horse drawn cart. She used to sneak carrots when her mother wasn't looking, loved the way the big gentle animal nuzzled them off the palm of her hand.

She wasn't sure that he understood much of what she was saying, but it didn't matter. As long as he understood that he was safe.

He lay back. Lily dabbed at milk on his chin.

"My jacket?" he said in English.

"It's in soak," she said. "Some of your other clothes too. In cold water, to remove the blood stains. Later I'll wash everything for you."

"In the pockets…"

He stopped. Of course: the gun.

"My husband emptied the pockets, put the photographs, money, everything in a safe place," she said. She emphasised the word everything. "Please don't worry. You must rest."

His exhaustion took over; he was having difficulty keeping his eyes open but he made an effort.

"What is your name?" he said.

"Lilian. I prefer to be called Lily though."

"Like the flower, yes? I'm Paolo, Paolo Bonora. Thank you for…"

She was about to say she'd done nothing, but he was asleep again, so abruptly it was as if he'd been switched off. She smoothed his blankets. It was nice having someone who needed you. Nurses must get this glow of satisfaction all the time. And those wonderful women who run soup kitchens for the families of men on strike. Or who fill their homes with stray cats. So, of course, must mothers; what needs more attention and help and loving than a new baby?

She wished… what did she wish?

That she'd married a different man, one who would encourage her rather than stifle her. But no, she loved James, didn't she? Not a different man, then, but a different James.

She wished she could grow her fingernails long, and have the courage to get her hair cut into a bob like in the magazines.

And she wished they'd never come to Italy. Not because she hated it – she didn't, quite the opposite – but because there was something about this place that was unsettling; about the people and the breathtakingly beautiful coastline and the light and that enormous ever-changing expanse of sky that somehow made her feel like... what? Like the strings of a violin, that was it. Taut, quivering.

Ten

$\mathcal{S}$he didn't need to find an excuse for going down towards the beach. The lower piazza was where everyone went if they needed the post office or bakers, or to buy groceries, or visit either of the two churches nearby: the little Chiesa dei Mulini or the one they could see from their window, the Chiesa Madre.

Sometimes Lily found herself walking alongside women carrying fat canvas bags that looked almost too heavy to lift, though they made no fuss. There was a public washing place reached by descending a flight of rough steps from the piazza, and though many women now had running water in their homes, they still liked to go there occasionally. To catch up with all the village gossip as they scrubbed, Lily supposed. Though snippets of news were exchanged on the road going down too, some too important to keep.

"*Titina e ancora incinta.* She's walking today to the church at Sant'Agnello."

Incinta meant pregnant. So why, Lily asked, was Titina walking to Sant'Agnello which was miles away, possibly a couple of hours walk each way.

The women glanced at each other, smiled.

"To be sure she has a son, yes?"

Lily smiled back, nodded. Boy babies were still preferred, boys being more useful, stronger, they would help provide food for the family. Many from the village went north, to other parts of Europe and even to America to work in factories and hotels, and sent back money. Good money.

Or there would be scandal. Don Giorgio, who was standing in for Don Federico whilst he visited the Vatican, was found asleep by the horse's water trough up on the main road, even though it was morning and he was due to take mass within the hour. His bloodshot eyes and stale breath gave him away. But then, everyone had their weaknesses and drink was a common one. It was understood and forgiven. After all, he may be a priest but he was also a man.

Or Lucia up in the mountains was marrying again, her fifth husband and her getting on for sixty, all the others at rest in the cemetery overlooking the sea, surrounded by cypress trees and peace.

"She's a witch, that woman. Her husbands, poor men, how hard she works them! Then, when they're exhausted, of no further use, she kills them."

More exchanged looks.

"*Il malocchio*, you understand?"

The evil eye? They didn't really believe that, surely? Maybe they just chose to, enjoying the thrill, like someone watching a horror film, alternating screams with nibbles of choc ice.

When they turned off Lily had that feeling she'd once had at school when she'd been left out of the Christmas nativity play. It had been for her own good; she'd had a chest infection, couldn't shake off a bad cough, and her teacher hadn't wanted to risk making her worse. But it had felt horrid, everyone else going for rehearsals, getting fitted for their robes. Even being allowed to paint the scenery hadn't helped.

Often Lily would stop for a drink at the cafe where she'd attended Natalia's party, sitting inside but near the door to get the breeze. Once she was joined by the grey plaited woman who turned out to be Austrian and a poet, and kept putting a hand on Lily's knee. Another time an elderly neighbour spotted her, asked if he could sit. Speaking slowly, waiting to make sure she understood, he told her of his concern about Italy's overseas policy, too aggressive, he said, lowering his voice before adding that people didn't want to be led into war by *Il Duce*. He looked behind him nervously. Someone should do something about him, he whispered.

Once she saw Sidney. Since their arrival he'd been away much of the time; gadding about, as he called it. She wished she was a writer, and had an excuse to gad about.

"Sounds more fun than it is," Sidney said. "All that travelling. Launches where you have to be polite to people you'd sooner punch. Parties that go on until the early hours when all you want to do is collapse into bed."

Looking closer, seeing more lines, a tightness around his mouth, Lily believed him.

"So now you're back you're going to take it easy, I hope?"

Sidney shrugged,

"For a bit. Must get started on the next novel, though. My publishers are already getting anxious to see something."

She'd forgotten how hard he pushed himself. He's trying to compensate for something, James had once said; an emptiness in his life. Even back then she'd wondered if James was talking about himself.

Most often she sat there alone, scanning the beach, the boats, the steps that led up past the cafe. If anyone had asked she'd have said she was just watching the world go by. When at last she saw Ernesto, though, she was embarrassed to feel a blush begin. He was walking past with two men; they were arguing, their voices loud, their hands going in all directions to emphasise points.

He saw her, nodded briefly, continued with his argument, and she felt her stomach drop. After some minutes she finished her drink and paid. As she pushed back the chair, he touched the shoulder of one of the men as though to say wait, walked across to her.

"*Signora Liliana*," he said. He didn't smile and she suddenly realised he hardly had that day of the picnic, two or three times at most.

"Ernesto. How are you?" she said in Italian.

"*Bene, grazie*. And you?"

How polite they were. Looking down she noticed his feet were still bare and thought how well formed they were, each toe perfectly straight. Hers were all scrunched up after years of being stuffed into shoes with high heels or pointed toes.

"You want to go to the island again?"

"No. I mean, yes. One day. It was lovely there."

He stared at her.

"I'll take you. Whenever you want to go, you say. I'll teach you how to swim."

They'd moved out into the sun now. She could feel perspiration on her upper lip, dabbed at it with a handkerchief.

"We must ask Natalia when she'll be free."

"Without her would be better. You and I."

"Oh I don't think my husband…"

Why did she say that? She was turning his innocent

invitation into something else. His expression didn't change.

"You tell him. Tell him I am an honest man, he can trust me."

Lily nodded, said she would do that.

"When you want," Ernesto said. He turned abruptly, went back to his friends who were looking on in silence. She'd been brought up to think it bad manners to stare, but here everyone did it all the time. She found it unnerving. But then, it was her own fault. She'd come to the beach in search of Ernesto. She'd put herself in a situation where she must expect to be stared at.

What on earth was she thinking of?

As she climbed the steps back up to the house she vowed to stay away from the beach.

It wasn't as though she had nothing to do at home. Paolo was getting stronger each day: he was able to sit now, even move about if he held onto things and took it slowly. Yet still he couldn't be left alone for too long. James had had what he described as a man-to-man with him, choosing his surgery as the setting to add the appropriate atmosphere. But as far as Lily knew, he still hadn't learnt much. Paolo's age: twenty five. That he came from Milan where he'd taught for a while, but then given up to concentrate on politics. He'd come to James because James was American. Did he think Italian doctors were inferior? Lily asked, and James had said no, it was nothing to do with that. She suspected then that he knew more than he was telling her.

"Do you like boiled eggs?" she asked Paolo "Our chickens are laying now. Not many, but that's our fault. We should feed them better."

Paolo was wearing James's dressing gown; he'd pulled it close around him, tied the cord belt twice.

"Boiled eggs. How English."

"Have you been to England?"

He nodded. Yes, three times. He liked England very much. And America, not that he'd been there yet but he hoped to one day. He would visit New York, and walk around the rim of the Grand Canyon, and listen to jazz in New Orleans. He couldn't imagine so much space, such freedom. Of speech, too. That was something he especially admired about both America and England: people being able to say what they believed without fear.

"Fear of what?" Lily was intrigued.

Paolo shrugged. "How do you say it – listening ears?" He smiled. "And yes, I would love a boiled egg."

It was pleasant, Lily decided, having someone else in the house. James was rarely there, or when he was he was busy in his surgery. Sometimes she wondered what he could be doing in there. On bad days she was convinced he was avoiding her, found her boring, preferring his books for company. Most days she accepted that she was being over-sensitive. He loved her, no question about it. But building up a practice in a new area let alone a new country, that was never going to be easy. Especially when the people were so poor. And even harder when, like James, you had ideals that meant you couldn't say no to someone in need, never.

She'd pulled the table close to the open door, though they couldn't eat breakfast out on the terrace. Paolo had said it would be better if no-one knew he was there. James said he'd already understood that. No-one mentioned the gun.

"And real English tea. My last packet."

The gold liquid steamed as she poured.

"You're very generous," Paolo said, sipping. "You know, you remind me of *mia fidanzata*, Lucia. Your husband is a lucky man."

Lily handed Paolo a spoon.

"Eat. Don't let the egg get cold."

His appetite was improving. In seconds he was scraping the inside of the speckled shell. Lily – who hadn't yet started her egg – passed it to him and after a half-hearted attempt to refuse, he ate that too.

"And this Lucia, when do you plan to marry her?"

Paolo sat back in his chair, gazed out of the door at the dazzling white world outside. A bee droned past, hovered as though about to come in and then was gone. He shook his head slowly.

"It's not so easy. There are problems."

He picked up his spoon, started to tap it against a plate, then suddenly aware of what he was doing he put it back down.

"It'll be alright," she said, wanting to comfort him but not knowing how. "I know it will. And you'll both have long happy lives together."

"Like you and James. I hope so."

Oh Paolo, she thought, how young you are. Or had she grown suddenly old? She poured the last of the tea.

An invitation came from Natalia. To luncheon. They would sit – her note said – in a cool room filled with the sounds of ice tinkling in tall glasses and fans whirring as they discussed Freud and opera and Taoism. At least, it said something like that; her writing reminded Lily of a scrunched up hair net.

James was of course included.

"Lily, you know I can't go off in the middle of the day. What if someone needs me?"

"You could leave a note saying where you are."

James was trying to repair the handle of his stethoscope which was coming loose. If he couldn't he'd have to order one from Sorrento, possibly from Rome, which would take forever.

"You go."

He was infuriating. Back home, when he'd had invitations he felt obliged to accept, she'd never once refused to accompany him, had attended so many boring functions she'd joked about the fixed smile on her face needing to be surgically removed. Yet when she asked him to go somewhere with her, he made excuses.

And this encouraging her to go alone was new. Was it because they were far away from the people who mattered, those who would have judged it as odd, him letting his wife go gadding about without him? Or did he not expect her to go?

Well, he was in for a surprise.

Following instructions she found the house easily, the heavy wooden door left ajar as promised. Her shoes clipped on the wide white staircase as she spiralled upwards. When Natalia had said she had a flat, Lily had imagined something small and modest. She should have suspected.

At the top of the house, another door, also open. Tentatively, Lily peered inside. Natalia was standing silhouetted against the window, came towards her with arms outstretched, on her shoulder the infamous monkey, a shaggy golden creature with eyes that were disturbingly human. Delighted, Lily reached up to it, but it screeched, bounced down and across the room and then up onto the table where it crouched looking sulky. After a moment it picked up a salt cellar and began banging it. The table, Lily noticed, was set for eight.

"What a beautiful room!"

As described, it was cool, spacious. Huge green plants

filled corners, their leaves shuffling as electric fans – one each end of the room – whirred silently overhead. Above the table a chandelier that looked as though it weighed a ton hung on a very long chain from a ceiling that was painted with angels, clouds, rainbows.

"It used to be a palazzo," Natalia said handing Lily a glass of something with leaves floating in it. "Part of one anyway."

She retrieved the salt cellar from the monkey who bounded off to sit on the head of a tiger skin rug, yanking at the ears. He reminded Lily of a spoilt child seeking attention. What he needed was a good spanking.

"Hello there."

A head from around a door that presumably led to a kitchen, if the food smells were anything to go by. It was one of the two young men who had been with Natalia on that first day. A moment later the other one appeared.

"Hans and Dieter. You've met, of course. They, darling, are the most divine cooks."

Natalia gently nudged the monkey with her foot. It made an angry clicking sound and started on the tiger's whiskers.

"Which is wonderful, as I'm the world's worst."

There were more arrivals: a shy young couple, the girl like a doll with freckles across her delicate nose, eyes that kept blinking, the boy very thin, his cropped hair revealing large pink ears. They were Dutch, Natalia said. Musicians. Behind them came the woman with the grey plait. Nodding hello she kicked off her shoes, sat cross legged on the sofa, and lit a cigarette.

Lily was relieved that everyone seemed to be speaking English, well, most of the time. Flattered to think they were doing it for her, she suddenly realised it was the one language they all shared.

Natalia clapped for attention.

"Food's ready!"

There were names written on pink card – each with a pink rosebud attached – showing everyone where to sit. Lily ended up between Dieter and the shy girl who looked unwell, as though she was anaemic or on the verge of a nervous breakdown. Lily ought to send her to James.

The last guest arrived, an older man, long grey hair, rings on every finger. He was breathless, claimed to have run all the way which had made him sweaty; he lifted his arms, attempted to sniff under them, grimaced and then took his place at the table. Lily thought she detected a Scots accent.

Natalia leant towards her.

"Donald is a hypnotist. So if you want to explore your deepest feelings – if you dare – he's your man."

"Or who you were in your last life," Donald said through a mouth full of bread. "Or any of your past lives."

Plates of curling green pasta were passed along. The shy couple gave each other encouraging smiles.

"I know who I was," grey plait said. "Joan of Arc."

"Darling, wasn't everyone?" That was Natalia.

"Or Florence Nightingale, Julius Caesar, Shakespeare. Strange that, whenever someone claims to remember a past life they were never a plain, ordinary nobody."

"Could it be the other way round? That you only get to come back again if you've done something worthwhile with your first life?"

"Black pepper. Who has the black pepper?"

"Tell you what I'd like to know." It was the shy girl. Though her voice wasn't much more than a whisper – or maybe because of it – everyone paused to listen.

"Not who I was in the past, but who I'm going to be next."

"Ah." The hypnotist looked at her for a moment, then went back to twisting tagliatelle around his fork, cramming it

103

into his mouth. Easy to see how he got that paunch, Lily thought.

"You're going to be a world famous concert pianist," Natalia said. "Trust me, I know these things. You have so much talent, it's sure to spill over into your next life. Like Mozart."

"And me?"

"What about me?"

The two young men had emerged from the kitchen to join the table.

"You, Dieter, are going to be a rich, fat capitalist with servants and a yacht and…"

Lily stopped listening. She let the sound of voices, the sudden soft laughter, wash over her like waves. She thought to herself, here I am sitting at an elegant table with all these lovely people, my bohemian friends, having delicious food served to me, drinking from heavy crystal glasses, and feeling cool as a cumber whilst the world outside sizzles.

Under the table she eased off her shoes.

She was drinking too much again, but it wasn't her fault. Life here seemed to revolve around food and drink. Eating, drinking, talking. The drinks helped her relax, of course. She'd always been a little tense in company, too aware of herself, worried she might say the wrong thing.

"…for turnips. They say that was one of the biggest expenses, supplying the turnips that they had to eat on stage each night. Raw turnips. Can you imagine?"

Lily knew at once what they were talking about.

"My husband, James, he saw it. Tobacco Road. When he was in New York a few years ago."

"Lucky man. What did he think of it?"

Suddenly she knew she had to be careful. James had thought it went too far, was too realistic. He was so conventional. These people weren't; they pushed boundaries.

"He… he was very impressed."

The conversation switched to books. Lily hadn't heard of half of them, had read next to none. At home she'd read magazines, the occasional twopenny library romance. She'd tried the classics but found them mostly rather hard going.

She recognised the names though: Hemingway, D. H. Lawrence, Virginia Woolf, William Faulkner.

"I don't read much," she said, finding herself suddenly on the spot, her opinion being sought. "Keeping house, helping James with his work…"

"Darling, you must make time." Natalia shook her head in mock disgust. "Let the dust gather, leave the bed unmade. Tell handsome James he must cook his own tea."

Really, Natalia did have some shocking ideas.

And then, after what seemed like hours, the meal was over and everyone drifted away from the table. The shy girl was steered towards a piano, Grieg's piano concerto in A minor was requested, and after sorting through a stack of sheet music, the girl began to play. Lily wandered over to the window, watched two boys who were sitting on a doorstep below, dark heads touching, plotting some naughtiness no doubt.

Natalia stood beside her, whispered.

"Come with me. I want to show you something."

She led Lily to her bedroom, started to rummage in a chest of drawers. Lily walked around the room noting the bedside lamp with its heavy fringe, the tapestry bedspread, ornate bottles on the dressing table. On the walls were a series of what she took to be prints. She looked closer, then pulled back. They were starkly drawn nudes, stick thin girls wearing stockings, with sad, dull eyes, many with their legs spread wide.

"Egon Shiele. Do you like his work?"

Lily suspected she didn't.

"Yes. To be honest, I don't know it."

Natalia laughed.

"Success," she said.

She'd found what she was looking for, a paper package that she handed to Lily. Inside was a pair of stockings, pale, the colour of pearls, their texture unlike anything Lily had seen before.

"They're not silk, are they?"

"No. They're nylon. It's the very latest thing. A friend sent me two pairs from America so I thought, why not give one pair to Lily? Here, sit on the bed."

Lily did as she was told.

Natalia knelt at her feet. Carefully she folded one of the stockings down into a coil, then she slid it over Lily's toes, her heel, gradually unfolded it up over her calf, her knee, up along her thigh. Gently she ran her hand the length of Lily's leg, smoothing the fabric with her palm.

"Doesn't that feel amazing?" she said.

Through the half open door came the sound of the piano. It was dim in the room, the shutters drawn, airless. Lily felt a bead of perspiration slither down between her shoulder blades.

"It does," she said, the words catching in her throat. She rearranged her skirt, stood and crossed over to a mirror where she could see the effect of the stocking.

"But Natalia, they were a gift to you."

"Please, I want you to have them. You have such fine legs, a beautiful body too, and you hide it away and seem to be ashamed of it rather than enjoying it. Such a waste."

She met Lily's eyes in the mirror.

"Take the stockings. Wear them one evening when you're dressing up for a very special occasion. Will you do that? For me?"

But it's wrong to take pride in your body, Lily wanted to

say. Worse still to take pleasure in it.

"I will. I promise."

Whatever happened she would treasure them. She took the stocking off carefully, folded it, replaced it in the paper.

"Now I really must be off."

She hadn't noticed how late it was getting. Soon James would start feeling hungry, then anxious. Then, when she did appear, he'd drop hints about her absence, how he really didn't ask much of her, and she'd feel guilty, and the day would be ruined. And she couldn't bear that.

"Of course."

No-one else seemed to be in a hurry to leave. Donald was stretched out on a sofa, eyes closed, snoring. At the other end of the same sofa the monkey too was asleep, curled up on the lap of the shy girl who was deep in conversation with Dieter. Or was it Hans? The young Dutch man was now sitting at the piano playing Christmas carols using two fingers.

"Wait," Natalia said, and hurried back to the bedroom. She returned with three books.

"Read them. You'll enjoy them."

"So many gifts!" Lily said. It felt like a birthday. "And Natalia, we must go over to the island again, have another picnic. If you really think we won't get into trouble for trespassing."

"Darling, we might well get into trouble." Natalia shrugged sharp shoulders. "Taking risks. It's what makes life worth living, don't you think?"

Running down the white stairs, Lily clutched the books to her as though they were kittens, precious little lives that had to be protected at all costs.

Eleven

*W*hen she got back to the house, there was an envelope. It had been pushed under the door as both she and James were out, and Paolo – James had stressed the point – wasn't to answer a knock, no matter how urgent it may sound.

Though it was addressed to James, Lily opened it.

> *Gentile signor,* it said. *The carabinieri are searching for a man called Paolo Bonora who they wish to question about acts against the state. We believe you may know of his whereabouts. If so, we want only to warn you so that you can take appropriate action on his and your own behalf.*
> It was signed, *Your friends in freedom.*

"You're wanted by the police?" she said.

Paolo turned away.

"Yes," he said quietly. "For trying to stop what Mussolini is doing to this country and its people."

"Not for… anything else? You haven't stolen anything? Or hurt or killed anyone?"

She hated asking the question though she knew she had to. She knew the answer too. He was not the kind of man to use physical violence; he was a thinker, an idealist.

"No, Lily. I swear to you. How can I make you…?"

There was a sound at the front door and for a moment they both held their breath. It was James. Lily handed him the note without speaking. He read it quickly.

"OK. As soon as it's dark we'll get you moved further south. It's too soon, but we have no choice."

Paolo started to thank him but James held up his hand. He had to go out again, he said. There were some people he needed to contact, plans to be made.

"Lock the door," he said. "Don't answer it to anyone."

Lily didn't ask any more questions. Instead she went to the kitchen to make sandwiches for Paolo to take with him; the bread wasn't that fresh, but it was all she had. He probably wouldn't eat them anyway, but it was what women did when their loved ones went away. Made sandwiches.

He was sitting on a chair by the window, his favourite position. As she went up to him he turned to her, pressed his face against her waist, and after a moment's hesitation she put her arms around his shoulders, smoothing the back of his neck. His hair was getting long; she'd thought about offering to cut it, but too late now.

"I'm going to miss you," she said.

For a long moment he didn't speak.

"I'll miss you too," he said, his voice thick.

She pulled away, took his hands and sat facing him.

"Paolo, will you get in touch with us, when you can? I'd like to know that everything is OK. Please?"

109

He held the back of her hand against his face, touched it with his lips. He looked so much older than he'd looked that first morning.

"Of course."

Then he stood, said he must gather his few things together.

James returned to say it was all arranged. He would go down with Paolo to the road where they'd be met. There was a farmer outside Salerno who would take him in for a week or two, give him time to get stronger, though then he would have to move on again.

After the two men left, Lily found the gun. She was confused: James must have given it back to him then. And if so, why hadn't Paolo taken it with him? It was wrapped in a checked handkerchief and had been left beside their bed. With it was a note; everyone is writing notes today, she thought.

> *I have no money to pay for your help and kindness, so please take this instead. There is, I believe, no way it can be traced back to me. It will be easy to sell, and should fetch a fair price. I won't forget you, either of you, ever.*

She balanced it on her open palm. It was a small gun, square in shape, lighter than she expected, the dark wood handle warm to touch. Beretta it said on the side. Was it loaded? Did it take bullets or a cartridge? She had no idea how to tell. Tomorrow, she'd take it, go up above the village and throw it where no-one would ever find it.

Meanwhile, she wrapped the gun again, put it to the back of a drawer.

By now they'd be down on the main road, Paolo huddled

in the shadows on the steps even though it was dark, not even a moon tonight. James would be sitting on the wall on the other side of the road, looking out for the truck that was to dip its lights three times, a signal he was to acknowledge by switching his torch on and off three times. If any of the villagers saw him waiting there, what would they think? That he had a secret lover, probably. It was what everyone who behaved suspiciously was accused of here. *Perché no?* the gossips would add with a lift of the eyebrows and a shrug. Why not?

Lily wasn't worried about the gossips, not right now. It was Paolo she was thinking about, closing her eyes and asking a God she wasn't quite sure she believed in to please keep him safe.

Twelve

"So tell me about him."

"Lilian, it's late, I'm exhausted. Couldn't we sleep now and talk about it in the morning?"

"How can I sleep? I've been lying here, my mind going round in circles since he left. You got me involved when you got me to help care for him. I have a right to some answers."

She paused. They were stretched out side by side on the bed, not touching.

"You know, don't you? What happened, why the police are after him. You've known for some time."

She heard James sigh, felt him reach up and link his hands behind his head.

"Yes. Not at first, but bit by bit. I've been unsure about telling you. The less you know, the better, should anything happen. You know, if anyone should start asking questions."

"James, for heaven's sake! I'm your wife. We vowed to share things, remember?"

In sickness and in health, for better or worse, she recited silently. And they were getting worse, that was for sure. Each day the space between them seemed to grow wider.

The rare impatience in her voice worked.

"OK. Like a lot of young, intellectual Italians, Paolo cares passionately about his country and the way it is now. Like young intellectuals everywhere, I guess. Anyway, that means he's anti-fascist."

"And anti Mussolini."

"Right."

She thought of recent conversations she'd had, and overheard.

"Aren't most people?"

"Some, yes. Not most. Despite his recent blunders he's still a powerful man, people shouldn't underestimate him. They shouldn't make their discontent too obvious either."

"And Paolo did?"

"He planned to. He'd read about someone back in the early thirties, I've forgotten his name. Anyway he – this hero of Paolo's – had flown over Rome dropping leaflets denouncing the government as corrupt and tyrannical, and encouraging everyone to fight fascism, not to attend ceremonies, to give up smoking."

"Why give up smoking?"

"I'm not sure. Something about the regime using the revenue from cigarette sales? You get the idea anyway."

"What happened to the man?"

"No-one knows. Never seen again. Some believed he ran out of fuel, others that he was shot down."

"And so Paolo thought he'd do the same?"

"Exactly. Only he didn't even get as far as Rome. He had a pilot license already so that was no problem. He hired a plane down in Sicily. Others in the movement helped pay, he said, for the leaflets too. They'd had literally thousands of them printed."

Lily pictured it: early morning and misty, a small plane on an airstrip in a remote part of Sicily. She saw Paolo, pale and yet calm, refusing to think about the risks, the very real chance that he might fail, might die even. Would Lucia have been there? Would she have clung to him, pressing her face into his shoulder so as to hide the tears?

A donkey brayed as it passed nearby, stumbling under a load of hay. In the air, a smell of wild herbs; a breeze brushed against the olive trees making them ripple and glitter, as though someone had attached silver streamers.

Disentangling himself from the girl, kissing her lightly on plum red lips, Paolo would have climbed into the cockpit, pulled on his helmet, goggles. Someone started the propeller turning, the engine caught, the sudden noise startling a flock of birds. She saw the plane trundle along the flat dry land then lift off, light and fragile as a moth. It circled once and those left on the ground saw him quite clearly, his hand lifted in a wave.

Lucia would have looked away.

"And?" Lily said.

"He hadn't been flying long, was still over water, when he became aware of a plane following him. A government plane, he suspected. When it got no closer he thought maybe he was mistaken, imaging things. But just south of Naples he was fired at, a direct hit, his plane started spinning."

"Good heavens."

He must have been petrified, Lily thought, convinced this was it, he was going to die.

"He said all he could think about was what a waste. That he had all those leaflets to deliver yet."

"It's a miracle that he survived, surely?"

"He was thrown clear, the plane exploded. It still had a fair amount of fuel in the tank, of course. He thinks the explosion saved him, reckons his attackers probably figured no-one could survive it."

"They didn't check?"

"Seems not." James chuckled. "He said leaflets were everywhere, and still fluttering down as he lay there. He thought, well at least a few of them might get read."

"But his injuries, all those cuts, the broken leg. How did he manage to get here?"

"A peasant and his son were working on their vineyard nearby. The peasant piled Paolo onto a cart and took him home, got his wife to patch him up. But they could see that he needed proper medical attention. Besides, sooner or later officials were sure to check out the wrecked plane. When the leaflets were discovered, and no body found, the police would…"

"Start looking. Of course. But so why bring him here?"

"God knows how they knew about me, but it seems they figured an American would be more likely to have the same political bias. They took the risk, left him down on the road. Somehow he managed to drag himself up the steps."

Lily didn't like to think about it, it was too awful.

"Will he be alright?"

"Hopefully. He has friends, they'll get him back down to Sicily where he can go into hiding until he's well again."

Lily sensed James turning towards her, thought for a moment that he might reach out and hold her but he didn't. She wished he would.

"Lilian, we have to face the fact that the police may well find out he came here. There'll be no point in my denying it, but I can insist I knew nothing about him. As I doctor I have a duty to treat anyone who needs help, even they can't dispute that. I'll say I did what had to be done, that he was here for a week or so and then went on his way, I've no idea where to."

Lily felt her pulse quicken.

Betrayal, police, planes being shot down in flames. It was another world. She'd known there was political unrest in Italy, that the fascist regime was becoming increasingly unpopular, that some people were openly rebelling. But that was all happening elsewhere, in the north, the cities, not here. Here in the south they would be immune. And apart from the fascist emblem carved onto the stone portals of some doorways, the drab little government office alongside the Chiesa dei Mulini where one bespectacled man sat behind a desk and shuffled papers, there had been nothing to make her think otherwise. She didn't want her paradise to be spoiled, dragged into the real world with all its turmoil and fear. It wasn't fair.

"James…"

Suddenly she was frightened.

"They won't arrest you, haul you off in the middle of the night, will they?"

James gave a small dry sound. It could have been an attempt at a laugh. If only he'd put his arms around her. Like a child she longed to be hugged, to feel the warmth of another body, the strength of two arms about her. After bad dreams her mother used to tuck her up with a piece of liquorice as a treat. She wanted liquorice now.

"Of course not. I'm an American. Besides, I've done nothing wrong."

James pecked at her cheek.

"You mustn't worry, Lily. Promise me you won't."

Even before she replied he'd turned away from her and she knew their conversation was over.

"I'll try," she said.

Outside a dog started barking, the sound echoing across the valley, and Lily imagined it chained up somewhere, thin, hungry, wanting someone to fuss and love it.

Thirteen

The hibiscus flowers lasted just one day. Each morning there were new blossoms, buttermilk white, large flowers that could have been made of satin, their stamens like fine gold tassels. They had no smell. By evening they would be folding, shrivelling, and some time during the night they would drop. Lily was convinced she heard them.

In the morning there would be new flowers.

Such brief lives she thought, sad in a way. And yet that was what made the beauty of the flowers so much more precious.

She was sitting out on the terrace under the bamboo shade they'd had put up. Antonio had arrived one morning, a ladder over his broad shoulders, insisting she would fry if she didn't have shade. Like fish, he said, making a sizzling sound.

The sun through the shade drew stripes across her flowered dress, her legs, her bare feet resting on a chair.

Maybe that's what's wrong with marriage, she thought. It

goes on too long and people expect it to stay as it was to begin with, full of wonder and magic, when how can it? It's like a flower that has gone past its best. It grows brown around the edges, it droops, begins to smell stale.

"*Un buon matrimonio.* You have a good marriage, you are lucky."

He'd said it, Antonio, balanced above her, the sun a halo around his head so that she had to squint to look up at him. He reached down; she passed him another nail.

He'd been talking about his parents, married thirty years that very day. They had a good marriage too, he said. Sure they fight sometimes, but then they have an excuse to make up again afterwards. He'd winked.

"It's important for a man to have someone to share his life," Antonio said.

"True."

"A wife who is there when you come home, who cooks for you, cleans, grows flowers. And makes babies, lots of babies, yes?"

He'd come down the ladder, winked again.

Did he know she and James had none? Maybe he thought they'd children back in England. She wasn't going to say anything, it was none of his business anyway. She'd excused herself, gone inside.

And her parents; was theirs a good marriage? She'd always thought so. At least they'd grown to look more like each other as the years went by, their eyes fading to the same pale grey, their hands freckling, a gentle curve to both their spines. Not that looking alike proved anything.

Cissy was scared of getting married. She denied it, but Lily knew better. She'd turned down a number of proposals, always with some pathetic excuse or other.

"Admit it," Lily had said more than once.

119

"What rubbish, of course I'm not scared. But I'll tell you one thing. You think having a man to run around is the key to happiness…"

"I do not!"

"Whereas I have no intention of being someone's unpaid housekeeper. I'm going to be independent, even if I meet the right man and get married. He's going to have to understand that."

Lily had always considered herself to be nothing like her sister. Nowadays, though, she began to suspect differently.

The sun had moved round to drop down behind the mountains but it was still hot, the air thick and heavy. Lily picked up the fan James had bought for her from a travelling salesman, a pretty thing with geisha girls and bridges, but it didn't make much difference.

She went back to reading.

It was one of the books Natalia had given her, and she thought it the most moving story she'd ever read, full of jealous rages and sulky silences and hearts beating like bewildered birds. Women in Love, it was called. One phrase stuck in her mind: a dark flood of electric passion. She'd no idea what it meant, but it sounded wonderful.

Of course, real life wasn't anything like that, not even today, and the book was written over fifteen years ago. How many of her friends back home believed in free love? How many were actually excited by the idea of making love with their husbands?

Lily had seen more than enough of the women who used to come to James, working class women old before they were forty, thirty even, their sagging bodies sucked dry by the hoards of children who trailed around behind them, silent urchins with runny noses and empty eyes.

She remembered some of the things the women did to try

to avoid getting pregnant again, things with chunks of lemon, or vinegar washes, or cotton wool daubed with Vaseline. For them sex must be worse than a duty; it must be a nightmare. Lying in bed waiting for your husband to return from the pub; hearing him clumping up the stairs, cussing as he stumbles; telling the children to go off to the other room and shut the door, just for a bit, you'll give them some bread and jam later, and the children scuttling out, tittering nervously.

Where was the passion in that?

A flickering movement caught Lily's eye: a flower had dropped from the hibiscus, and she reached for it, held it against her face. She went back to her reading.

When she looked up again it was evening and getting dark. She rested her head against the back of her chair and studied the sky, the blue now fading to a soft grey, but still not a cloud in sight. For the briefest moment she missed the English summer with its persistent drizzle that she used to complain made her hair frizz, but that also made the roses more fragrant, trees greener, the blackberries plump and sweet.

She went inside feeling suddenly dizzy, blaming it on the book. Reading could do that, could disorientate you. She would have a splash with cold water, that would bring her back to herself. Then she'd start preparing the fresh sardines she'd got for their evening meal, the tiny silver fish that tasted nothing like the tinned ones they used to have on toast back home. James liked his meal to be ready when he returned.

She took off her blouse, poured water into the bowl in the bedroom and splashed it over her neck, her shoulders. Glancing at herself in the mirror that hung above the commode she stopped, fascinated at the way the beads of water slithered across her skin, little rivulets joining up with each other. Her brassiere was getting soaked and – after a moment's hesitation – she reached behind her and unfastened it. Still watching herself she put her hands under her breasts, felt their weight, their soft warmth, the dampness in the fold beneath them where she'd been perspiring. The skin was very white, her nipples brown as berries. Even as she watched they seemed to harden.

What was it Natalia had said? You have a beautiful body. You should enjoy it, not be ashamed.

In the distance she could hear church bells tolling for evening mass.

Fourteen

*E*rnesto's hands.

Had she thought of Ernesto's hands that day? Lily couldn't remember, she doubted it. Now though she saw them: the short square nails, the scar on the inner wrist of his left hand. From a fight, he'd said; a drunk with a broken bottle. Now she imagined the smell of them, the feel of them.

But first, Ernesto's hands catching the lizard.

He'd come to the house one afternoon; James had been off helping to deliver a baby. There had been a knock at the door, a confident knock, and her immediate reaction had been it's the police come to arrest James. She'd debated not answering, had waited for a while hoping whoever it was would give up, assume the house to be empty. Then, the knocking again.

When she found it was Ernesto, she was overcome with relief.

"I'm sorry, my husband isn't here."

"I know. He's with a neighbour of mine."

Again she felt nervous, as though the ground had shifted slightly. So why was he here? She reached out and rested her hand on the door, as though about to shut it.

"May I come in? For a few minutes only? To talk?"

He was so polite. She opened the door again.

"I'm sitting out on the terrace," she said. "It's cooler out there."

He followed her and she thought how strange it felt to have him here with her in the house. On her territory, so to speak.

Outside, she turned to face him.

"So why are you here?"

"To see you. I wanted to see you."

She was furious at the small tingle of pleasure that made her want to smile, though she managed not to.

"Why?"

"Because I think of you all the time. Because I think you too feel something special for me."

There was little or no emotion in his voice; he was simply stating a fact. How arrogant of him, she thought, trying to put aside the fact that he was right. And what did he expect her to say?

And then, a scratching sound above their heads. Lily looked up, saw the outline of a small animal passing quickly across the bamboo shade. As it darted down the wall beside her she took an involuntary step back.

"*Una lucertola*," he said. "You're not afraid of lizards are you?"

"No, of course not."

Ernesto turned and, as the lizard reached the tiled floor, he pounced. Lily thought of a cat, so quickly had he moved.

He held his cupped hands out to her.

"*Tieni*," he said. He was calling her bluff, wanted her to hold it.

She stepped close, peered down as he opened his hands a crack and she saw a small head, one foot emerging between his fingers. Tentatively she reached, touched the foot; it withdrew.

"Poor thing," she said. "It's petrified."

"I let it go?"

She nodded, and he dropped it onto the terrace rail where it scuttled along briefly before plunging from sight.

"You too. Are you frightened of me?" he said, looking straight at her.

"Should I be?"

She made herself meet his eyes.

He caught her hand, lifted it. For a moment she thought he would brush it with his lips, a formal kiss, but no. He took the tips of her fingers into his mouth and touched them with his tongue, a flickering movement, his mouth hot and moist.

"Like a lizard, yes?" he said.

Lily was mesmerised. Part of her was indignant, as she knew she ought to be, as any decent woman would be. At the same time she felt strangely excited.

"Please stop," she said. "My husband, your wife…"

He laughed, removed her fingers from his mouth but held onto her hand.

"Your husband, yes. But me, I have no wife."

The sound of a distant door thumping shut made Lily jump. Still Ernesto held onto her hand and she had to pull it free, did so just as James peered out.

"James, you're back quickly. How did it go?"

She hoped he didn't notice the quiver in her voice.

"Fine, a nice easy birth. A boy too, so everyone's delighted. I've never seen so much black curly hair on a new baby."

She knew she ought to explain Ernesto's presence, was struggling to think what to say. Turning to him she was relieved to find his attention now on James.

He'd come for some cough medicine, he said. He'd always had a cough, probably because he smoked too much, but lately it had got worse. It was keeping him awake nights.

James beckoned and the two men went back into the house. Lily stayed where she was, nodded goodbye when Ernesto put his head around the door to say he was leaving.

It was as though she'd been given a gift. Pearl earrings in a box lined with velvet the colour of Devonshire soil; she'd been to Devon and thought it the most beautiful place in the world, before she came to Italy anyway. Or chocolates too pretty to be eaten, each one topped with a candied violet.

Ernesto. She said his name to herself.

James was telling her about yet another case of the evil eye, an old man taken to his bed in the belief that he was seriously ill, though there were no symptoms, he was amazingly well considering his age.

"You might find it amusing," James said. "But people die simply because they believe they've been cursed."

Lily hadn't realised she was smiling.

"I was thinking of something else, sorry. So did you manage to convince him?"

"I doubt it. The mind is more powerful than anyone ever realised. Up until now, that is."

He talked on, mentioned Freud, Jung, dreams. New thinking on hysteria, which was what this was in a way: a hysterical response to fear of the supernatural. It would be interesting to go into the effects of the evil eye in this area, he said. If he ever had time he would do some research, write up his findings. He might even get them published.

"I wish you would," Lily said.

James looked up, surprised.

"You do?"

"Yes."

"Because?"

"Because you'd do a brilliant job, and I'd be even more proud of you than I am now."

He looked genuinely pleased, though it could have been because she'd actually been listening to his ramblings. Just a few hours earlier she'd been thinking how it wasn't surprising she was flattered by Ernesto's attentions; James had long ago given up complimenting her, or even noticing her. He may still love her, but he took her for granted.

Now it occurred to her that this worked both ways.

Still, at least if he felt neglected he wouldn't be off flirting with another woman. He wouldn't sink to that.

When Lily called on Natalia – uninvited, but Natalia had said to call in any time and she did want to return the books – Ernesto was still on her mind. Not that she would tell Natalia that he'd come to the house, that was between him and her. But Natalia knew him, could tell her things.

"Darling. What a splendid surprise."

Natalia was wearing what looked like a silk nightdress. Had Lily got her out of bed? But it was nearly midday.

"Come on in."

As last time, the room was like a green oasis, and Lily thought how she'd never go outside if she lived here, at least not during the day. There was a smell of coffee; on a low table, a jug and cup. Lily dropped down onto the sofa beside what looked like a dead bird, but turned out to be a hat. Natalia was decorating it with feathers. Feathers gave it panache, she said.

"Look. What do you think?"

She settled it on her head at an angle, rested her hands on her hips, sauntered across the room. It was the most ridiculous outfit, yet somehow, on Natalia, it looked stunning.

"I'd be sneezing, with all those feathers!"

Natalia laughed, dropped it onto the table, went to the kitchen and returned with a matching cup. She pushed the jug towards Lily, picked up her own cup and drank thirstily.

"So how is everything with you and the handsome doctor?"

"Alright, I suppose."

"Suppose. Ah. There's a damning word."

Natalia lifted her feet up onto the sofa, looked intently at Lily over toe nails that this time were painted gold. Lily noticed how bumpy and misshapen her feet were; if she had feet like that she'd keep her shoes on.

"You haven't had a row, have you?"

"No, we have not." Lily could hear how defensive she sounded.

"I can't imagine the good doctor losing his temper. He might scowl, make tutting noises."

Natalia didn't like James. But she should realise that Lily would stand up for him. It was what wives did.

"You're right. He's from Boston. His parents weren't rich, but he was their only child, and they were determined that he'd have a good education, be brought up a gentleman."

"But Lily, men who behave like gentlemen are so boring."

The monkey, who'd been sitting quietly on the back of the sofa, now edged along and started picking at Lily's hair grips. She tried to shush him away.

"Not all men can be like those in your books. Take Gerald in Women in Love. Would you really want a man who got so carried away by love that he'd go and sit in the snow and die for it?"

"Absolutely."

Why was it that Lily was never quite sure if Natalia was serious or teasing her?

"Passion, darling. It's what makes the world go round."

She picked up a cushion and threw it at the monkey who jumped away just in time.

"That's what's so wonderful about Italian men, especially here in the south. Not only are they stunningly beautiful – well, the younger ones anyway, before they let themselves go – but they're so... what's the word? Intense?"

Sidney came into Lily's mind. You couldn't call him beautiful. Nor passionate, nor intense. Had she got it wrong when she imagined he and Natalia had been lovers? Or was Natalia just saying things, stringing Lily along, trying to give the impression she had a more exciting life than she did?

"Come on, confess. You must have noticed one or two of them."

"Natalia, I'm a married woman."

"Does that mean you're forbidden to look at other men?"

Lily sipped her coffee even though it was still too hot.

"I'm not in the habit..."

"Oh darling. Then maybe you should be. Find yourself a lover. Give that husband of yours something to worry about."

Lily put her cup down with a clunk.

"For heaven's sake, Natalia."

Surprised at her own reaction, Lily stood, walked to a shelf, picked up and started turning the pages of a book though she had no idea what she was looking at. She snapped it shut.

"I'm not like you and your bohemian crowd. I'm sorry, I'm not. You may think I'm dull and provincial, but I still have some values. I believe in marriage and in being faithful, I know it may sound ridiculous, but I just do."

"And in being unhappy?"

"What makes you think I'm unhappy?"

When Natalia didn't respond she waited a moment, then turned to see Natalia had poured some of the coffee into an ashtray for the monkey to lap.

"I do not need a lover," Lily said. "I don't want one. What can I say to make you believe me?"

Natalia lifted her head and smiled pleasantly.

Fifteen

A moth was trapped inside the hut, a flimsy freckled creature fluttering in panic against the dusty window. Lily lay there watching it, feeling her pulse fluttering too as Ernesto lifted her skirt, calmly and deftly removed bits of her clothing as though she were a child. She didn't try to stop him, but neither did she help; it was as though she had no choice, and in a way that was true. She closed her eyes as he pulled off his shirt and dropped it on the floor, unbuttoned his trousers. She felt his breath on her face, his lips on the side of her neck. Using his legs to gently push hers apart, he lowered his body down onto hers. He was heavier than James; she could feel the fishing nets on which she was lying cutting into her flesh and thought for a moment how she would be patterned, her skin marked into squares.

There was a smell of salt water, sun bleached wood, of seaweed and fish. Would she go home smelling of the sea?

When he entered her she gasped. He reached for her legs,

lifted them and wrapped them around behind him. He caught her wrists and held her arms up above her head; she could feel sand against the back of her hands. He was arched over her and there was nothing she could do.

And then she made herself stop thinking, let her body take over, as though hypnotised, hurting and yet not wanting him to stop, lifting so he could reach deeper inside her, her fingers now gripped tightly around his, even her toes curling. When Ernesto trembled, let out a long moan, then pulled free and flung himself onto his back beside her, she wasn't sure if the ragged breathing she could hear came from his lips or hers. Or did it come from both of them?

Outside, the sea crashed against the rocks. The hut shook.

Of course. The wind, the Scirocco, wasn't that what Ernesto had called it? A wild hot wind from Africa. Very dangerous to be out in it, he'd said when he saw her struggling to make her way back up the road, realising she'd made a mistake by coming out. Potted plants fall off ledges, he'd said. Trees topple. Once a chair was knocked off a balcony and crashed down onto a woman and broke her neck, he said. Come to my hut, it's on the beach, no distance. Come and shelter until the wind calms a little.

What had made her say yes, give in so easily?

Had he hypnotised her? She could believe it.

Or had she simply lost her sanity?

Now he reached and pushed her hair from her forehead, touched his lips to her nose, her chin. His stubble was softer than she'd imagined.

"Liliana," he said. "In Italian your name is Liliana."

"I must go," she said feeling suddenly shy, awkward.

"No, no, no," he said, catching her in his arms, a bear hug, his face buried against her neck.

He looked up then, gave her one of his rare smiles. A smile

of conquest, she thought. He'd done what he set out to do. She'd been seduced and his masculine ego had been satisfied, not to mention his bodily needs. He would tell his friends, no doubt. You know *Signora* Hogan, the doctor's wife…

"Let me go, please," she said, scrambling to her feet, suddenly angry – though whether with him or herself she wasn't sure. Getting dressed she kept her back to him, could hear him also pulling on his trousers, his sandals clumping on the wooden floor.

She combed her hair with her fingers, retrieved clips. There had been a tortoiseshell slide; she needed that to hold her hair up but it had gone. She bent to look for it and when he asked her what she'd lost she had no idea of the word, used her fingers to illustrate how it would grip her hair.

Ah, he said. And of course he found it first. And wouldn't let her have it, hiding it behind his back, teasing.

She burst into tears.

"*Cara, carissima!*"

Again he held her and she fought to be free, but only for a moment. Sobbing against the pad of his shoulder with his arms tight around her she felt herself growing calm.

"You didn't like making love?" he said. "It was too quick, I know, I'm sorry. Next time will be better, I promise."

"There won't be a next time," Lily said.

"But yes, of course. There must be another time, many times."

"Ernesto, this is wrong."

"*Perché?*" He looked genuinely perplexed.

"I'm a married woman."

"*Non c'é problema.* Your husband works, true? He can't watch you all the time. And what he doesn't know…"

"He'll find out. Someone will tell him."

"No."

Now he released her, held her at arm's length, his expression serious.

"No-one will know. We will be very, very careful."

The wind suddenly rattled the door and for a moment Lily's heart stopped, sure that someone was trying to get in.

"Ernesto, I can't do it."

"You don't like me?"

"Yes, I do."

"I like you, Liliana. I like you very much."

He was determined not to understand.

"I must go."

"But wait. The wind… it isn't safe out there."

Lily yanked at the door, leaving it open in her hurry to get away, stumbled across the craggy rocks trying her best to avoid the sea that bubbled in between them, yet slipping and soaking one foot just the same. And then she was on the path that skirted along the cliffs towards the beach, the café, and beyond that the road that led back up through the village.

Suddenly she remembered she'd promised herself that she would catch the moth, put it outside, though in this wind it wouldn't survive for long. Poor thing. Either way it was doomed to die.

It was exhausting trying to walk against the wind; Lily would pause when it was strongest, move forwards in the lulls. Everything was covered with a fine layer of sand. Once she had to jump into a doorway to avoid being hit by a barrel that was on its side and careering down the hill like a bull; minutes later she heard a crash of breaking glass. Overhead, birds were being blown about like scraps of paper. Though it was only early evening and still light, the place seemed deserted, most people having the sense to stay indoors. Lily was relieved. She didn't want anyone to see her. They'd know, just by looking at her. They'd know what she'd been up to.

As she reached the house she took off her shoe, dried her foot on the hem of her skirt.

There were two strangers in the drawing room, men in dark shiny suits and hats. They were standing side by side facing James who had his back to the window. Though she'd heard them talking from the hallway, they stopped when she appeared; the silence, broken only by the almost human howling of the wind, was unnerving.

"James? Is something wrong?"

"These gentlemen are asking about that young man we took in a month or so ago. Paolo Bonora. You remember him?"

She nodded, not trusting herself to speak. So it had happened. Whilst she'd been with another man, James was about to be arrested, hauled off, charged with collaborating with an enemy of the people. He'd be found guilty, of course, probably kept in solitary confinement, locked in a tiny cell for a year or longer, being forbidden to speak to anyone, not even the wardens. She'd heard talk of such severe sentences being passed. Making an example, they called it.

She tried to keep her voice steady.

"Yes of course. But how can we help?"

The two men turned to her. Neither of them were very tall, and their suits hung on them, and yet somehow she felt intimidated. It was all in her mind, of course.

"They've come down from Rome," James said. "It seems he's suspected of being involved with an anti-fascist group."

"Not suspected," one of the men said. So he spoke English. "We have proof that he is involved."

"Surely not? We didn't talk much, but he seemed far too sensible to do anything he shouldn't."

"We've been watching him for some time," the same man

said. "Now he's disappeared. We know he came to the south, that he was injured and that your husband treated him We were hoping you could tell us where he went when he left."

Lily looked at James, widened her eyes, shrugged.

"I have no idea."

"I've already explained to these gentlemen," James said, a hint of impatience in his voice. Lily was impressed, she'd never thought he could act. "When I qualified as a doctor I vowed to help anyone in need, and that's what I did. Once he was fit enough to leave, he was no longer any concern of mine."

There was a pause. The man who'd done all the talking scrutinised first James then Lily. The other one was presumably there for support. She wondered if she should offer them a drink, but before she could make up her mind their interrogator gave a small, sharp sigh. He was sorry for bothering them, he said. He thanked them for their time. He hoped he wouldn't have to return, but assumed they would be available for more questions if necessary?

"You're not planning to leave Italy?"

"Not for a long time, I hope," James said.

"You like our country?"

Was he pleased? Or suspicious? It was impossible to tell. James led them to the door, Lily listening as they talked briefly in hushed tones in the hallway, then were gone. She should have felt relieved, but she didn't. It had been too easy.

"What awful men. They must have been roasting in their suits, and those hats!" She paused. "Do you think they believed us?"

"I doubt it. But as long as they can't prove anything…"

For a moment she'd felt close to James; they'd stood together against the enemy, man and wife, and she wished it could be like that more often. That they could be a couple instead of two separate individuals sharing meals, a house, chores such as watering the plants, writing letters home. Like children at boarding school. No wonder she was lonely. Was that why she'd done what she did that afternoon? Was it out of loneliness rather than lust? Lust; even the word made her feel uncomfortable.

"You look a mess," James said, but not unkindly. "You shouldn't have been outside in this wind, it's far too risky. Couldn't you have waited at the café or somewhere, at least until it died down?"

Lily went to him, put her arms around his waist, keeping her eyes lowered. His shirt was damp with perspiration, his heart thumping.

"I hope a tree falls on their car," she said. "Or a gust of wind shoves them off the coast road and they're smashed to smithereens on the rocks below."

"Very nice," he said. She could tell he was smiling. "Very charitable."

He kissed her forehead. Gently he disengaged himself.

"Lily, dear, I must get on."

"I know," she said. "I'll start getting tea."

That night there was a sickle-shaped curve of moon that could have been made of metal, it looked so sharp. Lily was nervous of anything sharp – razors, needles, bread knives – her mother stressing how even the smallest cut could result in uncontrolled bleeding and eventually death. Her mother warned her about other dangers too: wasps, sitting on cold stones, dogs with black tongues, dark alleyways, eating unripe plums, telling lies, taking sweets from strangers. No wonder she'd grown up so cautious.

Her mother hadn't warned her against taking a lover; no doubt she'd considered such a situation beyond the realm of possibility.

Lily lay in bed thinking about him. My lover, she thought. And then, I am an immoral woman. Already the flood of pleasurable memories was diluting her guilt. What had happened had felt so right. Inevitable in a way; she'd been attracted to Ernesto from that day on the beach, she could see that now. To his solidness, his strength, the supple way he moved. To his quiet manner. He was an uncomplicated man living a simple life, close to nature, and what could have been more natural than making love in a shed on a stormy afternoon?

But it couldn't happen again, it mustn't. No matter how much Ernesto wanted it, how much they both wanted it. To see him again would be putting too much in jeopardy.

Fearing that she might dream of him, might say his name aloud and give everything away, she found another of Natalia's books and tried to read it, to fill her mind with someone else's life. But her concentration kept wandering, her eyes closing.

Eventually she dropped off. She didn't dream of Ernesto.

Lily stayed home. It was safest, she decided, not wanting to see Natalia, nor Sidney, nor Ernesto. Especially not Ernesto.

Determined to make herself useful, she decided to clean the house thoroughly, top to toe. It certainly needed it. Pulling out furniture, getting down on her knees, she spent three whole days dragging a stiff brush back and forth over stains that had been on the tiles for years and were near impossible to remove, climbing on chairs to dust the tops of cupboards, cleaning cobwebs from dark corners. Her back ached. She had blisters on her hands.

It was no more than she deserved. She'd been unfaithful to James and she was going to make it up to him. His house was going to be spotless, she would cook delicious meals even though the kitchen was unbearably hot, she would stitch on buttons and starch his collars and never complain.

In bed, though, she moved to the edge, not wanting to be touched. When, one night, he shuffled close, kissed her bare shoulder, and she knew he wanted to make love, she said it was too hot. She got up, splashed her face with water, went out onto the terrace, oblivious to the mosquitoes that whined around her. Other people also were out on their terraces: she could hear the murmur of voices, sudden laughter. She liked the way people used the outdoors as part of their home.

There was lightning out over the sea, silent white zigzags in a black sky, a storm that she knew was unlikely to come inland. How often had a promise of rain come to nothing, the ground now so parched you could wiggle your fingers in the cracks. Though the village below was in darkness, Lily stared over the rooftops towards the beach.

"Lilian? What are you doing out there?"

"I'm coming."

And thought that a little way along to the left, beyond the end of the path, beyond the flat grey rocks, was Ernesto's hut.

It was inevitable that she would see him again. She couldn't stay house bound for ever; there was food to be purchased, letters to be posted or collected from the post office, messages to be taken.

She'd just passed the oil-press, the blindfolded donkey going round in circles, its hooves clipping resignedly on the stone floor, when she saw him sitting on the low wall that ran alongside the road. It was as though he was waiting for her, though sitting watching the world go by was a common pastime here. Everyone did it, even the children.

Too late to turn away, she managed a casual smile.

"Hello," she said.

He didn't speak, but nodded. Feeling she had to say something Lily remarked on a lovely smell, could it be the blossoms of a nearby tree – a linden, wasn't it? She'd only ever seen one in England, the climate was much too cold.

He waited for her to run out of words.

"When will you come to my hut?"

His directness reminded her of a child. Concerned that someone might hear, Lily glanced around, but there was no-one, only a skinny dog sprawled flat out in the shade.

"It's not possible."

"Only to talk," he said.

He didn't really think she would believe that, surely?

"You remember how to find my hut? I'll be there this afternoon, I'll wait for you."

"Please don't. I won't come."

He said nothing more but stood, sauntered off. There was an air of confidence about him that for a moment irritated her.

It was all so easy for him; he wanted something, he saw no reason why he shouldn't have it. Of course she wouldn't go. How could she?

Then fate took a hand. James – who'd planned an afternoon going through his medicines, checking stocks, listing in his strong, upright handwriting what he needed to re-order – was called out to see a child with measles. Whilst he was over the other side of the village, he said, he'd stop off to visit an elderly French countess who he'd treated recently, aware that what she needed more than medicine was company. He didn't mind; he could spare an hour or two. Lily sat in the silent bedroom watching dust motes dancing in the rays of sunshine that had wheedled a way between the shutters. Alone again. Always alone. Sometimes she felt he'd prefer to be with almost anyone than with her.

She didn't have to be alone, of course.

And he'd never know.

Just one more time.

Having made up her mind, Lily changed quickly into a clean cotton dress, put on lipstick, tiptoed out of the house and down through the sleeping village. Siesta time. She thought of the song about mad dogs and Englishmen as she half ran down steps, along the road, down more steps, keeping to the shade whenever she could.

What if Ernesto had taken her at her word and wasn't there?

He opened the door for her before she knocked, closed it behind her, slid a bolt across, and she tried to recall if he'd done that last time.

He'd made a bed for them, blankets or something soft anyway under a white sheet, took her hand and led her towards it but then stopped.

"Take off your clothes," he said quietly, standing back. Shyly she began, dropping things onto the ground, aware of his eyes on her the whole time, her skin tingling. Naked, she took a step towards him but he held up a hand, and she felt an urge to fold her arms, to curl away from his unblinking gaze.

"Your skin is so white," he said. "Like milk."

It wasn't like last time; there was none of the frenzy, the lack of control. This time he made love to her as though he'd planned it, step by step, moving her into positions that felt strange but exciting, that she'd never tried before, not with James. Touching her with his stubby fingers, his tongue. Encouraging her to touch him. After a while they were both so slippery with perspiration that their bodies made small sucking sounds as they pulled apart, and Lily thought how she'd never before known what it was like to be with a man. Not really known.

"I thought we were going to talk," she said eventually.

"*Si*. Why not?"

He thought she was teasing.

"So tell me about your life. Where do you live?"

"Furnillo, you know where I mean? Up along the road and then down again."

"With your mother?"

"Yes, with my family."

She imagined him sharing one of the houses you could just see from the road with its familiar domed roof, paint peeling from the walls, an old chamber pot full of geraniums by the front door. Probably he had brothers and sisters, all of them dependent on him for the fish he caught, the money he brought home from doing odd jobs for people like Natalia and other visitors to the village.

His voice was flat and she sensed he was reluctant to talk about himself, that it wasn't something he was used to doing.

Slowly, struggling to find the words, she told him about her life back in London, realising he'd most likely never been in a big city, never seen double deck buses and department stores, and pavements so crowded you can hardly move. She said she had a mother, father, an older sister, a dog; that she loved dance music, going to the pictures. She didn't mention James.

"You must excuse my Italian. I'm trying to learn but…"

"You speak it very well. Much better than I speak English."

"Can you say anything?"

He shook his head, reached into the pocket of his trousers and took out a blue cigarette pack, offering her one. When she declined he lit one for himself, lay back down beside her.

"I'll teach you. What do you want to say?"

"*T'amo,*" he said.

"I love you," Lily said in English. Ernesto repeated it.

"*Come sei bella.*"

"You are beautiful."

"*Voglio fare l'amore con te.*"

She lifted her head, looked at him. He inhaled, blew smoke rings, watched them curling slowly upwards.

"Wouldn't you like to learn any useful phrases?" she said.

"These phrases are very useful." He smiled.

And suddenly it came to her that she wasn't the first foreigner he'd made love to here on the floor of his hut. All sorts of people were drawn to the village. Though it was unsophisticated and virtually impossible to reach – or possibly because of it – its reputation was spreading. Bohemians, artists and intellectuals gathered here, out of sight of the world, free to be themselves, to do whatever they wanted to do.

Free spirits who believed in free love.

How could Ernesto resist? He was young, virile, single. And here was a continuous supply of women looking for something to do to fill the long, languid summer afternoons. He would tell them all that he loved them, would gaze at them, his dark eyes melting. He would mean it when he said it.

"It's getting late," she said, sitting, reaching for her clothes.

"No, it's early."

Quickly he stubbed out the half smoked cigarette.

She was determined; she stood. He gave up, lay there watching her.

"Next time I'll bring music," he said. "You like music, yes? We'll listen as we make love."

He started to hum what sounded like a Neapolitan folk song, slightly out of tune though he seemed unaware of it, and Lily couldn't help but smile. The one thing she resented though – that, if she was honest, terrified her – was the power he had over her. He was so sure that she'd return. And he was right; she had no choice in the matter.

As she moved to the door she spotted the moth, caught in a spider's web like an autumn leaf, brittle and dead.

Sixteen

$\mathcal{O}$n the main piazza one morning there was the sound of someone giving instructions, a man, his voice reminding Lily of a sergeant major. She couldn't resist going and looking.

Young boys in black shorts and white shirts, a dozen or so of them, were lined up facing a short fat man who was obviously putting them through some kind of exercise session. The expressions of concentration on the boys' faces brought a smile to hers.

Others stopped to watch.

"It's not good," a man carrying a wooden box full of eggs muttered, shaking his head.

"Why not?"

It reminded Lily of the Women's League of Health and Beauty. She'd gone to classes one whole winter, paid her sixpence, taken along her uniform to change into in the cramped little room beside the cold main hall with its splintery floor, all the girls giggling, smothering themselves in talc. Hers had been Lily of the Valley and whenever she smelt it afterwards she'd remembered that winter.

"*I balilla.* You know what that is? The young fascists."

Of course. Wasn't there a similar youth movement in England?

"*Il Duce* catches them when they're young. Only eight years old, some of them. It's all wrong."

He turned away in disgust, and even as Lily moved on past them the boys gave the fascist salute, their arms straight, heels together, and the class was over.

At once they became small boys again, their energy far from used up, wheeling around the square, careering off in all directions. One bumped into her, tripped, fell and she bent to pick him up, brushed at the dirt on his legs. He was smaller than the others, his hair light brown; his smile revealed a tooth missing at the front.

"*Scusi,*" he said, then rushed off to a safe distance before stopping and turning to stare. Next time she looked he was still watching her.

She'd gone a short way up the road when she heard someone calling. *Signora, signora.* It was the small boy clutching three poppies. They were the exact same colour as the trickle of blood on his leg.

"You hurt yourself?" she said, searching in her pocket for a handkerchief, bending to dab at the graze.

He thrust the poppies at her, then made it clear he intended to tag along beside her, and she thought they start young, these Italian gigolos, though of course she was flattered. When a donkey loaded up with hay overtook them and the boy ran off to speak to the woman who was leading it, drawing attention to himself, Lily realised that he too was pleased to be sharing her company, that he wanted everyone to see. He scratched the donkey's nose before skipping back to her.

"Are you English?" he said.

"I am."

"I'm Italian." He grinned, and she couldn't resist ruffling his hair. The sudden pang of jealousy she felt was a shock: his mother was so lucky to have him. All three of the babies Lily had lost had been boys. Would any of them have turned out like this one? She doubted it. Neither she nor James were spontaneous, outgoing. But he'd have been kind, her son. And intelligent, if he took after James. And an excellent student. And hopefully he'd have had her colouring and her eyes, because she knew – shy as she was to admit it – that she was quite nice looking. In an ordinary kind of way, anyway.

Ernesto had asked her if she'd had any children, and when she said no, had asked why not. What was miscarriage in Italian? She said instead that her three babies had been born dead. The sympathy in his eyes was real.

But you're young, you can try again? he'd said. She'd shrugged. She couldn't possibly explain.

It had been on her last visit to the hut, a few days before. They'd been dancing together, shuffling really, his arms around her waist, hers looped behind his neck. As promised he'd brought a gramophone to the hut, though just one record, a jazz classic, which wasn't at all romantic. She wondered where he'd got it from, decided he'd probably borrowed it from Natalia. Had he told her why he wanted it?

The record was Cream Puff by Artie Shaw.

"What is that, cream puff?" Ernesto had asked. A sweet pastry, she replied, and he'd said *dolce* like you.

When eventually he'd lifted her and carried her over to the bed on the floor, she suspected he remembered about the dead babies and was determined to impregnate her, to make things right. Next day she found bruises on the inside of her legs and had to be careful to keep them covered, especially when James was around.

"*Signora?*" The boy was tugging at her skirt.

"Have you ever ridden on a donkey? *Nonna* has one."

"No, I never have," Lily said. And then remembered her own childhood, a day out at the seaside, Brighton was it? A special birthday treat. She'd hated it all. The hoards of people, the noise. The Punch and Judy show, everyone laughing and jeering, and her not wanting to watch, counting the black and white stripes of the tent instead. The donkey ride was to have been the highlight of the day and yet she'd been petrified that she might fall, had clung onto the animal's scraggy greasy mane longing for the moment when her father's strong hands would lift her down. On the train going home Cissy had teased her, and she'd ended up in tears.

No wonder everyone considered her the baby of the family, the timid one, the one who'd never take a dare, never do anything she shouldn't in fact. No wonder James treated her like one of those caged birds she used to hate walking past in the market: fluttery, pretty, their lives absolutely pointless.

"I'll ask *Nonna* if you can ride her donkey, if you like."

"Perhaps," she said. "Another day."

He seemed satisfied. It was better than a definite no, she supposed. Before he ran off he said his name was Dino.

That evening she wrote to her mother:

> *A young man gave me flowers today, three poppies that are on the table beside me now as I write. Don't be concerned – he was only eight years old, nine at the most! The children here are very different from the ones at home, so much more sure*

of themselves. Maybe that comes from living such free lives because they are left very much to fill the hours in any way they choose. It enables their mothers to clean and cook (and look after the latest baby!) whilst dad is off planting veg on his little bit of terraced garden, or putting out swill for the pig, or up in the mountains collecting spring water. Also, of course, because everyone seems to not only know each other, but be related in some way, and because there are no cars, it's quite safe for the children to roam around like little gypsies.

How I wish you could come and see this place! I'm sure you'd fall in love with it, just as I have, and with the local people, with everything.

She hesitated, tapping the pen against her teeth, added that James was well and busy, and finished with a line of kisses.

When James accepted the invitation to the christening, Lily was surprised.

"It's from Titina, the woman who dropped the terracotta pot full of spring water, remember? Twenty stitches, she needed. Anyway, it's her daughter's baby. We won't have to stay long, but I really should put in an appearance I think."

He was polishing his shoes as he spoke.

Was he changing? She'd always thought of him as a man people looked up to, a bit too serious possibly, but caring, reliable. A good man. And he was those things, all of them. But nowadays he seemed somehow pompous. Puffed up with his own self-importance. Even the way he dressed, with his pristine white shirts, his socks, black shoes that were polished every day. No doubt everyone took him to be much older than he was too.

It's me, she decided then. He hasn't changed, I'm just seeing him with different eyes.

Unsure about what to wear for the christening, she chose a rather formal navy dress with white lace cuffs and collar, even though it was taking place in the afternoon, the hottest time of the day. As they entered the vast church, with its twisted marble columns, stark wooden pews, the smell of incense blending with that of the pink carnations that were everywhere, even on the alter, she could see she'd been right to do so. Amidst the crowd gathered up near the alter were men in dark suits and high collars, most of whom looked distinctly uncomfortable, their wives in silks and satins with shawls draped over their heads.

The priest mumbled, the congregation joined in, the baby whimpered briefly whilst his parents exchanged anxious glances. Lily found herself looking upwards to where the sun streamed through the stained glass windows, the rays criss-crossing above their heads.

She remembered a story Natalia had told her: how just before Easter the villagers trap birds, hundreds of them, skylarks, quails, chaffinches, whatever they can, to be released as a celebration of the resurrection of Christ. Only they're released inside the church not outside. Trapped, they flutter around for days, battering themselves against the walls, the windows. Eventually the church is littered with tiny bodies, some with broken wings or legs, some with hearts still beating.

"That's horrible," Lily had said. She'd found it hard to believe.

"That's religion, darling. A lot of our circle agree with you, of course. But only Hans felt strongly enough to do anything about it."

He's been so incensed that one night, after dark, he'd thrown rocks at the windows, broken a number of them. For most of the birds it was too late, but some escaped. There had been an outcry and Natalia had offered to pay to have the windows replaced. Her offer had been accepted, of course.

Now everyone was standing, shuffling into the narrow aisle, moving slowly towards the doors at the back of the church through which could be seen the square, blindingly white, as if covered in snow.

Outside people gathered in small clusters and James moved from one to another, smiling, exchanging a few words, Lily following him as she was used to doing in such situations. A small hand grasped her elbow. It was Dino, the boy from the other day, and when she said hello, used his name, his face shone with delight.

She introduced him to James and the boy held out his hand and James shook it politely. He had a way with children, she had to admit. Which was just as well as a lot of his patients were children. Somehow he managed to get them to confide in him, to give him the information he needed to diagnose the problem. They'd take their medicine for him too; he didn't indulge tantrums.

When Sidney appeared, said he had a small problem he wanted to discuss with James and would she mind, Lily said of course not. Dino was still there, patient as a pet dog.

"You're not alone, are you?" she said.

"No. With mama and papa." He tipped his head towards the church steps.

He was telling her about how he and a friend had caught a snake when Lily heard a woman's voice calling his name. He didn't seem to hear it, or chose not to.

"I think your mother wants you," Lily said.

He pulled a face but went, pinching the arm of a fat girl in a white frock as he passed, pushing his way through the forest of legs.

Lily saw a woman bend to speak to him, to catch his hand. She was slim, had a frizz of dark curly hair. Her other arm was linked through that of a man who was turned away, talking to an older man. Her husband? Instinctively Lily pressed her hand across her mouth. Even from the back of his head she knew at once who it was.

She went across to the wall, sat down heavily. She felt sick, was trembling. She thought she might faint, and someone else must have thought so too because James was summoned and he came at once, bent down beside her.

"Lily? What's wrong, dear?"

"I... I'd like to go home."

"You don't want to come back to the gathering at the house?"

She couldn't speak, shook her head.

"*Fa troppo caldo*," a woman said, and Sidney agreed, said it was ridiculously hot, especially in the square where the heat seemed to bounce off the stone walls. We English aren't used to it, Lily heard him say.

"You go," she said to James. "I'll sit here for a bit and then make my own way home."

But he wouldn't leave her. He took her arm and encouraged her to walk slowly, not speaking but watching her out of the corner of his eye. Probably he was glad of an excuse, she thought. Glad not to have to talk any more about the weather, the rock fall up above that had blocked the road for a whole day, what the Americans thought about Mussolini.

She collapsed onto the bed, and he pulled the shutters and dabbed at her face with cold water.

It was only when he'd tiptoed out and she lay there listening to the village noises – people emerging after their siestas, kitchen utensils clattering as yet another meal got under way – that she let the tears flow.

She couldn't believe it. And yet she should have known. She was stupid, stupid, stupid.

She'd hoped she would fall asleep, forget everything, slip into a black velvety abyss. But she didn't. After a bit she got up and went to prepare some food. James said there was no need, she should rest, but she insisted. As she washed salad, grated cheese, sliced tomatoes, she could feel his eyes on her. He was worried, of course. He didn't understand.

Never again would she go to Ernesto's hut.

She should never have gone in the first place, and now – now that she knew he was married and had a son – she knew she had to stay away.

Whatever she was, she wasn't a home wrecker.

It was a few days later that she changed her mind. She would go to see him, just one more time.

Inside the hut it was like being inside a stove. Lily stood with her back pressed against the door, as far away from him as she could be. He stood facing her, confused by the way she was acting, by the anger in her eyes.

"You lied to me," she said.

A look of doubt flickered across his face.

"Me? No, Liliana, I love you."

"You told me you weren't married and you are. You have a son called Dino, probably other children too."

"Ah." He shook his head.

"But *carissima,* I lied for your sake. So you wouldn't feel bad."

"No. You lied because you thought I wouldn't come with you if I knew you were married."

He shrugged.

"And what about her, your wife? Is she sitting at home

alone wondering where you are when you're here with me? How can you be so…"

It was infuriating, not being able to think of the right word. She wanted to say cruel, would have made do with heartless or inconsiderate.

"Of course I love my wife and my son. I love you too."

It was all so simple. He loved everyone and that made everything alright.

Lily crossed to the window. The sea today was smooth, motionless; overhead a tiny plane slowly crossed the sky, quiet as a shadow, and Lily thought suddenly of Paolo. She'd lost him, he'd gone out of her life, and now Ernesto too.

He came up behind her, put his arms around her

"No," she said, as shocked by the anger in her voice as he was.

His hands dropped to his side.

"Liliana, forgive me. You're right. I didn't tell you because I didn't want to lose you. Yes, I love my wife, but we have troubles, we argue. It's normal I think? Here, with you, it's as though we're in another world. A perfect world. You understand me?"

He was saying the things he knew she'd want to hear, playing her like a fish on a line, waiting for her to tire, to stop struggling.

"We must never see each other again," she said.

"Please, Liliana." His voice was low, almost begging.

"Never," she said. She walked across to the door, opened it, thinking somewhere in the back of her mind that he would come after her, stop her. He didn't.

For a moment there was the feeling of elation that comes with cutting ties, the freedom, but it soon passed. Once round the corner and no longer in sight of the hut, Lily sat down on a rock. Seaweed had caught around the base of it and she pulled at a strand, wound it around her wrist, thought how it was fine and feathery like a boa stole. Though she'd never seen anyone on the path to the hut, people did use it; there was a smell of urine as proof. Courting couples, she thought. After dark. Did they lie on the beach to make love? She'd never done it in the open air, like an animal. Wouldn't have wanted to.

She saw his boat moving away down the coast. He wouldn't be gone long, an hour, two at most. Mostly he went fishing at night – the catches were better, he said – and then he didn't return until the morning. When he'd tried to explain how much he enjoyed his nights alone at sea, surrounded by black water and nothing else, she'd promised that one night she would go with him.

Now she stood, paused, undecided, knowing she should go home to her husband – that she was acting outrageously, like a strumpet, a whore – yet wanting more than anything to be with Ernesto.

She went back to the hut.

When she heard the sound of a boat clipping the rocks she had a moment of doubt. Suppose it wasn't him? Or that he'd taken her at her word and didn't care, knew that soon there would be someone new to lie with on his wooden floor?

The sun had now slipped behind the cliffs casting long shadows that enveloped the hut.

As he opened the door Lily turned to face him, didn't speak but slowly unbuttoned her blouse. She removed her skirt. Still he didn't speak. Only when she was naked did he let out a small moan and go to her, falling onto his knees, pressing his face against the curve of her stomach.

He does love me, she thought. In his way. He really does.

Seventeen

*W*hen eventually it rained, it bucketed down, flights of steps turning into waterfalls, rooftops sprouting leaks and everyone rushing for bowls, the dust becoming mud and then that too being washed away. It had been threatening for hours. Lily had watched it coming from out at sea, from the south; it was as though someone was pulling a grey curtain across the sky.

That was also the day James was arrested.

She could remember it all, every detail.

The frantic knocking at her door, and her thinking instantly of the time it had rained and she'd found Paolo collapsed on her doorstep. This time it was a young woman she didn't know huddled under a large black umbrella.

"The police have taken your husband away to Sorrento. In a car. I saw it, down in the piazza. He asked me to give you this."

The woman handing her a note and then hesitating,

obviously having something more she wanted to say.

"*Ha fatto bella figura, il dottore.*"

So he made a good figure, so what? Everyone was always on about the importance of putting on a good show, of being a real man. All that mattered to her was that he'd been taken away, and was in trouble, and that she had no idea what to do next.

Then reading the two words he'd written:

TELL SIDNEY.

She couldn't find an umbrella. She'd dragged everything out of the wardrobe, the cupboards, checked the empty suitcases and under the bed.

Giving up on her search Lily had set off, was soaked in minutes, the steps so wet and slippery that she took off her shoes and carried them. She could run more easily barefooted. If James thought Sidney would be able to help, she must get to him as quickly as possible. Maybe they'd take James somewhere else from Sorrento, further north, to Rome or even Milan. He could just disappear. She might never see him again.

Lily was breathless and doubled over with a stitch when Sidney opened the door. Around her feet, on the pale ceramic tiles, a puddle was spreading, in it threads of bright red. She must have cut her foot.

"My dear!"

He pulled her inside, found a towel, placed it around her shoulders and sat her on a stool. He went for a bowl of water, some bandages. Through an arched doorway she could see the Dutch couple, the musicians, who seemed to be talking animatedly though all she could hear was the rain lashing against the windows.

"I'm sorry, I've interrupted."

Sidney shook his head, concentrated on cleaning the cut

on her foot as she told him the little she knew about what had happened. She'd no idea what he could do to help, but if he could at least try to find where they'd taken James.

Should she mention Paolo?

"It's to do with that young pilot I suppose? I did advise him about not getting involved. Stubborn, that husband of yours."

Good, he knew. He ran a hand through thinning hair, stood up and his knees cracked.

"I'll do what I can. First I'll drop you off at your place."

She sat beside him in the car, silent, stunned. This couldn't be happening. It was all her fault, a punishment that she deserved.

"Lily? Are you alright?"

Sidney had parked and was waiting for her to get out. She rested her hand on his, and he put his other hand on top of hers.

"I am now. Sidney, I can't thank you enough."

"Nonsense. It's my duty, I persuaded you both to come out here, didn't I?"

He leant across, pushed open the door.

"Do you think you'll..."

"I'll do all I can. You go home and keep your fingers crossed," he said, giving her a peck on the cheek..

She waited until the car had pulled away before starting up the steps. The rain had stopped, the heat of the sun making the ground steam.

They'd been longing for it to rain, both of them. James hadn't said a lot, but Lily knew he was finding the work hard. One problem was getting around the village – he rarely used the bike now, most of the places being easier to reach on foot. Then there was the difficulty he was having obtaining the drugs and equipment he needed. So many things he ordered just never arrived; he suspected they were being stolen, flogged in the back streets of Naples.

But the heat, that made everything twice as hard. It sapped your energy so that even first thing in the morning you felt tired, listless.

The house seemed strangely silent. Lily poured herself a small brandy. For the shock, she told herself, sitting at the kitchen table with the glass in front of her. None of this would be happening if Paolo hadn't come into their lives. Yet she wasn't sorry that he had. He believed in fighting evil, really thought he could change the world, and good for him. He wasn't like the villagers who muttered over their coffee and card games, but did nothing, closing their eyes to the terrible things that were happening in the north, the Germans taking over Austria, the fear about who would be next. Wanting only to be left in peace. To fish, drink wine, make babies.

Then again, maybe they had the right idea. What could anyone do to stop what seemed to be inevitable?

She rested her elbows on the table, rubbed her temples. They were driving her mad, all these thoughts, buzzing around inside her head like so many trapped bees.

What would James be thinking? Would he regret getting involved or be proud that he had?

Would they give him something to eat and drink? Would they handcuff him, throw him into a cell? Would they ask him about Paolo and when he couldn't give them any answers, would they punch him and kick him until he crumpled into a bloody heap? Would he beg them to stop?

She poured another brandy, a larger one this time.

She was sound asleep when the front door opened, still seated at the table, her head on her arms. It was pitch black until he switched the light on. For a few moments she couldn't recall where she was, hardly recognised the haggard man standing beside her chair.

"James, you're back!"

She jumped to her feet. It was the first time they'd clung to each other, really clung, since coming to Italy, even longer ago than that.

When his father had died, killed instantly in a horse riding accident, and James had been shattered – much more so than she'd have expected – Lily had been shocked at the joy she felt at his need for her. And after the babies, then they'd turned to each other, though she'd understood that the loss was more hers than his. Except for the last one. It had been weeks before he went back to work; he'd vowed that until she was well and on her feet again, he would stay by her side. He'd made her cocoa and brought her magazines, Woman's Own and Photoplay, magazines he usually considered frivolous. And he'd taken her to see a new Busby Berkeley musical.

"I need a drink."

He pulled away from her and she hid her disappointment, went to get a glass.

"What happened? What did Sidney say to them?"

James yawned, drank the golden liquid in one go. There was a unfamiliar smell about him: stale, unpleasant.

"He didn't give me the details. I gather he threatened them with spilling the story to the US press. You know, innocent doctor arrested by fascist police. I suspect some money might have passed hands too, but he wouldn't say. Just said I should stop asking questions."

"He's a good friend."

"The best."

"Apart from the fact that it's because of him we're here, of course, instead of nice and safe back in London."

James gave a weak smile.

"I guess a safe life can be a little bit dull sometimes."

He reached for the half empty bottle and Lily caught his hand.

"Why don't you come to bed, James?"

"You go. I want to sit for a bit."

He picked up his glass and the bottle and walked towards the terrace door.

"James?"

He turned.

"I'm glad you're safe and back with me."

"Me too," he muttered.

Through the gap in the bedroom shutters Lily could see him sitting out on the terrace, motionless, staring into the dark. Or maybe he had his eyes closed, was thinking, or even sleeping.

He didn't need her, not this time. She couldn't help.

"I love you, James," she whispered, but the words didn't sound right.

The sun reappeared, so powerful now that it bleached the blue from the sky. James was called out to a man who'd injured himself whilst up in the hills shooting rabbits, to a boy who wouldn't stop vomiting; Lily was given some baby tomato plants and spent ages finding tins, filling them with soil, moving them around to try to decide where best to stand them. Evenings they sat out on the terrace to catch any slight breeze there might be, watching the stars switching on, chatting about local gossip or sometimes the news from further afield, stories gleaned from one of the three wirelesses in the village and passed on, like Chinese whispers. James wouldn't talk about his arrest and after a while Lily gave up asking. And one night they made love, slowly and tenderly, and Lily thought this is completely different from what I do with Ernesto. This is two people who share a life and a past confirming their love, strengthening the bond that makes them a couple. That, what I do in the hut, is passion. Raw passion.

Sometimes it disgusted her even to think about it, what she did with Ernesto.

When James said they'd been invited to a wedding and had said of course they would go, Lily was delighted. She'd always loved weddings, everyone putting on their glad rags, family tiffs being set aside for a day at least, the guests somehow touched by the optimism, the promise of a long and contented life for the happy couple. Weddings were a tonic that everyone should take regularly.

If only she'd known.

If only she'd been able to see ahead as she sorted yet again through her wardrobe; found a lilac dress in crepe de chine, tied a red sash around her hips, sprayed 4711 behind her ears and on her wrists.

If only she'd developed a migraine, or twisted an ankle, and stayed home instead.

James cursed about having to wear a suit in such heat. She assured him he looked very handsome – which was true – and that he'd be able to remove the jacket as soon as they got back to the reception, though she thought he probably wouldn't.

As they walked down to the church they could see smoke up in the mountains behind them, great black balls of it. A forest fire. Despite the recent rain the ground was still rock hard, the undergrowth yellowed and brittle. It occurred to Lily that if it wasn't contained the fire could eventually reach one of the smaller villages higher up in the hills, maybe even this one. Then what?

The bride was tiny. All that could be seen of her face was a crimson bow of a mouth beneath an embroidered veil. The groom, a young man James had treated for a dislocated thumb, looked nervous. When he repeated the vows it was in no more than a mutter, whereas the bride's voice was strong and confident. Everyone smiled at everyone and some of the women dabbed at their eyes.

Afterwards, the crowd stood outside and threw sugar almonds and coins at the couple, which were immediately scooped up by the children, whilst the church bells peeled and dogs barked.

Then everyone trudged up the steps. The smoke from the mountain fire looked thicker and was the main subject of conversation; already a group of men had gone up to see what they could do to stop it spreading. Lily wondered if Ernesto was amongst them; if so, she hoped he'd take care. If it spread it could be serious. *Un disastro*. The story was told of a grandfather of twelve, burned to death in just such a fire years ago, his charred body being carried down on a stretcher. Someone else had nearly been trapped himself, talked of the animals fleeing before the flames: mice, foxes, rabbits, all running together. Even snakes.

"*Basta!*" A woman with a baby on her hip turned and glared. Enough. "This is a wedding, *una festa*, a day for being happy."

Eventually they arrived at the house. The meal was to be eaten at long tables set out under a vine covered trellis; the grapes were tiny still, like green pearls. On the white tablecloths were carafes of wine, bowls of olives, salami so pink it looked artificial. As Lily took her seat she felt the pleasure of anticipation. She glanced at James and he winked.

A stream of women emerged from the house, plates were passed from hand to hand.

"*Buon appetito!*"

It was as if a starting pistol had gone off. Everyone tucked in enthusiastically. After the second course James took off his jacket, after the fourth he undid his shirt collar and rolled up his sleeves. His shockingly white arms became, briefly, the focus of attention and some amiable jokes.

He was talking with the man sitting on his other side; they'd met him when they first arrived in the village though Lily couldn't recall his name. She was having trouble remembering other names too and put it down to drinking too much. Still, when more wine was offered and she shook her head, her refusal was ignored. A little girl knocked over a full glass and the stain spread violently across the cloth, the mother scolded, the girl started sobbing loudly. To stop her noise she was scolded again, then hugged, then given a sliver of *panettone* dipped in *anice*, and when that didn't work, one of the bridesmaids untied a blue silk bow from her hair and gave that to the child. Everyone applauded.

"James?" Lily wanted to ask him if he was as happy as she was.

"Sorry, dear, what was that?"

She'd interrupted his conversation.

"Nothing."

After the meal someone brought out a mandolin, handed it to a skeleton of a man with a sharp nose and very little hair, who took it, handling it as if it were a very old, very valuable Stradivarius. He crossed his legs, perched the mandolin on his knee. His gnarled fingers plucked lightly at the strings, he sang a few words in a high voice. The guests hushed. Then he began.

Shyly and reluctantly the bride and groom moved out onto an open patch of ground set aside for dancing, stood face to face, began turning in stiff circles, and Lily thought how young they were, hardly more than children. Two men joined in, dancing together, then more men got up, linked arms. Those watching started to clap in time with the music. The rhythm quickened.

A new song was started. Women joined the dancers and when their landlord took Lily's hand and pulled her to her feet, she couldn't refuse, found herself caught up in the crowd, bobbing and laughing.

Thinking she ought to go back to James, she looked around but couldn't see him. He was probably still putting the world to rights. Red faced and puffing audibly, her partner indicated that he had to sit down and passed her over to another man, a younger one this time. Lily kicked off her shoes. She'd never danced like this before, feeling the music rather than listening to it, not caring that her hair had come loose and her feet were dark with dust.

The sun, lower now, filtered through the trees and it was as though the branches were strung with diamonds.

When James stepped into the circle she thought for a moment that the impossible had happened and that he was going to join in. As his hand tightened on her wrist though, she knew she was wrong. He pulled her and the crowd parted to let them through, closed again behind them. She was aware of faces turned in their direction, but only for a moment.

"We're leaving," he said.

"James, please don't be angry. It's a party, you're meant to dance and…"

"I said we're leaving. Where are your shoes?"

She stood there trying to catch her breath, imagined herself refusing. What right had he to treat her like this? Instead she went and found her shoes, realised she'd lost the sash from her dress and was about to go and search when James said to forget it. There was something about his tone;

she did as he said. The sounds of music and laughter faded as he strode down the steps, never once looking back, Lily doing her best to keep up. She called to him to slow down but he ignored her.

In the drawing room she collapsed onto the sofa, thinking how good it would be to have a cold water splash, which she'd do in just a minute.

"James, what is it? What's wrong?"

He pushed open the shutters, stood looking out.

"There's a word. *Cornuto*. Do you know what it means?"

"*Cornuto?* No."

"In correct Italian it means horned. Here, though, it has another meaning too, a somewhat derisory one."

Now he turned to look at her, his face blank, impenetrable.

"It's slang for a man who's wife is being unfaithful to him. A cuckold, isn't that what we say?"

Lily felt as though the room had tilted.

"I… I don't know what you're getting at, James."

"What I'm getting at is that everyone in the village, it seems, is calling me *un cornuto*. Pitying me, laughing at me. No-one can believe that I don't know my wife is having an affair, that whenever my back is turned she's off chasing after some man, like a bitch on heat…"

"Stop it!" Lily put her hands over her ears. How could he say such things? It was horrible.

James stepped forward, caught her wrists, made her stand.

"What's wrong, Lilian? Am I upsetting you? Dear me, how cruel of me. After all, such a good and devoted wife deserves better than that, wouldn't you say?"

He released her so abruptly that she almost fell.

She didn't know what to say. For a moment there was just the sound of his breathing, heavy now, uneven, and outside on the steps, a cat miaowing plaintively.

"It's not like that, like you said," she whispered. "You don't understand."

"I don't? Then help me to."

How could she explain? There were no words to capture how it felt being with Ernesto: the excitement, the freedom, the feeling of being alive. Truly alive. So alive that she could hear the blood surging through her veins, the hair growing on her head, her eyes blinking.

But it had nothing to do with how she felt about James. For all his faults, James was her husband.

Had she developed a split personality? There was a term for it, schizo something. It was a kind of madness.

"Who told you?"

"Someone. That's not the point."

She should have known he'd find out. Ernesto had said he'd tell no-one, and she believed him. But the villagers had eyes and ears and tongues, and not much to do except gossip. Hadn't she herself been guilty?

Another long pause. She'd have liked to go to him and put her arms around him, but she didn't dare.

When he spoke again his voice was controlled.

"I don't care what you do, Lilian. If you choose to take a lover that's up to you. What I do find unforgivable is that you seem to have no idea about the importance of being discreet. That's both naive and extremely selfish of you."

He sighed, turned back to face her and she was suddenly a small child again.

"Whilst you're my wife, and whilst you expect me to keep you, kindly remember that if I'm going to be a successful doctor, I must maintain a position of respect. If with your... your dalliances... you ruin my career, then we will both go hungry. Remember that."

He moved towards her and instinctively she stepped aside.

She expected him to slam his surgery door but he didn't. It closed with a hushed click.

One thing: she'd never lied to him. She may have kept something from him, hidden the truth, but she'd never actually lied. Not once since they'd been together.

Eighteen

Lily had promised James that she wouldn't see Ernesto again, had insisted that she didn't want to hurt him or cause him embarrassment, that that was the last thing she wanted. James had said she could do whatever she liked.

The house now were filled with thick, uncomfortable silences.

At night, James took blankets and a pillow into his surgery and slept on the floor.

The bed seemed vast without him, and at first Lily cried without being sure why, or who she was crying for. It was just the hopelessness of everything.

She tried to carry on as though none of it had happened, but it was impossible. Though James had determinedly dropped the subject, it was there in the house with them, following them around, like a shadow. When they passed close to each other he stood aside to avoid any contact. Conversation was kept to a minimum. He ate his food in the surgery, or out on the terrace; if Lily followed him he got up and moved away.

"We can't go on like this," she said.

"Like what?"

"We have to talk, sort things out."

"You think it's going to be that easy?"

"Couldn't we at least try?"

She grew brave; went and put her arms around him and he didn't push her away, but neither did he hold her. He stood there, his body wooden, unyielding. She longed to be held by Ernesto, to just be with him for a while. He'd be wondering where she was; she must let him know what had happened. What if he came to the house and James was home?

She promised herself she would contact him one day soon. Tomorrow or the day after, no later.

Sidney arrived at the door one afternoon. Did he know about her affair? Lily wondered as she ushered him in. He'd known about Paolo. But then, James had been proud to help Paolo. This was different. He was embarrassed, hurt, angry, all of which was understandable. It saddened her though that his main concern seemed to be what people thought. Not that she'd been lonely; not that she'd let another man make love to her because James so rarely wanted to. The only thing she'd done wrong was being found out by the village gossips.

"James has someone with him. He won't be long."

"No problem, I'm not in a rush."

She took him out onto the terrace. The chickens seemed to be finding the heat too much; they moped about, clucking miserably. James had said they might as well eat them now, before the pathetic creatures became skin and bones. When Lily said but look at all the eggs they'd been laying, James had said he didn't much care for eggs. It was because she was fond of the chickens, of course.

"Haven't seen you two around much lately," Sidney said.

"No." Lily shrugged. "It's too hot. Besides, James is kept so busy these days. By evening he's exhausted."

"Don't let him be too exhausted to come along to the *Festa della Madonna* next week. It's the big one."

"What is?"

James joined them; it was the first time she'd seen him smile for days.

"The festival of the year. There's a procession, the Madonna is paraded along the beach, then there are stalls, music, and later a splendid firework display. You mustn't miss it."

James said certainly he'd try, but Lily knew he had no intention of going. She decided then and there that she had no intention of missing it.

"You'll be going, Sidney, won't you?" she said.

"You bet."

"Then I... we can come with you?"

"You'd be most welcome."

That was settled then. James changed the subject, asked Sidney if he'd had any luck tracking down a bandage supplier who didn't charge the earth and Sidney said no, but he'd got the name of a new contact.

Lily excused herself.

Should she go to this festival? James wouldn't, she was sure. But she so much wanted to; she needed to get out, to get away from the atmosphere in the house that was suffocating her.

She went on her own, left James sitting in the drawing room. He'd started drinking too much and it worried her. Though she rarely saw him with a glass in his hand, his breath was tainted with the metallic smell of wine, or sometimes the richer one of brandy.

The road down was packed with people, visitors from the city or even further afield, peasants in long skirts down from the mountains for this special celebration, a few familiar faces dotted amongst them. Church bells peeled, as they had done on and off all day. Gradually the light faded, street oil lamps being joined tonight by candles that were set in windows, on ledges, everywhere, making the whole village sparkle.

Sidney spotted her before she saw him, waved energetically. With him were the usual crowd, everyone except Natalia, all eating lemon ices that were melting rapidly in the heat. Of course Lily had one too. Being with them was nice, it was as though she was with her family, but she wished in a way she could have been with the locals, taking part in everything that was happening rather than being an outsider watching it. She imagined if she were with Ernesto, her arm linked through his. It occurred to her then that of course he was there, somewhere. Everyone was there. What if she came face to face with him and his wife, and Dino? It would be so embarrassing. She must keep a look out, be ready to hop it.

The passing of the procession – the Madonna's statue hoisted high on a platform carried by six strong young men and flagged by priests and alter boys – brought a brief hush to the crowds. It was also a signal for the real festivities to begin. The brass band struck up a lively Neopolitan folk song. Stallholders enticed passers-by to buy thick chunks of watermelon, almonds, hazelnuts, to treat the children to a dragon kite, the wife to a new set of pans.

It wasn't until late in the evening – the Madonna safely back in her church, the beach cleared for the fireworks, a quiet buzz of anticipation – that Natalia joined them.

"I was in Sorrento. Have I missed all the fun?"

Lily wondered what she'd been doing there, but it was none of her business.

"And you, where have you been hiding yourself anyway?"

There was no time for Lily to reply. The explosions came one after another, the display so dazzling that for a moment it was as though someone had turned on a huge light in the sky.

"It's like the aurora borealis," Natalia said in a lull.

"You've seen it?"

"Last year. In London. Didn't you?"

Lily hadn't but couldn't remember why not. They were probably at some function or other.

After the sounds had died away – the whistles, the whoops, the staccato clatterings and then the cheers and applause of the audience – people started reluctantly to amble home. No-one wanted the evening to end. And besides, who could hope to sleep on such a sticky night?

"Let's go and look for some stones, shall we?"

Natalia caught Lily's hand, led her down onto the beach and along the waters edge; just visible out at sea were the two twisted rocks everyone called Mother and Son. Luckily they were walking in the opposite direction to Ernesto's hut

"Pierced stones. They're said to be lucky, especially today, after the Madonna has blessed them. Haven't you noticed how many of the women wear them on chains round their necks?"

"I'd wondered what they were."

"They soak them in water too, make some kind of miraculous potion. Personally I'd sooner have a pink gin."

They moved away from other stone seekers, further along the beach to where it was so dark they could hardly see what they were picking up.

"They're very rare, of course. That's why they're special."

Natalia was soon bored. She'd had enough, was going back to the others, insisted Lily stay on and keep searching. Lily didn't need persuading: the way things were at home, she needed some good luck. It was also nice to be away from the crowds for a bit.

"See you back at the café."

Lily even walked further along the beach enjoying the darkness, voices in the distance merging into an insect-like hum. Every now and again she picked up a handful of stones, sifted through them. They felt like marbles, cool and heavy.

"Here."

Even though she could see nothing more than the outline of a man, she knew at once that it was Ernesto. He pressed something into her hand: a pierced stone.

"Did you just find it?" she said.

"*Si.*"

"Where?"

He pointed.

"Back there. Up close to the rocks. That's the best place to find *le pietre della Madonna.*"

Just hearing his voice made her feel whole again.

"You found it, you keep it."

"No. It's for you. Come, there might be more."

She followed him, feeling the heat coming from rocks on which the sun had been pounding for days, weeks, rocks that wouldn't cool again until autumn.

"Here's one! And another."

And these she'd found herself; wasn't that even better?

"Now you have three. Lots of luck."

"But that's unfair. Please, Ernesto, take one for Dino."

Ernesto folded her fingers back over the stone she held out to him. Giving up she put them into her skirt pocket, turned to lean against the rock.

"My husband. He knows about us."

She heard him sigh.

"I thought so."

The sea, black and corrugated, was touched with flickers of silver that were reflections of the moon. Far out there was the light of a fishing boat.

"He is angry."

It was a statement rather than a question.

"Yes. No. I don't know. He's…"

Hurt; that was another word she didn't know in Italian. Pride, another one. Worried about what people might think.

"And if you see me again?"

She didn't know the answer to that either. Would James walk out? Beat her, beg or bribe her? She suspected he'd do nothing, say nothing, simply withdraw further into himself. He was turning into a tortoise.

"I can't," she said.

She sensed Ernesto look towards her, but he didn't move.

"We can't stop, not now."

Again he'd done just the right thing. If he'd touched her, implored her on his knees, she would have hated him for it.

"I don't know, Ernesto. It won't be easy. Maybe one afternoon next week…"

"I would be happy."

She promised she would at least try. Then, a thought.

"How did you know I was here?"

"I saw you with Natalia."

"And you followed us?"

"Yes. Are you angry?"

"No," she said. How could she be angry with him?

"But now I must go back," he said. And she understood that somewhere amidst the crowd his wife was waiting for him, his friends, probably Dino too.

"Me too."

He indicated she should go first, that he'd wait some minutes before following. As she moved away she heard him striking a match.

"So the wanderer returns," Natalia said.

"Look!"

Lily opened her hand and showed her the stones, and everyone congratulated her, as though she'd done something clever. It was ridiculous, such a fuss about a few stones, she thought. She tucked them deep inside her pocket.

It was late when she arrived back at the house, yet no sooner was she inside than there was a banging on the front door. She opened it. A young boy stood there, breathless.

"Please, the doctor must come."

"Wait here."

Lily hurried to the bedroom. James would have heard the commotion, he'd probably be half dressed by now.

The room was empty, the bed untouched.

She went out onto the terrace but he wasn't there. She looked in every room, then went back to the kitchen. He always left notes on the dresser when he was called away unexpectedly, weighed them down with a Wedgewood teapot with cherries on it that they'd brought with them. This time, however, there was nothing under the pot, nor on the table or his surgery desk.

Beside the sofa was a glass and an almost empty brandy bottle. She hoped the boy hadn't spotted it.

"He must be out with another patient. I believe there was a lady he said was very ill, Rosetta. He…"

"My mother is Rosetta!"

His face was puffed, his eyes red rimmed.

"And he didn't return?"

"No, no. Please, he must come now."

He rubbed at his eyes with grubby fingers, sniffed loudly. She longed to hug him.

"As soon as he returns I'll send him straight to your house."

The boy hesitated.

"I promise."

Lily pushed him gently towards the door.

"Tell your family the doctor will be with you soon."

She was relieved when he left, watched him go down the steps slowly, reluctantly. No doubt he'd been told not to return without the doctor. She closed the door, and then bolted it, not sure why, it was something she'd never done before.

She didn't dare go to bed. Instead she drank coffee and watched the hands of the clock move slowly around once, and then again, each minute feeling like an hour. Where on earth was James? It wasn't like him to let a patient down, something must have happened, something serious.

At one point she remembered the stones, took them out, washed them in clean water, found an old rag to polish them with. As daylight came she could see that they weren't just plain grey as she'd thought, but were subtle shades of cream, yellow, pink. Like the sugar almonds at the wedding.

She didn't know at what time the boy returned but his banging on the door now was frantic, full of anger. He shouted something but she didn't answer. After a while everything went quiet again.

Eventually she stretched out on the sofa and slept.

With dawn came a need to be busy. Lily swept around, plumped cushions, made coffee. She found some scrap for the chickens, talking to them as she cleaned their water dish, telling them not to worry, that James would be back soon. He'd probably been to visit someone, had too much to drink and decided he couldn't face the journey home.

The chickens took food from her hand now, their beaks hard and polished, though they never pecked her even by accident.

She had a wash, changed, did her hair.

But he'd never done this before. Should she go to Sidney? The police? She'd give him a little longer.

She was hungry. She'd go down to the bakery where, in the mornings, the *panini* were so fresh from the ovens that they were sometimes too hot to hold.

It was as she was returning that she the saw the man, a familiar face; he sometimes helped out in the post office.

"*Buongiorno*," she said with a bright smile. "How are you?"

When he spat on the ground in front of her, Lily couldn't believe it. He walked on and she stood paralysed, staring at the pale globule in the dust at her feet. She'd never been spat at before. What a horrible thing to do.

Again she bolted the front door.

Later there was more knocking, someone calling, a man's voice she didn't recognise. She went to the door, stood close but didn't open it.

"My husband isn't here," she said loudly.

"Then give him a message. Tell him my wife is dead and it's his fault, he killed her. He is *un'assassino*, a murderer, your husband. Tell him that."

The voice broke and Lily heard the man sobbing. She leant her forehead against the warm wood of the door, was about to open it and at least say a few words of consolation – though what could she say? – when she heard his footsteps going away, stumble and then gradually fade.

"James, where in heaven's name are you?"

She could hear the fear in her own voice, a voice that echoed in the high-ceilinged rooms, the empty house. She didn't know what to do.

She went to the bedroom, curled up into a ball, pulled the sheet up over her head. First a baptism, she thought. Then a wedding and now a funeral. She kept repeating it to herself, over and over, like a litany. Birth, marriage, death.

It was evening when the knocking started again, the room dim now. Tiptoeing, Lily approached the front door.

"Who is it?" she called.

"Lilian, open up. It's me."

She moved so fast she caught her finger on the bolt, winced at the pain, swung the door wide. He looked shattered. He had no jacket, his shirt was half undone, his hair dishevelled.

"James, where were you? There was a woman you promised to return to last night and she died and…"

He walked past her without saying a word.

*F*inally *the shelves were empty, battered books everywhere,
the only sound the occasional thump of a book sliding from the
top of a pile onto the floor. Lily plucked up courage.*

*"Whatever you think of me, I'm your wife, James. I have a
right to know."*

*She'd asked him before, more times than she could remember
over the past week since that awful night when the woman had
died. But his response was always the same: it was as though she
hadn't spoken. Maybe now though he'd tell her, now that he'd
exploded, got so much of the anger out from inside him where it
had been festering like a closed wound.*

"James, please?"

*He was crouching down now, his back against the wall, his
arms curved around his head, a stifled sound coming from him
that made her think for a moment that he was crying. When
suddenly he looked up and straight at her his eyes were dry. He
gave a small smile and for a brief moment she thought he was
about to ask if she was alright, to apologise.*

*"So you want to know where I was that night, do you? No,
I'm sorry. You have a right to know."*

*Lily nodded. Why did she feel suddenly shivery? She sat on
the edge of a chair, fixed her eyes on the floor, started to count
the tiles. One, two, three, four, five...*

*"I went to Naples. That's where men go when they want to
forget their wives, their lives, the fact that everything is a bloody
mess and there's no way out of it."*

*He waited a moment and when she said nothing, he went
on.*

*"Near the port I went into a bar, not a bar like the ones here
in the village, a bar for serious drinkers. There wasn't much
talking or laughter, no kids underfoot, no smell of pastries.
People were there to drink which was fine with me because so*

180

was I. That and to find…"

Lily turned to look at him, knowing that this was painful for him, half wanting to say he didn't have to tell her if he didn't want to. Or was it just that she didn't want to hear?

"To find what?"

His left foot was tapping up and down, up and down. For a moment he seemed to have forgotten she was there.

Then he blinked.

"Come on, Lily. Think. We both know you're not as innocent as you look, right?"

Did he mean…?

"A prostitute, Lily. I was looking for a prostitute, and I found one. She found me, to be more precise. How do they know? How can they pick one man out of a dozen and be so sure that he needs their… services? She was very young though all that lipstick and green eyeshadow made her look older. Well, more like a tart anyway. She smelt of garlic, and a musky perfume that reminded me of carnations."

"You went to a…?"

Lily couldn't say the word.

"She told me to follow her, led me through narrow back streets full of garbage, cats fighting over fish heads, washing hanging on lines overhead, you had to duck to avoid it. There was a man lying up against the wall, his head in a pool of vomit. He reached out a hand and groaned, drunk probably, though it occurred to me that he could be ill. I didn't stop, I just stepped around him. Can you imagine that?"

He ran a hand across his face and Lily thought how his skin looked like wax. She thought, who is he, this stranger sitting here in my home talking to me?

"Eventually we entered a house, went up some wooden stairs and into a room that I thought was a kitchen – there was a table and some chairs, dirty plates, that kind of thing. But then I saw

there was a bed against a wall with someone asleep on it, and on the floor a child curled up on a bundle of blankets. The girl touched her finger to her lips and we crept past them and into a small room with a mattress on the floor. She shut the door, found matches, lit a candle. I watched as she took off her clothes. She was so... liberated, at ease. I guess she understood how awkward I felt because she came across to me, unbuttoned my shirt, then my braces. Though she was slim, her breasts were full and very soft as she pressed them against me. And her hands too didn't seem to belong to her, they were large and rough skinned, though that was somehow exciting."

"James, that's enough."

"We made love most of the night, not that love had anything to do with it. In the morning she brought me coffee in a little silver rimmed cup with a matching saucer – it was obviously a prized possession – then lay down beside me again. I'm not sure how old she was. Seventeen, eighteen."

Abruptly, Lily stood.

"A woman died, James. Maybe it was inevitable, but maybe you could have saved her. At least you could have tried. At least you could have been there, like you promised you would."

James wasn't listening.

"I gave her the money we'd agreed, then I gave her some extra. When she smiled I noticed she had teeth missing, a sharp nose, that she wasn't as pretty as I'd thought. It didn't matter. She'd done what I needed her to do. I felt as if..."

Lily crossed to the door, walked out into the hallway and into the drawing room, wanting to get as far away from him as she could. She could still hear his voice going on and on.

PART THREE

Nineteen

$\mathcal{L}$ily remembered a trick her mother had taught her.

When something bothers or worries you, keeps demanding attention when you have other things to do, you just put it in a box, hammer down the lid, attach a label saying NOT TO BE OPENED FOR A WEEK, A MONTH, OR A YEAR, and tuck it away in the attic. Metaphorically speaking, that is.

Amazingly, it worked. There are so many things you can't change, nor do anything much about. Storing them like this is like giving yourself permission to forget them, for now at least, and get on with life. There's always the chance that when you do eventually open the box it might be empty, the contents turned to dust.

She would do it with the things James had told her. Put them aside knowing she could take them out and look at them again one day in the future, when she felt stronger, when time had taken away some of the sting. If she didn't stop thinking about what had happened, going over it again and again, she'd go mad.

Instead, she would concentrate on getting through each day. Now that James was home most of the time, ostracised, being punished for the worst sin of all, for breaking his promise, the days seemed to last forever. As though marking the seconds, his footsteps clicked across the floor, back and forth.

What would they do about money? And how would James survive not being able to work? Lily had long ago realised that he needed his patients as much as they needed him. The way the villagers avoided him, crossed the street, turned their backs, hurt him terribly. She could see it in his eyes.

Almost as bad as the pain he'd caused her, she thought.

The box in the attic, she reminded herself. Nailed shut.

If only something would happen to break the pattern, to shake them up, make them forget and forgive.

Her prayers were answered. Though it wasn't the kind of distraction she'd have chosen.

It would stay in her mind forever, that moment. Details like the smell of the yellow roses she'd bought from a man on the road early that morning. The taste of the fat, black grapes she'd bought at the same stall. The clicking of the bead curtain hung over the open doorway, there to keep out the flies though it wasn't much use. And Sidney standing in the hallway, mopping at the film of perspiration on his sharp nose and cheekbones, reluctant to accept even a glass of water.

"When was it?" Lily's legs were trembling.

"Eleven fifteen this morning. Chamberlain gave the German government two hours to suspend the invasion of Poland. As if Hitler would pull out now."

James was listening in the doorway behind her.

"God help us," he said quietly.

They'd known it was possible, of course, but had refused to believe it would come to it in the end. Someone would do something, devise a solution that was acceptable to everyone. This was 1939, people were civilised, had made so many advances since the days when war was the only way to sort out disagreements.

Lily thought of her mother and father, her sister, friends. It must be awful for them, their worst nightmare come true.

"What will happen?"

"Your guess, my dear, is as good as mine." Sidney shrugged. "I suppose in the end Britain will win. But it won't be easy, nor quick. Superior forces led by evil men, that's what they're saying about the Germans."

"One thing's for sure," James said. "A lot of people will die."

Lily could just about recall when the last war had broken out. Was she mistaken, or had there been excitement in the air, a surge of patriotism, young men impatient to serve their country, going off with high hopes of winning battles and medals, of covering themselves in glory, whatever that meant?

So few came back. Many of those who did wished they'd died out there in the muddy fields. Though Lily's mother had tried to shield her, she'd seen them at the hospital, hidden behind curtains, their bodies mangled and twisted, or with a leg missing, an arm cut off at the elbow. Worst of all were the ones who'd been burned, scarred, disfigured. Later, when she'd met James, he'd told her about the advances in reconstructive surgery and skin grafting techniques that had been developed after the war, the injured often undergoing a series of operations, the treatment agonising. They were tough kids, he'd said. The toughest.

"You look exhausted, Sidney." Lily wasn't going to let him

go. "Come in, sit down. Have some lemonade."

About to decline again, he changed his mind, followed James out onto the terrace whilst Lily went to the kitchen.

She would write to her mother that night, she decided as she found glasses, put them on a tray. She would tell her how anxious she was, and how she wished she was there with them, but it wasn't true, not entirely. How could she leave Ernesto?

She'd seen him again, of course, since the *Festa della Madonna*. Three times. Twice she'd been to his hut, slipping away in the quiet lull of early afternoon when it seemed a spell was cast over the village that made everyone disappear. They'd agreed she should teach him to dance, and he'd somehow managed to get his hands on some more records. He'd mastered the waltz but was having trouble with the quickstep. Though he moved well and had a good sense of rhythm, he didn't like the discipline of following a set pattern of steps, became irritated, then apologetic and then amorous. In the end they'd give up.

Last week she'd agreed to go night fishing with him, telling James simply that she was going out, not explaining. Why should she? He hadn't asked. He probably didn't care.

The boat had glided silently over the smooth water, the village lights fading behind them, ahead the soft black night. This time she hadn't been at all afraid of the sea, had stretched out feeling the warmth of the wooden boat beneath her, trying to pick out the Plough, the Great Bear, the Little Bear. Why was it that the stars here sparkled so much more than they did back home?

After a while Ernesto had lighted a lantern and suspended it out to the front of the boat. To attract the fish, he said. He'd started to sing what sounded like an aria from an opera she ought to recognise, but didn't, had then run out of words so hummed instead. She sat behind him gazing at the familiar curve of his back.

"I'd like to have your baby," she said in English

"*Come?*" He didn't understand.

She moved forwards, wrapped her arms around him, pressing her cheek against his shirt. As he half turned she felt his muscles stretch and contract.

"*Niente,*" she said. Better that he didn't know how she felt. The fantasies she had about them living together in a house in the mountains, chickens under the olive trees, cats everywhere, indoors the scent of herbs from bunches hung to dry in the cool domed ceiling, Lily sitting brushing her hair to look beautiful when he arrived home. And babies everywhere, beautiful fat babies with her chestnut hair and his dark eyes.

It was only a silly fantasy, of course.

She hadn't liked it when he caught fish, tossed them into a bucket at her feet, left them to squirm and flounder, desperately trying to breath, wanting not to die. She'd turned away, trailed her fingers in the warm inky sea.

But then, she liked to eat them, didn't she? She was becoming over-sensitive. Sentimental, that was the word. It was something to do with this place, and with Ernesto. She was not the same woman who'd arrived here in the spring, nothing like her.

He'd pulled the boat up onto a beach further along the coast, collected scraps of wood, found matches and lit a fire. He'd speared a couple of the smaller fish on metal forks, handed one to her, and they'd sat holding them over the flickering flames, turning them until the skin was dark and crisp. Following his example, Lily used her fingers to pull the fish apart, its soft flesh melting in her mouth.

Afterwards, they'd undressed and made love right there

on the sand, in the open air, Lily shy at first, not of Ernesto but of the feel of the air on her skin, of being exposed, vulnerable. He'd teased her. And eventually she began to enjoy the freedom, the feeling of being part of it all, this natural world around her. It felt right. Only when he was inside her, though, did she open her eyes, surprised to see that the sky to the east was beginning to take on the pearly sheen of dawn. And as she clung to him and the tension built up, tightening, waves of it surging through her body, and then, a sudden release that was shocking in its intensity, the words came back to her.

A dark flood of electric passion. Of course, of course.

Now she carried the tray out onto the terrace.

"Here, drink this."

Sidney took the glass, emptied it in a few quick gulps.

"Delicious," he said. "But I must be going."

She understood he had other people to tell, yet Lily couldn't bear to see him go. She linked her arm through his as he walked to the door. He squeezed her fingers, told her to try not to worry.

As she watched him hurry down the steps she heard James moving around inside. He too would be stunned by the fact that it had finally happened, but he wouldn't talk about it, not to her. They didn't talk these days, not unless it was absolutely necessary. She'd have given anything to be able to sit and talk things over with her mother, Cissy, her dad. Or a friend. She missed them all. There was Natalia, of course, but how often had she said politics were boring? Only artists and dressing up and sunbathing interested Natalia. She was lucky. Anyone who could ignore such dreadful things as war had to be lucky.

Lily put the glasses in the sink, went out onto the terrace. No sign of James. The chickens seemed pleased to see her, as they always did, getting up from their favourite corner spot, ruffling their feathers and then strutting towards her. She crouched down and held out some crumbs.

"It'll be alright," she said. The bolder of the two had already started pecking. "Now that Chamberlain's made it clear we're serious, Hitler will come to his senses, you'll see. He'll pull out of Poland and then they'll have lots of those interminable talks, and a new peace pact will be made."

From all around came the sounds of life in a small Italian village on a hot summer's evening, familiar reassuring sounds.

"Trust me, they won't let anything really bad happen."

Twenty

BRITISH LINER TORPEDOED.
ATHENIA SINKS OFF THE COAST OF IRELAND.
1,400 FEARED DEAD.

*N*ext to the newspaper, on the wooden table top, some red wine had spilled, and Lily's first thought was that it looked like blood. She didn't want to pick up the paper, but had no choice.

"*Ah, signora. E qualcosa terribile, non e vero?*"

The barman pointed to the headline, raised dark nest-like eyebrows. It was an English paper, over two weeks old. They'd already heard the news but seeing it in print made it real, no longer just a rumour.

She sighed as she started to read.

Despite the rules of submarine warfare that clearly stated no merchant ship may be sunk until the safety of all passengers and crew was assured – and just eight hours after war was declared – the Athenia had been attacked and destroyed shortly after starting its voyage from Glasgow to Quebec. There were 311 returning Americans amongst the 1,400 on board, said the article, a fact that had an instant effect on American public opinion. Already Roosevelt had made it clear...

"*Non capisco niente, io.*"

The barman put down her coffee, stood there. He too wanted to talk, wanted assurances.

"Nor me," Lily said. She didn't understand, and she wasn't going to try. The world had gone insane.

Soon she would pay, stand, step out into the white, shimmering air. Casually she would make her way along the beach, stepping carefully over the stones, moving away from the cluster of buildings, each step taking her closer to Ernesto.

With him she would find sanity.

Outside a boy went past with a black puppy in his arms. For a moment Lily thought it was Dino. Should she go out and talk to him, or turn away, hope he didn't spot her? Maybe he was on his way to the hut to show off the puppy, or with a message from his mother. What if he'd arrived when she was there with Ernesto? Would he be shocked, run away?

The boy turned to call to a friend; it wasn't Dino.

It occurred to her that it wasn't just Dino who would be shocked by the life she was leading now. No-one who'd known her back in England would believe it, not of her, the doctor's wife, a woman who took care not to sit around with wet feet, avoided too many late nights and would never cross a road without looking left, right and left again.

What would her family say?

They'd wouldn't be able to believe it. Her mother and sister would take it in turns to talk to her, try to make her see sense. Though her father would agree with them on the surface, she had a feeling that deep down inside he'd understand. He'd always had a soft spot for her, his little Lily.

It came to Lily suddenly that her father had had affairs. She'd not thought of it before, the possibility of it never entering her head. Why should it? Now, however, she recalled things. Her father coming home late, occasionally not coming home at all. Whispered rows between him and her mother that Lily couldn't help but hear, getting out of bed and tiptoeing past her sleeping sister to go and sit on the landing, her head pressed against the banisters, not understanding but still drawn to the drama that was going on downstairs. Gifts he gave to her mother when it wasn't her birthday or Christmas: fine face powder in a box decorated with a butterfly, a bottle of French champagne, a silver fox fur hat (which just last year she'd given away when she discovered that silver fox was all the rage with the prostitutes in Regent Street). Her mother had accepted them as though they were her due. Possibly they were.

Lily might be more like her father than she'd realised. She'd decided that the way she was carrying on now was the fault of the climate here, the casual lifestyle, and – as her mother would put it, her lips narrowing – falling in with a bad lot. Yet maybe it was something that was in her and would eventually have surfaced even back in England. She might have been having an affair with someone she'd met at the tennis club, or a teacher, or a member of the Household Cavalry.

"*Ancora, signora?*"

Even before she answered the barman had whisked her cup away to be refilled. He was a generous man, always smiling. He'd remained friendly, even when everyone else was treating James and Lily like criminals.

"*Grazie,*" she said, grateful.

In a minute she must go. Ernesto would be getting impatient.

When she arrived home the house was empty, a note from James saying he had gone to see a patient.

The relief made Lily feel faint.

"Thank you, God, thank you so much," she said out loud.

Someone had suffered an accident, or a heart attack, or was covered in boils, and because of their misfortune James and Lily would be able to stay on in the village, would be accepted again, invited to people's feast day parties, christenings.

Everything would be alright now.

Twenty-One

Two letters bearing English stamps arrived together, and in her excitement Lily opened them in the wrong order.

Dearest Lilian,

This is just to tell you that Cissy was married yesterday. It was a very sudden thing, needless to say. She only met Albert a few months ago, and dad and I certainly hadn't realised it was so serious – to be honest, we'd given up on her ever marrying, accepted she was going to be a spinster all her life, and that was that. Anyway, he's a bit younger than Cissy and very dashing, an officer in the RAF, so of course he'll be off to do his bit for Britain any day now, and he wanted to get married before he went. Everyone is getting married these days. I read that a jeweller in Camden Town sold thirty wedding rings in two days when he would usually have been lucky to sell three or four!

We're very happy, of course, but concerned that Cissy rushed into this without really thinking about what she was doing, and that when it is all over – which, please God, will be soon – she may regret her decision. He's a nice enough young man, but she hardly knows him. Dad and I were engaged two and a half years before we married.

Anyway, I promised to write and let you know at once, and to say she will write to you soon. Hope you and James are keeping well. At least you should be safe there for the time being, though goodness knows what will happen next.

Much love,
mummy

PS We miss Snooks dreadfully, more than we ever thought we would. You do think we did the right thing, don't you?

The second letter was dated over two weeks earlier.

Lily, my dear

I cannot believe that we are actually at war. Of course we've all known it was going to happen, all summer we've been holding our breath, praying for them to see sense. Now the worst has happened and everything here is in chaos, yet at the same time there's a sense of relief. Uncertainty is a dreadful thing. At least now we can get it over with.

Not that anything has happened so far. We thought the Blitzkrieg would start at once, and everyone has to carry a gas mask and hang carpets over the doors because of the chemical poisons they say the Germans will be using, but the waiting game it seems is still going on. The theatres and cinemas have been closed, bus services cut to a minimum. So many of the young children have been evacuated, it's strange not to hear them racing up and down the streets, what with the weather being so nice still.

Dear, we made a decision that I hope you'll agree with. Our neighbour Ida Hills – remember her? she has arthritis and a son living in Australia? – she said the papers were advising people to have their pets put to sleep. It will be terrible for them when the bombing starts, of course. So dad took Snooks down to the vet yesterday. He said he went very peacefully. I'm sorry, Lily, I know how fond you were of that little dog – we all were – but I'm sure it's for the best.

Cissy sends her love. She has joined the ATS and is working in the quartermasters stores which keeps her busy as well as helping to keep her mind off her new young man. His name is Albert. We've met him twice now. He's waiting to be sent overseas, of course, and already she's worrying herself sick about him. I keep telling her there are plenty more fish in the sea.

We're wondering what things are like there for you. Spain is keeping out of things, very wisely. If what the newspapers say is correct, Mussolini isn't rushing to offer his support to Hitler either. That's one thing we can be grateful for. Let's hope Italy keeps out of the war for as long as it takes, and that you and James can stay hidden away there until the world is once again a safe place. Please write and let us know all is well. I don't know if letters will get through but we must try to keep in touch.

We all send hugs and kisses

Your loving mummy
(missing you terribly)

Lily found her eyes filling with tears, not sure if they were for that scruffy old dog she'd always loved, or her sister, or all of her loved ones back in England sitting there with their gas masks and carpet over the door, waiting. Or were they tears of relief that she was so far away from it all?

Twenty-Two

James still hadn't woken.

Lily watched him sleeping, his forehead puckered even now, his chin in need of a shave. It was unlike him to sleep late; he must have been out most of the night. A young girl had come to the door as they were about to go to bed, said her grandfather had collapsed. James collected his bag and left at once, the child catching his hand to show him the way. He'd been out most of the day yesterday too, picking up supplies from the hospital in Sorrento. It was good for him to get away from the village, to meet colleagues, better still to catch up with what's new in the medical world over lunch. Just the same it made her nervous when he was away, the death of the woman still very much on her mind, the thought that there might be another death that could be blamed on him.

She slid gently out of bed, trying not to disturb him. Was this heat never going to let up? The air was humid and her nightdress clung to her back as she stretched, then headed out onto the terrace as she did each morning, to take her first look at the village below, a sea like green glass, and above her, mist caught like cotton wool on the mountains. Still the sheer beauty of the place took her breath away, even after all these months.

Should she wake James? After she'd washed, she decided.

In the bathroom she ran water into the basin, water that was cool now, though in the evenings it was much warmer. It came from the tank on top of the house and was heated by the sun.

She took off her nightdress, rubbed her hands on the hard white soap until she had a thick lather that she smoothed over her face and neck before splashing with water. She made more lather and rubbed it under her arms, across her breasts.

"Sorry."

She hadn't heard him approaching and when he opened the bathroom door it knocked against her. Once he would have come in. Now he hesitated, though his eyes remained on her, looking her briefly up and down, then he reached and rested his hand on the back of her neck before turning away.

"I won't be a minute," she called after him.

She found him sitting at the kitchen table.

"You look exhausted," Lily said.

"I feel it."

"And the old man?"

"He'll live, I think, for a while anyway. It was a slight stroke. Not much I could do except stress that he must rest. These old timers are so used to working they don't know how to stop."

Lily checked the kettle on the stove, poured the steaming water over the coffee, stirred.

"So if you couldn't do anything, what kept you so long?"

As soon as the words were out of her mouth she regretted

them. He'd think she was checking up on him, or implying something. The truce between them was fragile; one wrong word, even the intonation in her voice, could shatter it.

"Talking," he said. Good. He hasn't noticed.

"All night?"

"There's a lot to talk about."

"Oh. The war."

"It's amazing how often people come up to me, even in the streets, to ask my opinion on what's happening. What's really happening, they say. As if I know things they don't."

Lily could understand it. He had that way about him: a quiet confidence, a thoughtful expression. When he talked people listened.

"They must be getting the news, though. From the papers or the wireless."

"Sure. It's making sense of it all that they're finding hard."

Lily poured the coffee into cups, put one in front of James.

"I can hardly believe there's a war on," she said. "It's as though we're living on an island in the middle of an ocean, miles away, safe."

"If only."

"You think Italy will get involved?"

"Eventually, yes. We mustn't underestimate Hitler. He's a manipulator, he's dominated Mussolini for years When he needs his backing you can be sure he'll get it."

"But what about the Italian people? No one around here seems to like Mussolini…"

"Popularity isn't important. Power is what matters, and he's powerful. When he says go to war, they'll go to war. Wait and see."

"But if you're right and they do, we'll be the enemy, you and I, won't we?"

Just putting it into words made Lily's mouth go dry.

"I guess so."

And then what? They would have to leave, give up their life here, go back to England or maybe America. She'd have to give up Ernesto.

But she couldn't.

She picked up her coffee, turning away so that James wouldn't see her hand was shaking.

She wasn't ready for that, not yet.

Please God don't let it happen.

Much better, she decided then, to talk to the Madonna. The Madonna was a woman too. The Madonna would understand.

Long shadows stretched across the road, a few crisp brown leaves swirling in a sudden breeze, the sky pink above where just minutes ago the sun had dropped behind the mountains. Lily walked slowly, enjoying the first taste of autumn in the air, in no hurry.

Inside the church, a service had come to an end.

Most of the congregation had left, a last handful of elderly women in black shawls crouched over, whispering, sliding rosaries awkwardly between stiff fingers. The sacristan stood in front of the altar, reached up with an extinguisher that was just long enough to snuff out the flickering candles, one by one. Someone closed one half of the heavy doors at the back of the church and the loud clunk it made echoed.

Lily stopped half way down the aisle, edged into a pew and got down on her knees, crossing herself as she'd seen others do. She pressed her palms together, closed her eyes. Praying had always seemed a strange thing to her; how can you pray to someone that has no face, no form, is just a nebulous spirit that lives up there somewhere? The Madonna, though, was different. She was real; her pictures were all over the place.

Praying to her would be more like having a chat with a kindly neighbour.

At first Lily was unaware of the noises outside, the shouting.

Then there was the sound of someone running up the steps towards the church door and she turned to see the figure of a man pause briefly, couldn't see his face because the light was behind him, but knew from the way he gasped for breath, his shirt half out of his trousers, his dishevelled hair, that he was in trouble.

"*Padre, dov'é il padre?*"

It was a young voice, high with panic.

A couple of the women now turned, one of them stood, then another, and they scuttled away to a side door that opened and shut silently.

There were more shouts outside, heavy footsteps coming rapidly closer.

Where was the priest? He'd been there a moment ago. Had he too gone scuttling off, avoiding trouble, not wanting to be involved, to be a witness even?

The young man started to run towards the alter, stumbled and caught hold of the pew on which Lily was sitting.

"*Aiutami, ti prego.*"

Instinctively she pulled back from his outstretched hand. As he straightened up there was a rush from behind, uniformed *carabinieri* surrounding him, grabbing hold of his arms, his hair, whatever they could. He struggled, kicked out, and was punched once then again, no-one saying anything, the thud of fists making contact with bone, his gasps of pain sounding loud and incongruous in the vast silence. One of the policemen gave her an apologetic shrug.

"*Scusi, signora.*"

He was only half conscious as they dragged him out,

blood pouring from his nose, his feet bumping on the flagstone floor.

Now from outside came a single scream, sharp, piercing, a woman's scream. His mother? His girlfriend? Lily closed her eyes tightly.

"These are terrible times. Terrible."

She hadn't noticed the sacristan standing behind her, his voice made her jump. He sighed, moved away and continued extinguishing candles.

Why didn't you help him? she wanted to shout.

It was some time before she had the courage to leave the church. Outside in the twilight the piazza was calm, normal, as though nothing had happened. Two girls sat on a wall swinging their legs, giggling. An old man leant on a stick and gazed out to sea. A group of children were sharing out what looked like strips of brown leather.

"*Vuoi una carruba, signora?*" a boy said, chewing one as he held out another for her. It was some kind of dried bean.

"*Grazie,*" she said, taking it but not eating it, walking on with it in her hand, her mind elsewhere.

Had no-one outside realised what was happening? Did no-one care? It was sensible not to get involved these days, of course. Sensible to say nothing. Though most of the villagers seemed completely disinterested in politics, you could never be sure. After twenty years of fascism the authorities had their spies everywhere. They knew how to track down the flies in the ointment, and what to do with them.

Sidney had told her things.

"They hold official trials, it all looks above board and fair. But you know in advance that anyone who's even suspected of anti-fascist activity is going to be found guilty."

"And sent to prison?"

"If they're lucky, yes. Some just disappear, are never seen

again. Others are publicly executed."

"Truly? How barbaric."

"When Mussolini said anti-fascist activities wouldn't be tolerated, he meant it."

Sidney had paused.

"A fellow I know who lives in the north told me a story. A seventeen year old boy was arrested, pink faced, a kid and petrified. Naturally, who wouldn't be? Two of the *carabinieri* were seen whispering, then they smiled. One of them said to the boy they were going to give him a second chance, told him to go home."

"They set him free?"

"He was scampering back towards his house, laughing with relief when they took out their guns, shot him in the back. He fell at his mother's feet. They saluted her before they drove off."

"OK, that's enough. I don't want to hear any more," Lily said.

She thought about the terror in the face of the young man in the church, how he'd turned to her for help and she'd done nothing.

She thought about Paolo. She hoped he'd got back to Sicily and was now in hiding, safe, living in a remote farmhouse with his books and dreams and his pretty *fidanzata*. Or had he too been tracked down by the *carabinieri*, or by plain clothes officials who'd come for him in the dead of night and caught him unawares? Was he even alive still?

Sleep, that night, was impossible. Lily tossed and turned, got up for a drink of water, tried again. When she did eventually fall asleep it was to have dreams full of unseen terrors, threats she couldn't quite remember when she woke, though she knew it would be best to stay awake. As dawn came she heard a single bird trilling; she hoped it wasn't in a cage hanging on someone's wall.

She felt stunned with fatigue.

For the past week or so James had been sleeping beside her again. She found it disconcerting, had got used to being alone. In many ways she preferred it. Now he turned onto his back, one arm flung above his head. So he too was awake.

When he suddenly moved towards her and put his arm around her, drew her close, she didn't resist. Whilst his lips sought and found her neck, the lobe of her ear, his hands were pushing at her nightdress, his body pressing against her hip. She could feel he had an erection.

"James, no…"

She didn't want to make love. She couldn't bear it. She didn't even want him to touch her.

She said his name again, sharply, but he paid no attention, one hand nudging, insinuating its way between her legs.

"I said no!"

Before she knew what she was doing, she'd shoved him away and pulled herself free, falling out of bed and onto the cold tiles, knocking her ankle bone which was agony.

"How dare you, how dare you?" she heard herself hissing, clambering to her feet, clutching her nightdress around her as though for protection. For a long moment James stayed propped up on one elbow, just looking at her. Then he sighed and turned his back to her. Though it all he hadn't spoken a single word.

Twenty-Three

The rest of the world may have seemed far away, but gradually stories filtered through.

In just one day of Polish cities coming under attack by German aeroplanes – and by a million German troops – over 1,500 people had been killed.

Now that Chamberlain had declared war, Britain would surely be next to come under attack. In readiness, the government was spending over £1,000 a minute on rearmament. Private and commercial vehicles were being requisitioned. Kerbs were being painted white to help traffic find its way in the nightly blackouts, and it was rumoured that supplies of black material were already running out.

The stained glass windows of York Minster and Canterbury Cathedral had been carefully removed and stored for safety, as had the art treasures of the National Gallery and other museums. Those pet owners who were reluctant to have their four legged friends put to sleep placed advertisements in The Times for new homes. In the same paper a concerned dachshund owner pleaded that these dogs should not be persecuted, as they had been in the last war. They are just dogs, she said.

Airports were shut down, the Channel packets stopped running, petrol supplies began to dry up. Everything came to a halt whilst Britain sat and waited for the inevitable invasion. Defence experts calculated that – when the Germans did start bombing London – an expected 100,000 tons of bombs would drop in the first two weeks. Nearly a quarter of a million casualties might be expected in just one week.

Large manors and stately homes became auxiliary hospitals. Silent, empty, with rows of beds neatly made, they waited for the expected flood of wounded and dying.

Meanwhile, many of the city children evacuated to the country cried themselves to sleep and begged to be sent home.

In contrast to the black clouds of dread, the September weather remained warm, soft, golden.

Lily tried not to think about what was happening at home, about what they were going through, the people she loved. She couldn't do anything about it.

Here in the village it was harvest time. It had always been traditional for surplus food to be preserved for the winter; this year it was more vital than ever. Each family had its favourite methods, the women getting together to clean, chop, prepare tomatoes, aubergines, courgettes, peppers, mushrooms before packing them in oil or vinegar or alcohol. They smoked meat too, and salted fish. Often they sang as they worked.

Boys were sent shinning up trees to pick plump olives which were carried in baskets to the mill to be pressed, the thick green oil bottled and sealed.

Meanwhile the men took their guns and went up into the hills to shoot rabbits, quail, or exhausted migratory birds heading south towards Africa for the winter. Later they would drink too much wine and doze in the shade of trees whose leaves were now turning to gold, yellow, red.

"They remind me of trees back home," James said. "Especially the maples, which are just stunning in the fall. It's as though they're on fire."

"Really?"

Once, many years ago, Lily had wanted to know everything about the place he came from: his house, his family and friends, pets, every tiny detail. She no longer cared.

"Yes, really."

The look he gave her was that of a disappointed child.

The village gossip continued doing its rounds. At least it was a distraction from the horrors of life on the other side of the mountains, and beyond.

A hunting dog was bitten by a poisonous snake and lay groaning, frothing at the mouth for a whole day until his distraught owner took up his gun and put him out of his suffering. He then got blind drunk.

Two Russians, an artist and his friend, were spotted dancing naked on the beach at dawn. Soon a small crowd had gathered to watch them, everyone agreeing that the dance they were doing wasn't so very different from the tarantella. An old man even joined in to prove the point, thrashing around in the sand, though he refused to remove his clothes.

"*Fa troppo freddo per uno vecchio,*" he said. It was much too cold.

A woman had twin girls, pale skinned babies with carrot coloured hair, and two pink bows were tied on the front door of the house to announce the good news.

It was only when, during the *Festa di San Gennaro,* something very unusual happened, that the villagers began to understand that whatever it was that was threatening the rest of the world would eventually reach them too. Like a poison gas it would drift to the far corners of the world. Even here.

The man who came to sharpen knives brought the news.

"This year there was no blood," he said.

"*Ma non é possible.* There's always blood."

"Not this year."

"What did he say?"

"Christ's statue in the chiesa San Gennaro, in Napoli…"

"…his wounds bleed, just this one day each year…"

"I went there myself a few years ago. The church was packed, everyone anxious to see the sign. I was in tears. To be present at such a miracle is a beautiful thing."

"This year there was no miracle, no blood, nothing."

"I don't believe it, how is it possible?"

"God has despaired of us."

"And rightly so, the world is a wicked place, terrible things are happening…"

The news was passed on; people with anxious faces crossed themselves. Heads were shaken.

At evening mass there were more worshippers than usual, Don Federico officiating, ending with a special plea that everyone should pray for peace, for the world to be returned to sanity before it was too late, before the rivers ran red with blood and the streets were piled with the corpses of not just young men but women too, the elderly, and worst of all, innocent little children.

It was one of his most powerful sermons. Eyes were wiped, heads bowed, lips moving in silent prayer. One woman sobbed hysterically and had to be taken out. The collection amounted to nearly five times more than had been donated the previous evening.

"You're my wife," James said. "It's your duty."

Why had he suddenly brought up the subject? Lily wondered. Surely he couldn't actually want to? She carried on watering the tomato plants which were more like bushes now, the fruits still coming, more and more of them. She didn't speak as she moved around him.

He caught her wrist.

"You can't deny me, Lilian."

"And you can't make me," she said. Proud of herself.

It was dusk, the terrace in shadow now, the smell of fried peppers coming up from somewhere below, voices ebbing and fading.

James released her.

"But I can persuade you, can't I?"

He blocked the way back into the house, caught her face between his hands and started to cover it with small kisses.

"James, please stop."

But he didn't. Instead he backed her towards the wall, still kissing her, muttering as he did so.

"Come on, Lily, remember how it used to be between us? It was good, wasn't it? It can be like that again."

He ran his hands up the side of her body to her breasts, his thumbs circling her nipples, kissing along her collar bone, up under her chin. He began to unbutton her blouse.

"Leave me alone."

She pushed him away, angry now. And realising she meant it something snapped in him.

"Of course. I forgot you're used to a different way of loving now. So what is it your fisherman does that's so special?"

"For goodness sake, James."

He caught her shoulders, shoved her back against the wall again, its coarse surface scratching her bare arms.

"Does he play rough? Is that what you prefer? I can do that, too, Lily."

Now he was kissing her hard, at the same time trying to lift up her skirt. For the first time Lily felt a flutter of panic. She tried to wriggle free, but he wove his fingers through her hair and yanked her head backwards. She tried to loosen his grip but it was impossible.

"James, please…"

She could hardly get the words out, trapped, hurting, surprised by a strength she didn't know he had. His other hand now was high up under her skirt.

"Hey, you're right, this is fun."

With his body pressed hard against hers she had no chance of getting away. As he tore at her underwear, wedged his knee between her legs and then pushed himself inside her, she could sense the anger, the jealousy, the frustration. Making a final attempt to get him away from him she put her hands against his shoulders and pushed, pushed as hard as she could. He didn't even seem to notice.

"And outdoors, you like that too. Like animals mating, right?"

His voice was hoarse, he was thumping hard against her, and when she tried to speak, to beg him to stop, he released her hair and instead pressed his hand against her mouth, turning her face away as though he didn't want her to look at him. His nails were sharp, not short like those of a manual worker; his fingers tasted of disinfectant.

From a house higher up the steps she could hear two men arguing, then a woman calling to them both to shut up, then laughter.

Lily blinked back the tears and stopped struggling.

This wasn't James. He'd never hurt her, he hated physical violence of any kind. Had she done this to him, turned him into a slavering monster?

Twenty-Four

There seemed to be celebrations of one kind or another every few minutes. Bean *festas*, wine *festas*, saints' days galore. Any excuse would do. Much as she enjoyed them, Lily wasn't in the mood for another one. But she'd given in to please Natalia who'd insisted that – if she liked spectacles – this really was the one not to be missed. And that in any case if she stayed home all she would do was hang around the house trying to avoid James, and then getting upset when he avoided her, which was true.

There was also the fact that Sidney was in Rome for a few days, and that Hans and Dieter both had some kind of stomach bug.

Natalia admitted it.

"It's horrid going to these celebrations alone, darling. Do come with me. Please?"

Once again it was all happening on the beach; the local

equivalent of the village green, Lily decided. Natalia had got there first, bagged a space on the wall that curved around the side of the beach, and Lily squeezed in between her and a fat man in shorts and a panama hat, smiling at him apologetically, feeling the warmth of the stone beneath her though the sun had already set, the days getting noticeably shorter.

The *festa dei Saraceni* was the most exciting of them all, she'd been told, the most colourful with its re-enactment of the arrival of the Saracens, the fighting on the beach, the eventual routing of the enemy by the villagers and the celebrations that followed.

"So is James at home today, or off somewhere healing the sick?"

In a weak moment – immediately regretted – Lily had confessed that things weren't good between them. She hadn't gone into any details, of course, but Natalia would no doubt make them up for herself.

"He was at home when I left."

Natalia gave her a look that she ignored.

"You know who was asking about you the other day? Ernesto, you remember, the fisherman who took us to the island?"

"Was he?"

"Said he hadn't seen you around lately and that he hoped everything was alright."

Lily didn't believe her. He wouldn't talk to Natalia about her. Or would he? Sometimes Lily wondered if Natalia knew all about them too, not that he'd have told her, but she had her informers. Natalia collected gossip like little boys collected stamps. Sidney said it was good for her; meddling in other people's lives gave her something to think about beside herself.

A cheer, and the spectacle had begun.

Thank goodness. There was no way they could talk over all the shouting and grunting as the two opposing sides threw themselves into the action with enthusiasm. She liked the Saracens best with their rainbow-coloured robes, even though they were the enemy. When the dancing began she remembered once sneaking out with Cissy to visit a gypsy camp that had set up nearby. Their mother had warned them that gypsies were thieves and liars and stole children to sell as slaves, and Lily had been terrified as they crouched behind a caravan watching the dancing, the camp fire flickering. This time though she enjoyed it, a strange pulsating music coming from flutes, cymbals, some instruments she didn't recognise. It sent a tingle down the back of her neck.

She was disappointed when it stopped.

"And now, yet another firework display." Natalia sounded almost bored. "They do love their fireworks, the Italians."

In order to clear a space, those in the centre of the beach were pushed back so that the promenade became even more crowded, fathers lifting young children and perching them on their shoulders. Boys clambered up trees or swung like monkeys from the railings of balconies, whilst those at the far end of the beach climbed onto the fishing boats that had been dragged up there out of the way. It brought to mind Oxford Street at Christmas. Lily was grateful not to be in the crush.

"Afterwards, you must come and eat with me," Natalia was saying. "Stopping off for cocktails first, of course."

Like gunshots, the first volley of fireworks lit up the sky with fountains of colour, diamonds showering down to join their reflections in the black sea, more rockets going up, cries of delight mingling with the explosions so that for a moment Lily pressed her hands against her ears, closed her eyes. When she opened them she noticed that – over to the right, close to

216

the fishermen's stores that backed the promenade – something was happening. There was a sort of swirling movement in the crowd, like a whirlpool.

Natalia put her mouth close to Lily's ear.

"I wonder what's going on over there?" So she'd noticed too.

Lily shrugged. More bangs, and another burst of colour splattered the sky. It was probably nothing, one of those little dramas the locals loved to make a meal out of.

The fireworks seemed to be even louder, echoing back from the mountains. When suddenly they stopped, the silence was almost as deafening. Then came the cheering, and then the slow moving exodus edging away from the beach, people yawning, exchanging smiles, praising the *festa* which was without doubt one of the best one ever, *senza dubbio*.

Reports of the drama in the far corner were slowly rippling through the crowd, changing constantly as they were passed on.

"There's been an accident. Three people are dead."

"Part of a wall has collapsed and a child is trapped."

"Why bring a horse down here? Of course it would be driven crazy by such noise!"

"It's nothing, an old woman fainted."

Lily looked over her shoulder at Natalia.

"Should we go and see if we can help?"

"How exactly?"

"I don't know, it just seems…"

"Best thing we can do is keep out of the way," Natalia said.

They were nearly at the bottom of the steps that led up from the beach when the crowd parted, hushed now, shuffling to try to see and yet also pushing back to leave a narrow pathway through which came a man carrying the limp body of a child.

Natalia caught Lily's arm.

"I think we need that drink, don't you?"

"Was that…?"

"Ernesto. Yes."

Lily's head felt odd. She had difficult catching her breath.

"I must go to him."

"Don't be ridiculous."

"Natalia, I have to, don't…"

"Darling, it's nothing to do with you"

This can't be happening, Lily thought. Then, it may not be so bad, she thought. Dino had looked awful, but that didn't mean anything. He could have been hit on the head, knocked unconscious but not badly injured. He could come to and have nothing worse than a headache.

"But Ernesto might need me."

"Lily, he has a wife, a family. Why would he need you?"

The next hour or so was a blur. Obediently Lily followed Natalia to the cellar below the café, found a chair, drank whatever was put in front of her. She even managed to have polite conversations with a couple of familiar faces, though had no idea what they'd been about.

When she felt the gentle tap on her shoulder she started.

"*Signora?*"

It was the barman from upstairs.

"There is someone to see you. Outside. Come please."

For a moment she thought there must have been a mistake, then got unsteadily to her feet and followed him. The upstairs bar was also crowded with late night revellers. Two men on the brink of a fight were actually being encouraged by jeering onlookers; a little girl was asleep with her head on a table.

"Over there." The barman pointed.

It was like stepping into an abyss; there was no moon, and

218

at first Lily couldn't see anyone. Then, up the road she caught a movement as someone stepped out from a dark doorway, heard a murmur that could have been her name.

"Ernesto?"

She hurried towards him, wanted to put her arms around him, to hold him tightly, but she didn't. He pulled her back into the doorway, immediately took out a cigarette and lit it. In the brief flare of the match he looked old, weary.

"Dino, how is he? What happened?"

"Some of the railings on a balcony broke, came away. He was holding onto them. When he fell he... I don't know exactly what happened. Things landed on top of him."

His voice faded.

"Is he...?" Lily couldn't think of the word conscious in Italian. "Is he awake?"

Ernesto shook his head.

"Liliana, you have to help me. I went for *il dottore*, asked him to come and see Dino, to do what he could. He looked at me. Then he shut the door. When I called he wouldn't answer. Even when I begged."

"You went to James?"

She hadn't even thought about them summoning James; it was as though she'd already assumed Dino was either dead, or up and about again. Of course James wouldn't go. Why should he help the man who was making love to his wife, was the reason people pitied him, *un cornuto*, wasn't that the word? She'd heard it said that any Italian man who found his wife cheating on him was justified in killing both his wife and her lover.

But James was different. Taking life went against everything he believed. Even if there was nothing he could do, he should go and see Dino. He couldn't punish a child for what his father had done.

"Will you ask him for me?"

Now she understood why he'd come for her so openly. He was desperate. Natalia was wrong; there was something she could do to help.

"Of course."

He caught her face in his hands and kissed her, a kiss that tasted of desperation, of fear. Lily had to force herself to pull free. She ran up the road, got a stitch and walked for a bit, then started to run again.

The house was in darkness and for a moment she thought James had gone out, on another call possibly, to help someone else in trouble. Or had he gone to Naples again?

"James?"

She looked in his surgery, the bedroom and kitchen. All empty.

He was out on the terrace, a shape, the white of his arms giving him away. At first she didn't speak, just sat down beside him and waited for him to say something. After a bit she knew it was up to her

"James, don't do this. Dino needs you."

She kept her tone steady, dispassionate.

No reply.

"You wouldn't want him to die."

"I wouldn't?"

He didn't mean it. He might have changed – she shuddered at the memory of the night he'd forced himself on her, put it out of her mind as she'd resolved to do – but not that much.

"Maybe you hate Ernesto, and me too. But don't take it out on a little boy."

Silence again. He wasn't going to make it easy for her.

"Please, James. Will you go and at least see him?"

"I've already said no."

Was it because he loved her so much? Or was it just hurt pride, a need to retaliate, to make her suffer? Or was it Ernesto he wanted to punish? She wished she knew.

"You can't do this."

"I can do what I like, Lilian."

He stood, stretched.

"Just like you."

He went inside. Lily felt the anger welling up inside her. The accident had happened hours ago; every minute that passed lessened Dino's chances.

He was sitting at the kitchen table peeling an apple, the chair tipped back on two legs. He didn't look up as she entered. She too kept her eyes on the green spiral of skin.

"Whatever it is you want me to do, I'll do it, James. If you want me to promise I'll never see Ernesto again, I will. If you'd prefer me to leave, to go back to England, I'll go."

He bit off a chunk of the apple, munched noisily.

"If you want to give me – us – another try I'll be a good wife, I'll cook, I'll keep the house tidy, I'll do your washing and…"

He stood up so abruptly that the chair fell over backwards, dropped the knife and remainder of the apple onto the table.

"You can do what you like," he said.

Again he walked away from her, and she heard the door to his surgery slam shut. Should she follow him again, beg him? Surely he wouldn't say no if she got down on her knees in front of him?

The door swung open again, there were footsteps across the hall, the front door opened and shut. Lily ran to the surgery, looked in all the usual places, but it had gone. He'd taken his Gladstone bag.

She went across to the glass dome under which the Madonna stood in prayer. Carefully she lifted the glass, put it down, reached for the statue. It felt light, insubstantial. She kissed it, as she'd seen an old lady once do with a statue of Christ; it tasted of paint and dust.

"Thank you," she whispered.

She was asleep when James returned, stretched out on the bed, still dressed. For hours she'd walked back and forth, then she'd lain and stared at the ceiling. Eventually she'd dropped off though she'd woken more than once, got up to check the time, then collapsed back onto the bed.

The moment she heard movement in the house she was up, stumbling her way to the door.

"How is he?"

James sat, rubbed at his eyes.

"Not good. He ought to be got to a hospital, but I wouldn't move him, not yet. Not until he's conscious anyway."

"He's still unconscious?"

James nodded.

Lily didn't know what else to say.

"Would you like some tea?"

Another nod.

Tea, the answer to everything, she thought as she put water to boil. Even if it was herbal tea, the only kind she could get nowadays.

What if Dino died? Would Ernesto stay with his wife? When Lily had fantasised about him coming to live with her, Dino had always been in the way. She could imagine somehow Ernesto leaving his wife, but not his son, not the boy he obviously adored.

But if Dino died…

It was at that moment Lily realised James wasn't the only one who'd changed.

For the next few weeks James was rarely home. Sometimes he was called to other people: a girl with a plague of abscesses that needed to be lanced, a woman with chronic indigestion, a man who'd fallen whilst carrying water in an earthenware pot and cut his arm.

Often, though, he was at Ernesto's house.

Lily longed to ask questions.

What is his house like? Does it have pretty things inside, a large bedroom, views of the sea? What is his wife's name? Do other people live with them, parents, brothers or sisters? How are they together, Ernesto and his wife? Do they hold each other, get strength from each other, or is the worry tearing them apart?

Tell me everything, she longed to say.

James volunteered nothing. She managed to get out of him that Dino had gained consciousness, that he had a fever, his broken leg could leave him with a limp, there could be internal injuries. And then there was a slight improvement.

"He's a brave kid," James said. "A real little fighter."

Lily's feeling of relief was tainted with one of jealousy.

Whilst James was growing closer to Dino, she no longer saw him, she couldn't even go to the house to enquire how he was.

It was shortly after that James decided he should be transferred to the hospital in Sorrento.

"I think he's going to be alright. But I'd like him to have some X- rays and other checks, and besides, he needs twenty four hour nursing and his mother is just about at breaking point."

Another twinge.

"Can't anyone help her?"

"She won't let them. She's hardly left his bedside since the accident. If I can get him into hospital hopefully she'll trust he's in safe hands and catch up with some rest herself."

"And what about Dino's leg?"

"Not sure. Should be OK."

Lily could imagine the joy Ernesto must be feeling, the relief. And it's all thanks to *il dottore*, they'll say. A brilliant doctor. He can work miracles. None of them would know about the sacrifice she'd made in exchange for Dino's life, only Ernesto. And would he care, now that he had his son back?

"James?" She waited until he looked up. "Thank you."

He met her eyes briefly, looked away.

"I didn't do it for you," he said.

Twenty-Five

Lily couldn't stop crying. Think of something nice, she told herself. Anything. Autumn in England, the things you miss, like glossy fat blackberries, sweet juice staining your fingers as you pick them. Better still, a blackberry and apple pie topped with thick yellow custard.

Withdrawal symptoms, wasn't that what drug addicts suffered when they could no longer get their own particular poison? She'd read that they went through agony, both physical and mental. She was addicted to Ernesto, so what she was going through must be withdrawal symptoms. Every bit of her longed for him, craved his touch, even just his nearness. How was she going to live without him?

Autumn, she reminded herself.

Dog rose hips mixed with chrysanthemums and ferns, her mother's favourite combination, usually tucked into a copper jug. Cutting the lawn for the last time, the mower kicking up a fountain of green, then raking the grass into soft damp piles. Frosts that covered everything with a fine white film. Log fires, orange flames flickering, and that delicious smell of cut wood from the log basket.

Ernesto's hut smelt of wood. And fish, and that strange green smell that came from the nets.

No, no, no.

Something else, quick.

Soft blankets. Hot water bottles. Ovaltine made with extra sugar, and whisked so that it goes frothy on top.

The tears trickled into the corner of her mouth. She rubbed at her eyes with the back of her hand, not caring that she was making them red and sore.

They'd met by chance, a week or so ago, she and Ernesto.

She had walked down to the post office to see if there were any letters, been disappointed to find none. Though there had been no reports of bomb attacks on London, everyone knew it would happen sooner or later. When she didn't hear, she worried. Making her way back up the road she'd seen two figures sitting on the wall deep in conversation; as she'd drawn nearer one of them got up and walked off. The other was Ernesto.

"*Ciao*, Liliana," he said. He had dark shadows under his eyes.

"How are you?" she said, only too aware how formal that sounded. What she meant was how are you really?

He held up his hand, palm downwards, tipped it from side to side.

"*Non c'e male.*" Not too bad, all things considered.

"And Dino?"

"Better. He's coming home in a few days."

"That's wonderful news."

"Liliana, you know that you helped…"

Lily reached and put her fingers across his lips. He caught her wrist and held them there briefly, kissing them lightly, then let her hand go. She couldn't bear to look at him any more, gazed out over the sequined sea to the distant hump that was the island she and Natalia had visited so long ago. That was the day she'd met Ernesto. He'd never taught her to swim.

"And you, Liliana, how are you?"

She was determined to smile.

"I'm fine. Missing you, but I'm fine."

"We had some good times together, didn't we?"

He'd used the past tense.

"Liliana, I've been thinking…"

"Wait. There's something I must say first. When James agreed to see Dino there was a condition. I promised him that you and I wouldn't meet again, not…"

Not alone, she meant. Not as lovers. Now it was Ernesto's turn to avoid her eyes. He'd turned and stared up the road, waiting as an elderly man with a stiff-legged dog walked slowly past, then a boy on a bicycle.

Then he'd stood, held out his hand, formal, not smiling.

He wrapped both his hands around the one she gave him.

"What can I say?"

"*Niente.*"

There had been nothing more either of them needed to say.

Since then her resolve to put on a good show, keep a stiff upper lip and all that, had dissolved. If James noticed her mood he said nothing, simply stayed out of her way. She didn't mind, she preferred it. As soon as he left the house Lily headed straight for the surgery, for the cupboard where she knew he kept a bottle of brandy, poured herself a drop and drank it back at once. She hated its bitter taste but would think of it as medicine.

What was wrong with her? Why did she feel as though she was dissolving, like a digestive biscuit dipped into hot tea?

More brandy. More pacing the room. More questions without answers.Without realising how she got there she found herself hunched on the floor, curled tight, the tiles cold beneath her, unsure if she'd been asleep or had passed out. Someone was banging on the door. So that was what had woken her. Lily didn't move and after a bit the footsteps went away.

Where was James? How long had he been gone? She'd lost track of time completely. She couldn't even remember what he'd said as he left; was he going to see someone, or pick up supplies, or what? He might have gone to Naples to find himself another prostitute, assuming it was his right now that he and Lily didn't make love any more. It was fine with her. He'd probably get some terrible disease and his body would rot and he'd lose his mind and go doolalee, but so what?

If he ever touched her again she'd kill him.

All she wanted was one man, the one man she couldn't have. Forcing herself to sit up, she realised she'd got chilled. She couldn't stop shivering. Somehow she managed to get to her to her feet, her legs stiff, her whole body sore.

It was as she was rummaging in a drawer for a cardigan that her fingers touched something hard and unfamiliar.

For a moment she couldn't think what it was. As she unwrapped it she remembered Paolo, his sudden departure, finding the gun afterwards. She'd intended to throw it away, but so much had been happening back then. Obviously she hadn't. Sitting there holding the gun she thought how right it felt nestling into the curve of her palm. A perfect fit.

She slipped the gun into the pocket of her dress, held the

half empty brandy bottle close against her body, concealing both with the cardigan she'd eventually found. Outside there was a strong wind, clouds scuttling across the sky. Her hair was messed up in minutes, but it didn't matter, she didn't care what anyone thought. Besides, she hardly saw anyone, those she did pass had their heads down, anxious only to get where they were going. As she got closer to the sea she saw that the water too was grey, choppy, topped with ruffles of white.

The stones on the beach felt familiar under her sandals.

Would he be there? She doubted it. Certainly he wouldn't take his boat out in weather like this. It was weather for staying home, doing jobs around the house, for being with your wife and child.

Going into the hut was like going home. Lily shut the door behind her. In the gloom she could make out a pile of nets, some boxes stacked against one wall, a single shoe lying on its side. Then she noticed that the gramophone was still there, a record waiting. As though she'd been there recently, a day or two ago.

She went across, wound it up, carefully placed the needle on the outside of the dusty black disc. Cream Puff. Of course, hadn't they played it nearly all the time, until they both knew every note off by heart?

A splattering sound drew her to the window; it was raining, she could hardly make out where the sea stopped and the sky began. A brown spider scuttled down the inside of the glass.

Lily played the record again, then one more time. Then again. She drank the rest of the brandy.

She got down onto the floor, sat back on her heels, took the gun out of her pocket.

She held it up to her temple, her finger curled around the trigger. It felt awkward. Her arm began to ache.

The music was slowing, hardly recognisable.

What if the force of the explosion jolted her hand and she just got a graze, or blinded herself, or something equally awful? Better, she decided, to put it into her mouth. She looked at the gun, then made up her mind, closed her eyes, opened her mouth and rested the gun on her lower lip. It tasted metallic, cold, and made her retch.

Don't think, just do it.

The music had come to an end; there was the scratching of the needle trapped in the centre as the record continued to go round and round.

Do it now.

She lifted the gun to her mouth, shut her eyes as her finger rested against the trigger, the ringing in her ears growing louder. It felt stiff. She would have to use both hands.

"I can't!" she wailed then, letting the gun slide to the floor.

After a few minutes she got up, went across to the gramophone, took off the record and smashed it against the wall. There were slivers of black Bakelite everywhere.

Stupid. The music was stupid, she was stupid. What in God's name was she thinking?

Opening the door she stumbled out, then remembered the gun. She couldn't leave it there, anyone might get hold of it, someone could be injured. She dropped it back into her pocket, started again towards the village lights.

Afterwards she could remember little about her walk home, except that she'd again seen hardly anyone, and that at some point it had stopped raining, though now it was almost dark, the narrow, uneven steps difficult to negotiate. That must have been how she'd got the cut on her foot. And she'd been cold, she could remember that. Cold deep down inside.

Now her thoughts had turned to James.

He'd never really loved her, not for herself, only as Mrs

Hogan, someone to accompany him to dinners and answer the telephone and give him the respectability he needed if he was to be a successful doctor. And hadn't he fooled everyone else too, his patients, his medical colleagues, with his suits and his nice Boston accent and books all over the house. What would they say if they knew he went to prostitutes? That he risked his own health and that of his wife by having sex with poor sad girls who sold their bodies so they could eat?

What would they say if they knew he'd left a woman to die whilst he went off in search of sex? And if they knew how he'd treated her, Lily, the woman he'd vowed to love and honour, that would open their eyes too. It was no wonder she'd fallen into Ernesto's arms. She'd needed to be wanted and loved for herself, she had a right to expect that much at least, didn't every woman?

James. He'd brought her to this, him and his lies. His life was one long lie and he was destroying her.

At one point she'd passed a young couple, arms wrapped around each other, their bodies pressed into a doorway.

"*Buonasera, signora,*" the young man had said, though Lily didn't think she knew him. She hadn't replied.

The door to the house was open. She'd stepped inside silently, pushed it shut behind her. Now she had the gun out.

Though the hall light was on, James wasn't in his surgery. Nor in the drawing room, bedroom, or the kitchen. She felt confused. He could have rushed off on an emergency which would explain the open door. And yet she sensed he was there, could feel his presence.

Then, a small cough from out on the terrace. So that's where he was. Lily tiptoed towards the door that led outside, holding the gun with both hands now.

He was standing hunched over the railing looking out

towards the sea, his white shirt billowing as the wind caught it, his hair ruffled. It would be so easy. All she had to do was hold the gun steady.

He deserved it, God knew he deserved it.

Her heart was making so much noise she felt sure he would hear it. Holding the gun with both hands she pointed it at his back, kept her arms straight as she'd seen them do in films. Gently she pressed her finger against the trigger, steadily increasing the pressure. In a second it would give and there would be a loud crack, and even as she thought it she felt her arms begin to shake, her strength suddenly draining away like water from an upturned bottle.

"Lily?"

His voice was all wrong.

Twenty - Six

To think what might have happened.

Lily opened her eyes. The room was dim, though sunlight was filtering through the shutters and patterning the bedspread, so it must be morning. She could hear church bells, small feet clattering past on their way to school.

To think she might have killed Paolo.

He'd been wonderful so far, hadn't asked a single question in fact, had shown only concern.

Suddenly a black sheet had dropped over her. When she'd come to she'd felt someone tapping her face, saying her name over and over, and couldn't for a moment remember anything. When she'd finally managed to get her eyes to focus she was even more confused.

"Paolo? I don't understand. Where's James?"

"Never mind about him. How do you feel? Can you sit up?"

He'd tucked his arm around her, pulled her up to a sitting

position and the world had tipped again.

"Lily?"

"It's OK. Just let me stay here for a minute."

He'd crouched down beside her, holding her, and gradually the dizziness had passed.

"James…"

"He had to go out. I arrived an hour or so ago. We were having a drink and then someone came, an old man had been bitten by a scorpion, or a spider. Something poisonous anyway."

Probably the knocking she'd heard earlier.

"I thought you were James," she'd said. "I didn't hurt you, did I?"

"No. You fainted before you pressed the trigger." Was he smiling? It was hard to see in the dark. "Besides, it's not loaded."

He must have thought she'd gone mad. She should explain. And then there was the sound of footsteps in the hallway.

"The gun…" Lily suddenly remembered, turned, feeling for it across the floor, but Paolo put a finger across his lips.

"Shh. I've got it."

As James appeared in the doorway he'd looked up.

"She passed out. My fault. She saw a figure out here in the dark, then heard a stranger's voice. I should have thought."

She tried again to stand but James knelt down beside her, his fingers on her wrist, pushing back a strand of hair. Though she'd said she didn't want him touching her there was something comforting about his hands.

"Best thing for you is bed," he said.

Thank God she hadn't shot him, she couldn't believe she'd come so close to doing it. She may not love him any more, but she didn't hate him either. Not that much.

What if she'd pulled the trigger and he'd died? She'd have been arrested, found guilty of course, transferred to an ugly building with bars on every window. Her life would have been confined to four walls, to boredom, to indignities such as having to go to the toilet in front of other people, never having any privacy. She'd read a letter in a newspaper once, written by a woman in prison. The worst thing of all, she'd written, was never being able to touch or smell fresh flowers.

A tentative knocking at the door. Paolo, then. James wouldn't have knocked.

"*Poverétta*. How are you, Lily? Is there anything I can get?"

He looked anxious, and so pale. Did he ever have a colour? Maybe it was just that she was used to the darker, weather beaten skins of the locals. Lily patted the blanket beside her.

"No, nothing. But come and sit with me. I'd like that."

The bed dipped as he balanced on the edge.

"About last night."

"Lily, listen. It isn't necessary to say anything."

"But it is! I could have killed you. I thought you were James…"

He took hold of her hand.

"I'm serious, Lily. I don't want to hear. I know you didn't intend to kill anyone."

He smiled.

"If you had, you'd have made sure the gun was loaded."

He made it sound so simple. She smiled back.

"You haven't been reading Freud by any chance, have you?" she said.

Paolo shook his head.

"No," he said. "I will one day though, when all this is over. He died recently, did you know? In London, James said. We had a long talk last night. About so many things."

Which meant they'd been talking about her.

"James and I... well, things are not very good between us," she said.

"He said. He said you've been very unhappy and that he knows he's partly to blame, and that he'd like more than anything to put things right but thinks it's probably too late."

"He told you that?"

Lily couldn't imagine James talking to anyone about his feelings, his personal life. Though Paolo was a good listener.

"I think he meant it ."

"Possibly."

"And is it? Too late, I mean?"

Lily pulled her hand free.

"I don't know. I don't know much about anything these days. Except that you're right when you say I didn't mean to kill him, I hadn't even thought..."

"You know, Lily, I feel guilty too. I shouldn't have left the gun. I didn't know what else I had of any value that I could give to pay you for all you'd both done."

"Have you ever used it?"

"Me?" He grimaced. "No. I hate guns. That's why it's never loaded."

She wanted to ask the point of carrying it then.

"Where is it now?" she asked instead.

"I have it. This evening I'm going to go up into the mountains and throw it somewhere no one will ever find it."

"That's exactly what I was going to do. Can I come too?"

"If you feel up to it, of course."

He stood.

"But for now try to sleep. James said I have to make sure you stay in bed and rest."

"I'm in bed and I'm resting."

She snuggled back against the pillow feeling better than she had for some time. It was as though a fever had come to a head, and then passed leaving her weary and empty and yet somehow cleansed. Even as it came to her that she'd not asked Paolo what he was doing there, her eyes began to close. She didn't wake until mid afternoon.

James had brought home figs wrapped in leaves and tied with blades of grass, and a string bag of fresh walnuts. Given to him by a woman as he was heading home, he said. He didn't recognise her but obviously she knew him. It was just as well as there was nothing else to eat in the house except some ricotta cheese, and not very fresh bread.

"Unless you fancy roast chicken?" James said.

Paolo glanced at Lily.

"No, I'm not very hungry."

"Neither am I," Lily said, and it was true. She still felt a little queasy.

She'd hoped James had given up suggesting eating the chickens. There was no way she could bring herself to eat them. Other chickens, yes, but not those.

"Right. A snack it is then."

They ate, the three of them, at the kitchen table, hardly talking. It was like having a lost son back home, Lily thought. For the first time she was grateful for the heat of the stove.

Paolo yawned, stretched out his legs.

"I could do with a walk, some fresh air," he said.

"Me too," Lily said.

"Is that a good idea, Lily? After last night?"

"Don't fuss, James. I've done nothing all day. A short stroll will be good for me."

"Don't go too far then."

Lily followed Paolo up the steps, noticing for the first time how badly he limped. The few doors they passed – doors that had been propped open all summer – were now closed. They met no-one.

When they reached the road, Lily took the lead. If she'd been there alone she'd have been nervous. With Paolo, though, she thought how beautiful it was. Bats swooped above their heads, black darts against a rapidly darkening sky. There was a sliver of moon. A shuffling sound in the bushes made them both hesitate, Lily clutching Paolo's sleeve. Then a flash of golden eyes, a flurry of movement, glimpses of fur and a bushy tail and it was gone.

"What was it?" Lily whispered. "A wolf?"

She knew wolves were sometimes seen in the mountains. A shepherd had caught one in a trap a month or so ago, had carried its pelt around the village to be stroked and admired.

"Unlikely. They don't often come this close to habitation. Probably a fox, a youngster who hasn't learnt not to trust human beings. He better learn soon."

Lily felt both relieved and disappointed.

They walked on in silence.

"So how about here?"

Paolo had crossed to the side of the path, was peering over a low wall into a crevice amongst the rocks that was thick with shrubs and bushes, a real wilderness.

"Perfect."

"Right."

He climbed up onto the wall, took the gun out.

"Be careful," Lily said, having visions of him plummeting over the edge and being swallowed up by the jungle below.

Letting his arm fall back first, he used his whole body to propel the gun up into the sky. It seemed to hang there for a moment then dropped like a stone, disappearing instantly.

Lily clapped. Paolo turned and took a bow before dropping back down onto the path, wincing as he landed awkwardly.

"I didn't forget you," she said, linking her arm through his as they headed back the way they'd come. "I wanted so much to hear that you were safe."

"Believe me, if I could have got a message to you I would have."

"Was it terrible?"

She meant the journey back, the physical pain, the fear, everything.

"Yes. But I knew I'd be alright. I have friends. More and more people are coming to realise that we're living under a dictatorship, that we have been for years."

"But how will you ever get rid of him?"

"Mussolini? It'll happen, when the time is right. He's clever, he knows how to manipulate people, but they won't be fooled forever."

Lily remembered something.

"You know the one thing he did that made him popular with the English?"

They'd reached the steps that led down from the path. Paolo stopped.

"He's popular in England? *Perche?*"

"He banned the netting of song birds on Capri."

"Of course. You English!"

He shook his head, hesitated then leant against the stone wall, both of them looking out towards where the sea and sky had merged into a grey and pink dusk.

She couldn't put the question off any longer.

"So why are you here, Paolo?"

"I'm in trouble again. Seems like I'm always coming to you and James for help, aren't I? I was to meet someone in Salerno, he would arrange to get me up north to Florence, also he was going to give me money."

"And what? He didn't turn up?"

"I waited two days, sat around in a bar from opening to

closing. The owners were becoming suspicious. Then, early yesterday morning, a young girl came to the *pensione* where I was staying, a pretty child in a yellow dress. I hate it, getting children involved. She said I must go quickly. I climbed out of the window."

He paused.

"I'm sorry," he said.

"No, don't say that, Paolo."

"I'll be leaving tomorrow. Any longer will be dangerous for you and James. This place might seem out of touch with the rest of the country, but there are always eyes watching, someone ready to give you away."

They descended the last flight of steps carefully. Now they were home, a thin line of light showing under the front door.

"How will you travel?"

"By road. I'll have to hitch rides. It's dangerous because I'll be drawing attention to myself. The plan was to go by train, get lost in the crowd. But without money…"

She sensed him shrug.

"One way or another I'll get there," he said. "There are people waiting for me, things that need to be done, now more than ever."

The door opened, James silhouetted against the light.

"There you are. Enjoy your walk?"

It wasn't like him to worry. Inside the house felt warm, welcoming.

"If you two will excuse me, I'm going to bed," Lily said, feeling suddenly exhausted. At least she should have a good night's sleep.

But she didn't. Almost as soon as she closed her eyes she saw a small girl climbing up a long wooden staircase, each stair as high as a chair so that she had to clamber up on her hands and knees. Eventually she reached a door, knocked. When it opened there was a sudden loud shot, the girl looked down, and her eyes filled with tears as a patch of red on her dress grew bigger and bigger.

Lily forced herself to wake up. Why did she never have nice dreams? James still hadn't come to bed so it couldn't be late. She studied the ceiling, the cracks, the cobwebs in the corners. Closing her eyes she tried counting sheep: one, two, three, four, five...

How was Paolo going to manage without money? What if he didn't get a lift? She imagined him standing by the roadside in front of a petrol station in the middle of nowhere, cars driving straight past, horses pulling carts loaded with fruit, vegetables, farm workers perched on top like birds. She saw a long black car with darkened windows appearing out of nowhere, and as he turned to run men tumbling out of the doors, grabbing him, twisting his arm up behind him, marching him back to the car. He'd never be seen again.

And all for the sake of a handful of lire.

It was clear what she must do: she would give him her money, the money her father had pressed into her hand a few days before they left England.

"Here, love," he'd said. "Take this and put it somewhere safe."

She'd been surprised, touched, then confused.

"But why should I need money, dad? James will make sure that we're alright, you know you can trust him."

"This is nothing to do with him, Lily. I don't even want you to tell him about it. It's your emergency fund. Something might happen to him, we hope not but you never know. Or you might need money and not want to ask him."

He was a sensible man. And he was right. It wasn't much, but it was comforting knowing it was there, just in case.

She'd changed it into lire shortly after they'd arrived in Italy. They were in Rome; she'd gone sightseeing on her own – James was visiting a colleague at a hospital – and had felt very pleased with herself for finding a bank and making herself understood. She'd tucked the wad of large notes in a pocket at the back of her suitcase. And though she hated having secrets, she'd kept her promise to her father, hadn't let on to James.

Paolo wouldn't want to take it, of course. No problem. She would make him up a food parcel, tucking the money inside. He was sure to open it before he got to Naples, would be able to buy a train ticket straight through to Rome. She would add a note saying it was not a gift but a loan. One day, when the world was again a sane and safe place, she would expect him to come and repay it in full. What was Italian for sane?

Finally she slept.

Paolo left very early next morning.

They exchanged only a few words, and a hug. James had accompanied him down to the main road and Lily had been grateful, hating to see him go off alone into the chill mist that hung over the houses, absorbed noises so that the crowing of the cockerel that lived below sounded muted, as though it came from a great distance.

He'd looked so young. So thin and cold. He'd insisted he was fine but James had looped around his neck a woollen scarf that Lily had knitted, checking first with her that she wouldn't be offended, which if course she wasn't. She liked the thought of Paolo having it. She'd made him a food parcel too.

She sat drinking tea, waiting for James to return and feeling smug. It occurred to her that for the first time in years – possibly the first time ever – she'd made an important decision entirely on her own, had taken the appropriate action, and accepted that any consequences were hers alone to deal with. It was frightening in a way. What if Paolo was arrested, the note traced to her? What if James abandoned her and she had no money to fall back on? What if... so many things.

It was also exciting. All those years of thinking she needed James's permission, his approval, his advice for even the simplest things, and suddenly she'd discovered she'd been wrong. She didn't need him. She didn't need anyone.

Twenty-Seven

"Lilian, why didn't you say?"

James had gone white. He sat down heavily.

"I wasn't sure."

"And now you are?"

She nodded.

"I've had so many things to worry about lately, I lost track of dates. And I assumed I was feeling off colour because of... well, you know. Everything that's been happening."

She stared at her hands, counted three chipped nails. She'd never have let them get into this state back home.

"It's dangerous, Lily. You realise that. For you, I mean. Remember what happened the other times. And here the facilities are much more basic, you're further away from a hospital if there is an emergency."

Did he think she hadn't gone over that again and again?

She didn't speak. He sighed.

"It could be terminated. You could go to Naples, there's a surgeon I've been hearing about, he's Finnish I think.

Scandinavian anyway. He has an excellent reputation and I'm sure he'd be willing, seeing as to go ahead carries so many risks."

He paused.

"It would be much, much safer than going ahead, Lily."

She looked up now, waited until he met her eyes. She wanted to make sure he understood.

"I know the risks, James. I also know this is my last chance. I intend to have this baby, and nothing will go wrong this time, I won't let it."

Even she was surprised by the quiet determination in her voice. He seemed to lean back a fraction in his chair.

"Lily, I do understand how you feel. But this isn't the kind of decision you can take lightly, not without at least considering…"

"You don't understand anything at all about me, James." Again she kept her voice steady; he wasn't going to do his usual thing and accuse her of being over-emotional, needing to calm down and take some deep breaths before she said another word.

"You never have because you've never bothered to find out. For a long time that mattered to me, but now it doesn't. Not any more. All that matters is that I'm pregnant, I'm happy to be pregnant, and in time I'm going to give birth to a beautiful healthy baby."

He stood, walked across the room, ran his hand over his hair, walked back. She waited. She knew what he was thinking.

He sat down again, reached as though to take her hand and then changed his mind.

"Lily, my dear."

The words came out as a whisper. She could help him, but why should she?

"It's his, isn't it? Ernesto's?"

Lily closed her eyes.

"I don't know, James. I honestly don't know."

She'd have liked to add that she didn't care, it was her baby and that was the most important thing. But it wouldn't have been true. She did care. With all her heart she wanted it to be Ernesto's.

Twenty-Eight

An egg-timer, that was what the village felt like. Each grain of sand was a person, and they were slipping away a few at a time, the ones left behind shuffling around a bit before they too slipped through the hole in the middle and were gone.

First to leave was Donald, the hypnotist. Lily hadn't seen him often, yet when he told her he was heading back to Britain – it was his country, after all, and needed all the help it could get, even his – she felt strangely unsettled. The egg timer had been turned upside down. Dieter went next, not to Germany but to Sweden, and it suddenly occurred to Lily that he was Jewish. After he'd gone Hans got blind drunk and stayed that way for almost a week, starting fights, one night going berserk in a bar and smashing glasses, a chair, three full bottles of wine, and then weeping uncontrollably. Natalia had persuaded a couple of local men to help get him back to her flat.

The Austrian writer with the grey plait just disappeared, as did most of the Italians who'd come down from Rome or Florence for the summer and stayed on, enticed by soft golden days, reluctant to face the inevitability of winter. Before they left they put away the colourful parasols, closed the shutters, locked the gates, and the village took on a desolate look.

Then Sidney departed for America.

"There are some friends I've been promising to visit for ages, and in any case, I ought to do a couple of promotional appearances. The Americans, bless them, are still buying my books. They deserve the opportunity to see me in the flesh, don't you think?"

"Will you come back?"

"To Italy? Of course, Lily love. Not sure when. But this is my home, at least, the nearest thing I've got to one."

She hated the thought that he wouldn't be there; he was her rock, just knowing he was somewhere nearby made her feel safe. Besides which she liked him, he made her smile. She was going to miss him. Even James seemed sorry to see him go.

The temperature suddenly dropped, the locals now disguised in thick jumpers, some with coats on top though Lily thought that a bit excessive; it wasn't that cold. Trees lost their last few leaves, late buds withered. One morning on the terrace she watched as a wasp fell to the ground and spun around on its back, struggled to right itself, spun some more then went still. Lily brushed its body behind a pot.

Everything was going away or dying or shrinking back into itself. It was depressing. Or it would have been if she hadn't had that little secret glow inside her.

Up in the mountains there was more shooting than ever, the blasts echoing across the village all day long. A neighbour claimed to have had *volpe* for dinner. Fox? Lily thought she must have misheard, but no. Proudly the woman brought out its brush to prove it, and Lily remembered the one she'd seen with Paolo, the youngster he'd said was taking a risk coming so close to the village. Sounds like he'd been right.

Back home it was the fox hunting season, of course. Would people still don those red jackets and drink sherry and then clamber onto horses and go chasing around the fields, great packs of dogs leading the way, all in pursuit of one small animal? Or would the war at least do the foxes a favour?

It was unfortunate that they didn't hibernate along with hedgehogs and dormice. Winter in the country was best slept through. In winter she'd especially liked living in the city where there were street lights, and laughter, and you could go to the pictures with your two ounce bag of tiger nuts, or to Lyons Corner House, or on very special occasions to the Savoy Grill for half a dozen Oysters Mornay.

Here, she suspected, the people were going to hibernate even if the animals didn't. And so was she. It might be boring and a little bit sad, but it would be good for her, good for the baby, and that was the only thing that mattered.

She had another letter from her mother.

It said nothing was happening; that they were still waiting, almost wanting the bombing to start so that at least they'd know what it was going to be like, what they'd have to deal with. Waiting is a dreadful thing, she said. The biggest fear was the poison gas. Even if you go to the toilet you take your mask with you. She enclosed a cutting from a magazine, a picture of a debutante coming home from a ball carrying her gas mask in a specially made lavender velvet bag trimmed with white chrysanthemums.

If Lily was honest, it didn't seem real to her. It was as though someone was describing a film they'd seen. Things might have been different, she supposed, if Italy had also been at war. Though of course the Italians would be fighting alongside Hitler, so wouldn't have to worry about the Luftwaffe attacking; it would be British bombs they would be fearing. Everyone said it would happen sooner or later, that Italy couldn't stay neutral for much longer.

The thought dropped like a bombshell If – when – Italy entered the war, Ernesto would be sent off to fight.

How could she bear that? She missed him already: the way his face could be dour one moment and then would break into a smile as dazzling as a field of mustard. She missed talking to him in her stumbling Italian. Or listening to him describing life as it used to be in the village, or what Dino had done or refused to do more likely, not always understanding but not wanting to interrupt his quiet, hypnotic flow of words. She missed the anticipation when she knew they would be meeting later that week, or day, counting the hours, the minutes. And his hands, she missed his hands, chunky, rough skinned hands that knew her body far better than she did herself.

She imagined telling him about the baby.

She had no intention of telling him, of course. Not yet. If he had to go away to fight, would she tell him then?

She was glad that James knew. She'd been nervous about how he'd take her news, but determined to be honest, and to make it clear that nothing he said could change her mind. In fact, he'd said very little, about the baby or anything else come to that. Often though she sensed him watching her. Some mornings he brought her tea in bed, and toast, or a bowl of porridge; once, as she was struggling with an armful of logs for the stove, he silently took them from her.

She'd noticed he was around the house more than he had been lately. She hoped he was going to have enough work to keep going. In England winters had been the busiest time of the year: children succumbing to a variety of bugs, icy roads causing accidents, the persistent fog playing havoc with the lungs of the elderly, asthma sufferers, anyone poorly nourished.

"Everything seems to have gone very quiet," she said, peeling chestnuts. She was about to try out a local recipe for chestnut soup.

"Not that quiet. I'm still getting called out most days," James said. "Or else I see someone in the surgery."

"But you don't seem to be taking much actual money."

"True. That's because so many of the foreigners are leaving. They're the ones who pay cash. But we're not on the bread line yet."

The bowl of chestnuts on the table was payment for a visit he'd made to an elderly lady with a fever.

And when it reaches that point, Lily wanted to say, then what? She knew the answer. He'd leave. She suspected he was already considering it. Unlike her; she had no intention of leaving. She wanted to stay here, bring up her child to run around barefooted, to swim like a fish, speak both English and Italian fluently, a love child living a charmed life. She'd decided it must be Ernesto's child, and if so, it should of course remain in Italy. Exactly how she would live, where, what she would use for money, were details. If James wanted to go back he would go without her.

The tiled floors that had kept the house so delightfully cool in summer now felt cold and stark, even with the assorted and musty smelling rugs their landlord had brought them. Draughts from beneath the badly fitting doors and windows didn't help. Sometimes Lily stayed in bed all morning; most nights she was in bed by nine.

It wasn't that she felt unwell; she didn't. Looking back she wondered if the incident with the gun, the swings of mood, the feeling of desperation were due to the fact that she was pregnant, her body struggling to adjust to the changes. Things seemed to have settled. The dizzy spells had stopped, as had the queasy feeling in the pit of her stomach. She still had a dull back pain much of the time, but it wasn't so bad. In a way she liked it: it was a constant reminder that something was growing inside her, a new life. Her baby.

So when one morning she noticed a few spots of fresh blood on the back of her nightdress, it felt as though she'd been doused with ice water. She sat back on the bed and hugged herself, shivering, eyes tight shut as though unwilling to face what was happening, what might be happening. She was petrified to go to the toilet in case anything escaped, slithered out of her before she had a chance to stop it.

When James put his head around the door to see if she was still sleeping, he knew instantly that something was very wrong. He crossed to her, stood there, his hands hanging loose.

"Lily, what is it?"

She couldn't reply, simply shook her head from side to side. And then he understood.

"Right, let's get you back into bed." With his arm supporting her shoulders he turned her stiff body around, lifted her legs. His voice was gentle but authoritative, and Lily felt a tiny glimmer of hope. He was a brilliant doctor, everyone said so. He'd make it right, make it not be happening.

"OK, first we must keep you warm. I'll get another blanket from the cupboard. And Lily dear, I know it's easy for me to say, but try to stay calm, not to panic."

He arranged the blanket carefully, pulling it right up to her chin, then he lay down and put an arm across her waist, his face nestling against hers. A tear escaped and trickled down her cheek, tickling as it went. He dabbed at it with his fingertips, then rubbed his own face with the back of his hand.

Still she hadn't opened her eyes.

"It may be nothing, Lily. A false alarm. It happens more often than you realise."

"But after last time…"

"Forget about last time. Forget about all the other times. Concentrate on now, and on this baby."

Gently he touched his lips to her cheek.

"We mustn't give up hope."

It was later, much later, that she remembered his words. He'd said WE. WE mustn't give up hope.

*B*est to get things out into the open, get them off your chest. It was what James always said, and he'd obviously decided to take his own advice. And though Lily had hated having to listen, she understood. At least she knew him better now, the complete picture, the horrible as well as the holy.

But he wasn't finished, it seemed.

Not quite.

Despite the chill evening air, he was out on the terrace.

Lily pulled on a cardigan, went and sat alongside him on the bench. Neither of them spoke. It was peaceful, all the sounds she was used to hearing – kitchen pans banging, a knife against a chopping board, someone singing – now muted by closed doors and windows. A crackle of shots from up in the mountains reminded her of that same morning when she'd passed a hunter with his gun under his arm, his shirt bulging, who'd proudly shown her what was tucked inside: like scraps of brown rag, the limp bodies of ten or more tiny birds, bloody and dull eyed.

"Come sono buoni," he'd said, rolling his eyes.

How could anyone shoot song birds? Or eat them, come to that? It was disgusting. She'd left a vegetable and bean stew bubbling on the stove.

"What are you thinking about, James?" she asked softly. "You've been out here for almost an hour."

"Lily…"

The voice was hardly his.

"There's something I have to tell you."

She waited, her heart doing a skitter then settling. Out over the sea a light cloud drifted across the moon, like a net veil over a face. Lights from another small village on a peninsula further along the coast could have been the lights of a passing cruise ship.

James moved and though she couldn't see him properly, she realised he was drinking something from a bottle. Brandy probably. His hands stayed firmly clasped around it.

"That night three years ago. When you had the last miscarriage, remember?"

As if she'd ever forget.

"I had to go out and see an elderly man who'd fallen down stairs. His wife had come to the house. Strange how clearly I can still see her face. Of course I agreed to go with her. You said you'd have a cup of hot cocoa waiting for me."

Lily could remember the woman too. And kissing James goodbye, putting the wireless on and settling down to do some knitting. It was comforting, if unnecessary. The baby wasn't due for six months but already she'd got more than enough things folded in tissue: tiny matinee jackets, vests, booties, some she'd made herself, others her mother had knitted for her. Most of them had been made when she was first pregnant, and then the second time when they'd all been so sure nothing would go wrong. It wouldn't this time, she was determined. She'd made a bargain with God, promised to be the best mother ever, to put money in the poor box every week, never again to be jealous when James put his patients before her.

Feeling suddenly weary she'd realised it was getting late. The man's injuries must have been worse than James anticipated. She'd mixed cocoa and water to a paste, left it ready in a cup, poured milk in a saucepan so that when James arrived home there would be next to nothing for him to do.

She'd fallen asleep whilst going through names for the baby: she was up to the letter G. George or Grace then.

"The old man was in a state, but not badly injured," James went on. "I got him into bed, assured him that though he'd be bruised and stiff for a while, he was going to survive. His wife

was more shaken than he was, kept saying she didn't know how she'd manage if anything happened to him."

James took another sip from the bottle. Lily was confused; hadn't he told her that the old man had needed to go to hospital, and that he'd stayed to settle him in, to comfort him?

"Getting away from them wasn't easy. Then when I set off to walk home I discovered I had no gloves or hat with me, and a bitter wind had sprung up. It was a vicious winter that year, remember?"

Lily had been lovely and warm. She'd been dreaming she was paddling in a stream on a hazy summer's day, kicking up sprays of sparkling water, fish as colourful as clowns swimming around her feet, between her toes even, then the pains had woken her, and when she turned over she discovered the bed was sopping wet.

"I passed a café, one of those late night places. It looked bright and welcoming. I went in and ordered a mug of tea, took it to a table well away from the door. I didn't see her at first. Though the place was three quarters empty she came and asked would I mind if she joined me. What could I say? She was thin as a stick, pretty in a pale and fragile way. She looked frozen. I offered to buy her a cup of tea and she said I was a real gentleman."

Reaching for the bedside light, Lily had pushed back the eiderdown. She was lying in a pool of blood. James, she called, still groggy, unsure how long she'd been asleep. Where was he? He must be home by now. Was he in the kitchen? Dragging herself out of bed she'd felt a wave of nausea, the pains in her stomach so severe that she could hardly stand. Bent double she'd stumbled towards the door, aware that the bleeding was getting heavier, blood pouring out of her, sticky and warm and shockingly red. She made a wad of her nightdress and pressed it between her legs.

I'm losing the baby, she'd thought. James, help me.

Somehow she'd reached the door, grasped the white china knob, briefly concerned that she was smearing it with blood. Then the stabbing sensation had got much, much worse and she'd known that it was too late. Her baby was dead, nothing could be done to save it. Then, blackness.

"*She seemed so young and vulnerable. She spun me a story – I can't remember the details. A boy friend who beat her, an ailing mother who hadn't eaten for three days, the usual. When she invited me back to her room I knew I should be getting home to you. But then I thought, Lily will be asleep. And she, this woman, this girl... well, I was enjoying talking to her. I enjoyed the way she looked at me too, and the way she kept touching my hand lightly when she wanted to interrupt.*"

Lily began to understand.

"*You went home with her?*"

"*I didn't intend to stay more than half an hour, I swear to you. I thought...*"

"*That night? You were with another woman that night?*"

"*I'm only human, Lily. You wouldn't make love, hadn't for weeks, not since you discovered you were pregnant. You didn't intend to do anything that might risk the baby's life, remember? I assured you it couldn't possibly harm the baby, but no, you were determined. What I felt, what I needed, was no longer of interest to you. I'd impregnated you and that was all you cared about. Or seemed to care about anyway.*"

"*James, I can't believe you...*"

"*She was a prostitute, for God's sake. I did what I needed to do and I paid her, and everyone was happy.*"

Below the terrace, in the dark, a woman edged her way down the steps with a dog on a lead, the dog pulling, the woman chastising. Lily pressed herself back against the wall, closed her eyes, waited for the footsteps to fade.

"I wasn't happy," she said. "I was at home alone, dying. I probably would have if my sister hadn't called in on her way to work."

James took a deep shuddering breath.

"Do you think I don't know that? Do you think that I haven't gone over it time and again, wishing I could go back to that evening and do things differently?"

"I nearly died," Lily repeated, aware that her voice was getting higher and louder. "You were with some other woman and I had no-one…"

"Lily, don't. I promise you can't make me feel any worse than I do."

She heard another glug of liquid, a gulp.

"…I had no-one to even help keep me warm. You know the worst thing about that night? You won't believe it. It was the cold. I felt as though my whole body was going numb. I suppose that's what it's like, freezing to death in the snow."

"Lily…"

"Do you think it is? You'd know, of course, being a doctor. Do you just gradually lose all the feeling in your toes and fingers, then along your arms, your legs? Is that what happens?"

James shuffled on the bench.

"I guess so. They say freezing to death is one of the best ways to die."

"What a shame I didn't then," Lily said, though she didn't mean it. She wanted him to react, say what a terrible thing to think and that he would be devastated without her, life wouldn't be worth living, but he didn't speak.

"What is it, anyway, this thing about prostitutes?" she said then, changing the subject abruptly. "What's the attraction? I *thought what we had – what we did, you and I – was something special, maybe not exciting but warm and loving and… I was obviously wrong. What is it you need, James? The thrill of doing something frowned on by decent people? Something dangerous and dirty?"*

Even through the anger that was bubbling up at the injustice of it all, Lily knew she was on dangerous ground. He could turn the tables, accuse her of much the same. Except of course that her affair with Ernesto was based on a genuine attraction to each other. It was intense and emotional and real; a love affair, of a kind. It wasn't a financial arrangement.

"If I'd had any inkling of what was going to happen I'd have been there with you. You know I would. It was all so completely unexpected."

James tipped the bottle again and Lily couldn't stand it any longer. She reached and yanked it out of his hand and slung it along the terrace where is smashed against the wall, startling the chickens whose box was nearby. Ruffling their feathers they emerged with bits of straw on their heads, clucking anxiously as they picked their way through the glass shards.

And now Lily's eyes filled with tears.

"I'm sorry, you two," she muttered, starting to stand, but in one quick movement James was on his knees in front of her, his arms tight around her legs, his face pressed into her lap.

"Forgive me, Lily, tell me you forgive me, please?"

Lily folded her arms, didn't speak. She couldn't.

"I love you. I never meant to harm you, or the baby, or anyone else. Everything just keeps going wrong."

He started to shake, harsh dry sobs coming from somewhere deep inside him, his grip getting tighter.

"Please, Lily. Say it, say you forgive me."

But how could she, when he'd deceived her, deserted her

when she most needed him, when he'd destroyed everything that they had together? Sometimes, it seemed, you need to go far away to see what's happening right under your nose.

She couldn't think, her mind a blank. She didn't dare say a word, afraid she'd go too far. Instead she stroked the back of his neck, as though calming a child.

PART FOUR

Twenty-Nine

*I*t was a mistake; she shouldn't have come. Lily knew it the moment she tipped her head around the half open door.

"Darling, how nice of you to remember I exist," Natalia said, looking up briefly from where she was lying face downwards on a rug on the floor. A young oriental man dressed in white was crouched beside her, one of her feet nestled between his hands, was moving it from side to side, pressing the sole with his thumbs.

Natalia and her feet, Lily thought.

"If it's a bad time…"

"Don't be silly. Come in and sit down now you're here, Lily. Ouch."

Natalia pulled away from him and glared.

"My poor feet," she said, gazing at them mournfully. "Absolutely ruined by the dance of course."

With the grace of a child she stood – she always made Lily feel large and ungainly – and waved a dismissive hand.

"*Basta per oggi,*" she said, and the man nodded, and after quickly collecting his lotions and towels, was gone.

"So what exciting things have been keeping you so busy?" she said, taking some purple grapes from a ceramic bowl as she passed the table, joining Lily on the sofa.

Natalia's tone was beginning to irritate Lily who'd been looking forward to having a heart to heart with the closest thing she had to a friend. She missed her real friends.

"Nothing special. Cleaning, shopping, cooking."

Natalia popped a grape in her mouth, sucked it like a sweet.

"You're becoming boring, you know that, Lily? At first you were wonderful company, like a child, open mouthed with excitement and wonder, always willing to try something new. Now you're more like that husband of yours. Staid. Dull."

"I'm also pregnant."

She'd said it before she could stop herself. Natalia hesitated only briefly before breaking into a big smile, giving Lily a hug, saying what perfectly wonderful news. Then she held her at arm's length and scrutinised her face.

"And are you happy, darling?"

"I think so. Yes. I'm not sure. All I know is that I want desperately to have a baby, so yes, I must be. Mustn't I?"

"Oh Lily, you are funny." Natalia released her but continued looking at her.

"And is the doctor over the moon too?"

Somehow she always knew the right question to ask, or the most relevant one.

"He's pleased, yes."

Natalia sat forward, eyes glittering.

"Don't tell me it isn't his. Is it? Come on, Lily darling, you know you can trust me."

But could she? Lily hesitated a second too long.

"It's Ernesto's then," Natalia said with a touch of what could only be triumph in her voice. But that didn't make sense. And besides, how did she know about Ernesto? Lily hadn't told her. James had said that the whole village knew, of course. Seems he was right.

"I'm not sure," she said with a small shrug. "All I know is that it's mine. That's the important thing."

"Ah, the maternal urge."

Natalia stretched out, hands behind her head. Her hair had been cut shorter than ever, it looked like a man's.

"Be careful, Lily. There's that saying... how does it go? When a baby comes in the door love goes out the window."

No worries there then, Lily thought. It's already gone.

What was it James had said only yesterday?

"I've lost you, haven't I? For one reason or another, probably lots of them. My own stupid fault. But you still have the baby, and every day its chances of surviving are getting better. I guess that's the only thing that really matters."

Finally he'd begun to understand. Yet she felt a vague sense of unease: did he really think having a baby was the only thing she wanted out of the marriage? Worse, could he be right?

"Anyway, there's this party being held at the end of the week," Natalia was saying. "Jules is organising it to cheer us all up. He's French, a composer of some kind. Isn't it depressing these days, with nearly all the old crowd gone and the days so short and dreary, and all the absolutely dreadful things happening in the north?"

"Natalia, I'm not in the mood for partying."

"Which is exactly why you must come."

"But I have to be careful, you know, because of the baby. Besides, I won't know any of the newcomers. And I look a mess, my hair desperately needs a perm, and I've got nothing different to wear."

"Excuses, darling."

Natalia led Lily into her bedroom, flung open her wardrobe.

"There. Choose. Whatever you want."

"Natalia, I couldn't. Besides, you're half my size."

"Not nowadays, you've lost a lot of weight. Think of it as your last opportunity. In a few months time…"

She drew a curve with her hand over her own flat stomach.

She took out a dress, held it up to Lily, put it back and disentangled another.

"Here. This pink looks wonderful with your freckles."

"Natalia, do you ever listen to me?"

"Try it. Try all of them. It doesn't mean you have to come." She meant well, of course. In the end Lily chose a grey crepe dress, its scooped neck hung with beads. It felt very dressy but Natalia said not at all, not at that length.

"And don't forget to wear the nylon stockings I gave you," Natalia added. It would be the first time; up until now the weather had been far too hot for suspender belts and stockings. That was if she went, of course.

"Have you told Ernesto about the baby?" Natalia said as she folded the dress and slid it into a bag for Lily to take home with her. On the side of the bag was written Saks of Fifth Avenue; it looked very chic.

"Of course not."

"And don't you think you owe it to him to tell him?"

"No, I do not."

Lily looked around for her coat.

"And Natalia, promise you won't say anything either."

"Of course, darling." Natalia burst out laughing. "What is it you English say? Mum's the word."

Sometimes the sea now reminded her of the sea off Cornwall, choppy and grey, great waves thundering in, then pulling back to rear up and crash back down onto the beach, white froth blowing everywhere. Lily liked to go down to watch it. It was exhilarating, especially when it reached up as far as the promenade and she could feel the spray on her face, hear the stones rumbling as they were dragged back. James didn't like her going, made her promise to take care, also not to get chilled, which gave her an excuse to stop off for a hot drink at the café. Inside it felt familiar, like a second home.

It was as she was about to leave one morning that the door opened and two men and a boy entered, all of them wrapped in drab coloured blankets, a smell of goats about them, their hair long and matted, each holding what looked like bagpipes. As the few customers lifted their heads or turned to look they began to play, a thin harsh sound that had little tune or rhythm, an eerie sound, not just of another world but another time. When they'd finished one of the men walked silently amongst the tables, his calloused hand extended, eyes lowered. Everyone gave him a few coins, including Lily.

"*I ciociari*," the teenage girl who was helping behind the bar whispered. "Shepherds from the mountains. They always come this time of year. What a noise, huh?" She giggled.

It was beginning to rain as Lily headed up the hill. She didn't at first notice the figure approaching her. When she realised it was Dino she felt a wave of relief, even though he was supported by two crutches and hobbling like an old man. At least he was out and about.

"Dino, caro. *Stai meglio adesso?*"

"*Ciao, signora.* Yes, but I've been ill for weeks. Everyone thought I was going to die."

He sounded so proud. Lily put on a suitably concerned face.

"Poor you."

"And then I went to hospital in Sorrento. I was in a big ward full of beds, and had a photograph taken of the bones inside my leg. And one day I had tinned pears with tinned milk."

She'd forgotten how positive children could be.

"Did you like the tinned pears?"

"Unfortunately he did." Ernesto's gravelly voice made her jump, she hadn't heard him emerge from some steps to one side. He ruffled his son's hair. "We bought some as a special treat, but they're too expensive to have often."

Ernesto turned his smile from Dino to Lily, and for a moment she was lost for words. He looked different, scruffier, older in a faded blue sweater, baggy corduroy trousers, shoes for a change. She thought, he's nothing special, certainly no heart throb. His hair which needed cutting was curling onto his neck, and she longer to run her fingers through it, to feel its coarse texture. She longed to touch him.

"And you, Lily, how are you?"

"I'm OK."

"*Veramente?*" He ran the back of his fingers lightly down her cheek in that way that he had, his eyes determined that she shouldn't look away. And at that moment Lily knew that he knew. Had Natalia told him? Who else?

"The boy in the bed next to me died," Dino said, tugging at her hand. "He was my friend. They pulled the curtains around so we couldn't see."

"How very sad for you," Lily said, genuinely touched.

"His mother cried."

"Yes, she would."

"Lily, if there's anything you want, or need..." Ernesto said quietly. So many things, she wanted to say, but nothing you can give me.

"No, everything is fine. With your wife too I hope?"

She said it without thinking, wasn't sure why, probably to make him feel guilty.

"My wife?" He looked confused rather than guilty.

"And now I have to walk with these," Dino was saying, waving a stick about, wobbling dangerously.

"But not for ever," Lily said.

"For a long time." The prospect obviously delighted him.

"*Il dottore*, he saved my life," he said then.

"Did he?" She pushed back the damp sweep of hair that had fallen across his forehead. At least she could touch him, Ernesto's son. "Good, I'm pleased about that."

"Lily…"

Ernesto wouldn't stop staring at her, and for a few seconds she stared back. Hold me, she wanted to say. It wasn't that she wanted him to make love to her, not at that moment, she just wanted to be enveloped in his love. She was jealous of his wife, even of Dino, who was now watching the two of them intently. Her sister used to have a saying, whenever one or other of them discovered something they shouldn't have: children see more than grown ups realise.

"If we stand here much longer we're all going to be soaked," she said then, pulling her coat around her, stepping away, making it clear she was going. A little further up the hill she was tempted to look back, but she didn't.

But why would Natalia have told Ernesto she was pregnant? Especially when she'd asked her not to? It didn't make sense.

When James announced he was going back to England, it was almost a relief. Lily had been waiting for this moment, knew she'd have to face it sooner or later. She'd vowed to at least have a go at changing his mind.

"After all you've done here? People know you now, James, they trust you. And you're going to throw it all away?"

"There's a war on, Lily."

"But nothing's happening, not in England anyway."

"It will. It may be weeks, months, who knows. The only sure thing is that sooner or later the Germans are going to start bombing London. And when it happens they're going to need every doctor they can find."

"And when Italy gets drawn into the war, as everyone says it will? Then they'll need doctors here too, won't they?"

"Not American ones with English wives."

"Surely one doctor is…"

"Lilian, we'll be the enemy. Why can't you see that?"

"You're wrong, James. Whatever happens our friends in the village will still be our friends."

"Possibly. Yes, you're probably right. But it's more complicated than that. How are you going to feel if they join up with the Germans and start dropping bombs on London?"

Lily sighed. She was losing the argument.

"You're determined, aren't you?"

He dug his hands deep into his pockets.

"The way I see it is I don't have a choice."

"And me? What about me?"

He'd obviously planned what he was going to say next. He walked to the window.

"You must do whatever you want. I'd like you to come back to London with me, Lily, but I know you're reluctant to leave Italy and I'm not going to force you, or even try to persuade you. It's your life and your decision."

He turned back to her, tried a smile that didn't quite work.

"Whatever makes you happy."

He was doing what he thought was right. And wasn't this

what she wanted: to be independent, a free spirit? Instead she felt suddenly alone.

"Should you decide to stay on here, I'll do whatever I can to help support you, but I won't be able to make any promises."

Alone and abandoned.

"But you're not leaving yet, are you James? I'd like to think about things for a while. If that's OK with you?"

"Of course. Just keep in mind that I plan to be gone before Christmas."

Christmas. But that was only weeks away.

Thirty

Have you ever watched a cat playing with a mouse? That was what Sidney had said when he introduced Lily to Natalia, but of course she'd forgotten his warning. Now, though, it had come back to her. And suddenly everything made sense.

Natalia arranging the picnic, introducing her to Ernesto.

Natalia winkling out her feelings of discontent about her marriage, about James, encouraging her to look again at the little things she'd learnt to ignore. Encouraging her to see the worst in James.

Natalia lending her books. Carefully chosen books.

Natalia egging on her on to take a lover.

The worst thing was that Lily couldn't be sure what part Ernesto played in the game: was he another cat, or had he been used just as Lily had, wound up like a clockwork toy and then set in motion?

Lily was embarrassed at how stupid she'd been, how easily manipulated. Then she felt betrayed and hurt. Then, gradually, she became angry. Used to being the level headed, sensible sister, this was a new sensation for her. She was angry, and she intended to let Natalia know. In public. In front of the people Natalia considered so wonderful.

Jules was the name of the French composer, Lily remembered that. And that he had rooms in what used to be a palazzo once owned by a prince from Naples. Lily had passed the place often, peeking through the heavy wrought iron gates to admire the ornate though flaking façade, the palm trees and orchids in the lush garden courtyard, though she'd never dared step inside.

Even as she climbed the wide marble staircase, Lily could hear music. It led her to a heavy wooden door that was partly open so her fears about her knock not being heard were unnecessary. She pushed it, stepped inside.

The music was louder now – something classical on a piano and cello that she couldn't name, though James would have been able to. It suited the room, echoing back down from the high domed ceiling with its baroque golden twirls, and swirling around in all the empty space below; furniture was minimal, just some low tables, lamps dotted about, fat cushions with tassels. There didn't seem to be many people there either, though in the low lights and with the shutters drawn it was hard to be sure. The air was hazy with a strange smelling smoke.

Lily hesitated, then edged along the walls. No familiar faces so far. No sign of Natalia either. She was beginning to wonder if this was such a good idea.

"And you are?" The voice came from ground level.

"Lily."

"Ah. Natalia's friend."

About to say she wasn't so sure, Lily nodded.

"I'm Jules."

He was a large man wearing a purple caftan and sitting cross legged, and he insisted she come and sit with him, patting the cushion beside him. When someone put a glass into her hand she drank down the contents in a few quick gulps. She was thirsty, what with the smoke, and being so hot; she was still wearing her coat over an old skirt and blouse, hadn't dressed up. She'd no intention of staying.

Jules took her hand, his skin soft, as though he used creams on it. He said he'd learnt his English from a nanny he'd had many years ago. That wasn't all she taught him he added, moving his tongue across his lips in a way that told her more than she wanted to know. She soon realised he didn't expect her to speak, just to nod occasionally. She slipped off her coat, had another drink, half listening as she watched the door. With a sudden influx of new people his attention was diverted, and Lily made her escape, heading for the other end of the room. There was more noise now, a hum of conversation broken up by sudden laughter. Another record was put on the gramophone, a man she didn't recognise singing in French, a slow sad song.

"Here."

Someone held out a long wooden pipe, a young man with startlingly blue eyes and an accent, Swedish possibly. She sat down beside him but shook her head.

"No thank you."

"Draw it in slowly, take it right down."

He tipped his head to one side and she thought how pretty he was, like a girl with his pink lips and long eyelashes.

"No, really I…"

"Try it."

He held the end close to her mouth and reluctantly she did as he said, starting to cough as soon as the bitter smoke hit the back of her throat.

"Again," he said. "It'll be easier this time."

He was right; it was as though her lungs had got over the initial shock. She inhaled again. Gradually she felt her whole body becoming heavier, slowing down, her heart calming. When the young man eventually moved away she was almost disappointed. What was it she'd been smoking? Natalia would know. But there was still no sign of Natalia.

A man with long grey hair and rings on each finger joined her, gave her another drink. His name was Nicholas, he was English. The noise in the room was getting louder and then fading, like a radio. Lily stretched her arms up above her head and yawned. The man bent close, pushed her hair from across her ear and whispered. She didn't catch what he said. He laughed. Behind him she could see an older man with a vaguely familiar face who had taken what looked like a brown pea from a tin, was stuffing it carefully into the bowl of another pipe.

She wanted to ask Nicholas what it was, but it was too much effort. When she leant back against the wall he said why didn't they find somewhere more private and she nodded, managing somehow to get to her feet, following him as he lead the way into a second room which was much like the first only less crowded.

They found more cushions.

Nicholas took off his jacket, loosened his tie. The first young man reappeared bringing with him the pipe, sat down, and Lily took first turn.

"Errol Flynn swears by this stuff, says it helps him keep going all night," one of them said. Lily wondered what he meant. She thought she heard Natalia's voice, knew that she should go and find her, confront her, but she couldn't be bothered. Later. Another day. She kicked off her shoes.

When Nicholas leant towards the younger man and kissed him full on the lips, Lily thought how nice. She watched them for a moment until they pulled apart.

"Isn't he beautiful?" he said, turning to Lily.

She nodded. Everyone was beautiful. It was a room full of beautiful people.

"Would you like to kiss him?"

Lily thought about it for a moment.

"Oh no, I…"

The young man shuffled across so that he was sitting facing her. He was wearing some kind of cologne; it reminded her of early summer, her parent's garden.

"Please," he said. "Say yes."

He bent and lightly touched his lips to hers, then kissed her again, a longer softer kiss. She felt a hand on the calf of her leg, smoothing up and down, then on her knee, and when the young man paused she realised it was Nicholas who was caressing her leg.

Both men smiled at each other, and then at her, and she smiled back.

She lost track of time.

Looking around her she was vaguely aware of other people sitting or lying down together, kissing and touching each other. Some were only half dressed. She noticed one couple were naked and couldn't get over the beautiful golden sheen of the skin of the girl who had her back to her; it was like a copper jug.

When the young man started to undo the buttons of her blouse and then eased it down over her shoulders, she leant forwards to make it easier for him. Then he unfastened her brassiere, gently removed it and cupped her breasts with hands that felt surprisingly small and fragile. He gave a whimper.

"Liliana, *vieni.*"

The voice hardly registered, but when she felt her arms being gripped roughly, strong hands yanking her up onto her feet, her blouse being wrapped around her, she knew instantly who it was. How wonderful that he was here too.

"Ernesto, I didn't think you…"

"Don't talk. We're leaving. This is not a place for you."

She was up but unsteady, Ernesto holding her hand, pulling her as he tried to weave his way through the bodies on the floor. More than once she tripped, once she actually fell, until finally he muttered something she didn't catch and then scooped her up as though she were a child, and carried her towards the door.

Outside it was pitch black, a cold wind whipping off the sea. Shivering now, Lily felt his arms around her, his face against her hair, and she snuggled close.

"You came for me," she whispered. "You came."

"Shhh," he said.

Thirty-One

$\mathcal{L}$ ily had made up her mind: she would stay in Italy.

If she had any doubts they were small ones, as irritating as sand in your shoe but of no more importance.

She'd chanced upon Natalia in the café, and sitting beside a steamed up window drinking hot chocolate she'd demanded the truth. Natalia had given her an embarrassed smile. Yes, she'd sort of set things up, encouraged them along, encouraging Ernesto too, though that had been easy once he'd set eyes on Lily. But the last thing she'd intended was to harm her or make her unhappy. She just wanted to bring her out of her shell, to bring her alive. And look how it had turned out, Lily had got the one thing she most wanted. So surely she should be forgiven? Natalia had looked at her with wide pleading eyes, and Lily had to admit she had a point.

As for Ernesto.

When he'd heard about the opium den he'd shrugged, used to the foreign set and their ways. Until Natalia mentioned that Lily was going.

"I've never seen him angry before. He didn't say much, he just – how would you say? – smouldered?" She shook her fingers as though they'd been singed. "I didn't think he'd do anything about it though."

He had. He'd been her knight on a white charger, and proved how much he cared, and Lily knew that had to be enough. He couldn't give her more. She had no right to ask.

"We are still friends, you and I," Natalia said. "Aren't we?"

Lily hesitated. She'd never trust Natalia again, not entirely. But then she should have known better, she'd been warned.

"Yes, I suppose so," she said.

She was going to need all the friends she could get.

She'd enquired about renting rooms and found a place on the other side of the village, up near the cemetery. Basic but cheap. Her father, she was sure, would send her some money to keep her going for a while, until she could find work. She'd heard about an author living along the road towards Amalfi who needed a typist. Or she could teach English, or even take in laundry. Come the spring everyone would be back, war or no war; there'd be plenty of opportunities to earn the small amount she'd need. She planned to live a simple life, close to nature, her and her baby.

Of course, once the baby arrived everything would change. It might not be so easy.

She pushed the thought aside.

It was comforting to know Natalia and her crowd would be nearby. The local people were kind too; they'd help her if she was in trouble, she was sure. Though right now they didn't understand what was happening. Only the other day a neighbour had stopped her.

"We're so sad to hear you and *il dottore* are leaving."

"My husband is going, but I'm not."

"You're staying? On your own? Without him?"

Lily nodded. They'd prefer it the other way around, of course; it was a doctor they needed. Would they be as friendly when she was on her own? Or suspicious, confused? And what if they knew the father of her baby was Ernesto?

Meanwhile, the village was getting ready for Christmas. There were cribs everywhere: in the church a splendid one surrounded by candles; home-made ones in windows of houses where often the models were mismatched, chickens towering over cows. There was even one in a crevice on their steps. Preparations for the feasting were getting under way too. Pine cones like small brown pineapples were roasted whole, the children given the task of picking out the tiny white nuts tucked deep inside. Chestnuts were ground to make flour. Fruits preserved in alcohol were dug out from the back of cupboards.

Lily, having no preparations to make, took to walking on the beach.

She would walk one way, then back, never going as far as Ernesto's hut. One day she took with her the pierced stones, dropped them back amongst the others, spacing them out, kicking at them until they were well covered. Let someone else find them. Let someone else have good luck.

When she got home James was coming in from the terrace.

"I've fed the chickens. Which reminds me, you know the old guy up above, the one with the limp? He said he'll take them. Unless you'll have somewhere for them, that is?"

"No, that's a good idea. He's a kind man."

She'd miss them just the same. She went to take off her cardigan, changed her mind. It was almost as cold indoors as out, with the stark floors and draughty gaps under the doors that she hadn't noticed in the summer.

"Shall we eat?"

Lily had left a soup on the stove. She got out bowls, cut some bread. They sat either side of the kitchen table.

James took a few spoonfuls before he spoke again.

"Lilian," he said. "I'm leaving next week."

She felt a twinge of panic.

"So soon?"

"I'll make sure all your things are moved to your new rooms before I go, of course."

She didn't want him to leave, not yet, she wasn't ready.

"And about the baby."

He put down his spoon.

"There's a doctor I knew in Rome, he's recently transferred to Sorrento. If you're determined to stay, will you at least go and see him? I'd like someone to keep a check on things. And when the time arrives, go into hospital. Don't take risks, Lilian. Not with the baby's life, nor your own."

He'd got it all worked out. Unexpectedly tears of gratitude filled her eyes.

"Will you promise me?"

"Of course."

"Thank you," he said.

It's me who should be thanking you, Lily thought. She reached her hand across the table and he curved his hand over hers, gave it a squeeze, then carried on eating.

Just three more nights together, three more nights of having his warm body stretched out beside her, his familiar body.

She'd been woken by torrential rain. It had stopped but she could still hear water dripping from the gutters. Unable to go back to sleep Lily got up and wandered around, trying to ignore the tea chest full of books, the suitcase left open on the floor into which James had packed his lightweight clothes, things he wouldn't be needing over the next few days.

The chickens had gone. Many of her potted plants were either wilting or dead, though she was determined to take at least a couple with her to her new home. She needed something to care for, to talk to. It was ridiculous, talking to potted plants, but better than talking to yourself.

She'd never lived alone before. It was going to be strange.

A white line appeared under the bedroom door; so James couldn't sleep either. She wished they could have talked, like they used to. Talked, and listened to each other too.

She'd written a letter to her parents trying to explain why she'd decided to stay on in Italy. It had sounded trite. She would re-write it before he left so he could take it when he went to see her family. They'd be upset, would decide she was ill or having a breakdown. Her mother would write and beg her to change her mind and come home.

Lily imagined her mother standing there, touching her cheek with her laundry-roughened hand and sighing, like she used to when Lily was a child and up to something she shouldn't have been. Hurt, annoyed and forgiving all at the same time.

"Mummy, I know you won't understand," she whispered. "I'm not sure I do myself. But please don't stop loving me."

The light went off again. Lily waited a while for James to go back to sleep. Yet when eventually she slid into bed beside him she could sense that he was still awake. She'd have liked to feel his arm around her, but he didn't move.

It wasn't until the room began to lighten that she eventually fell asleep.

James had collected the mail from the post office. There hadn't been any for a week, and now there were three items:

a letter from a doctor, a postcard with a picture of New York skyscrapers and Sidney's scrawl saying he was having a wow of a time. And a letter with unfamiliar handwriting and an Italian stamp. He passed it to her.

"You open it," she said.

He used a paperknife to neatly slit the envelope, took out the single sheet of coarse paper. He read it slowly, put it down on the kitchen table.

"It's Paolo, isn't it?" Lily said.

He nodded.

"It's from Lucia, the girl he…"

"Yes, I know." She fingered the paper but couldn't pick it up.

"He's dead, isn't he?"

James nodded. For a moment Lily couldn't speak. It was as though she'd been punched in the stomach.

"Did he get to Rome?"

"Yes. She said that they'd talked on the phone just once and he was excited to be back there, had met up again with his friends, that they were making all sorts of plans."

"How? How did he die?"

"He and two others were shot. As far as she can tell they were only…"

"No, don't tell me," Lily said, changing her mind. She remembered how Paolo had hated guns. Through the window she could see a patch of grey sky, clouds scurrying past.

"He was something special, that young guy," James said.

It was all going, the magic, the sparkle, the laughter, slipping away as the chill and looming shadow of war edged closer and closer.

Everything was ready. Next morning, early, a hired car would take James and his luggage to Naples. Shortly afterwards two men with a horse and cart would arrive to transport Lily's few bits and pieces across the village. James had already paid them. He'd paid her first month's rent too.

Tomorrow, she thought, my new life will begin.

Why was she not excited?

Neither of them seemed to know what to do with themselves. Lily kept checking the bags and cases, unable to stay still. James sat in the kitchen, his chair tipped back and balanced on two legs, staring into space.

When she sat down opposite him he didn't look at her. She noticed he needed a shave.

"James, you do know I don't hate you." He didn't speak.

"Please say you don't hate me either."

Silence.

"James?"

There was a faint creaking sound as he tipped the chair forwards, back again.

"Despite everything that happened, I never wanted us to…"

The chair banged down onto the tiles. James entwined his fingers tightly, his eyes lowered.

"Come with me, Lilian," he said quietly.

Now he looked up, straight at her, and she thought how pale his eyes were, as though bleached in the sun. Had they always been that colour? He looked back at his hands.

"Lilian, I don't know how to say this. I want you, I need you. Life without you… well, I don't think I can stand it."

Lily couldn't believe he was saying these things. Not James.

"You want me to come back with you? To England?"

She'd thought of it, more often than she would have admitted, torn between staying and going, between living in paradise on her own, or a war torn city with the people she loved.

"What about the air raids, food shortages? There are sure to be diseases, and rats. What about the baby?"

"Lilian, nowhere is going to be safe. Why can't you see that? Even this place will be dragged into the war sooner or later. Looking after a baby on your own isn't going to be easy, far from it. Together, we can... well, he'll stand a better chance."

"And you don't mind that he's Ernesto's?"

She had to ask.

"You don't know that for sure."

"I do."

"Lilian, we talked about it, you agreed it might also..."

"It's Ernesto's. I know it is."

What she meant was that she wanted it to be his, needed to feel that though their affair was over something beautiful had come out of it, something she would have forever. Wanting, however, was not the same as knowing.

She was saying it to punish James. For a moment she hated herself.

He rested his elbows on the table, put his face in his hands.

"OK. Even if... even though the baby isn't mine, I'm still prepared to look after him. I want to look after him."

His voice was muffled.

"You're still my wife, Lilian. I know how you long for a child, and I promise I'll do everything in my power to make sure this time nothing goes wrong."

He looked up and his gaze was steady.

"I need some air," Lily said.

"Are you feeling...?"

"I'm OK. Truly."

She opened the door onto the terrace, closed it behind her.

She rested her hand on her tummy, sure that it was more rounded than it had been. She smiled to herself.

She'd had a thought. It took her breath away.

Her new start could be with James.

She'd accepted that their marriage was over, that no marriage could survive the dreadful things they'd done, both of them. But what if it made their marriage stronger? What if they could start again, as equals? Was it possible?

It was early evening, but already it was getting dark. As always at this hour the church bells were ringing, a dog barking from somewhere high above, children scampering past on the steps, late for their tea yet again because they were up in the hills getting up to mischief and forgot about the time. She didn't want it to change, ever. But it would, of course, it was inevitable. Everything was about to change.

A gust of wind tugged at her skirt, a cold wind. Lily hugged herself, shivered. And then, as she watched, the moon lifted up slowly out of the sea, a silver orb that was reflected in the still dark waters, so beautiful it took her breath away.

After a while Lily went back inside, sat down.

"Tell me about Christmas in New England," she said. "I'd like to know."

James glanced at her, momentarily confused.

"It's…" He hesitated, then smiled. "Well, it's cold."

"How cold? I mean, are there icycles? Do lakes freeze over?"

He nodded.

"It's why we kids could skate before we could walk."

And suddenly she remembered way back years ago when a new ice skating rink opened in Bayswater – everyone was going, it was all the rage – and James had insisted they try it, despite her protestations that she'd no idea how to skate.

She'd been scared. Scared of falling over and looking silly. Scared of the strangeness of this vast room with its slippery white floor, people whizzing past seemingly standing still, their calls and laughter echoing in the crisp air.

She'd strapped the skates on thinking how awkward they were, her heart thumping. Holding her breath she'd gripped his hand tightly and stepped out onto the ice.

Thanks to James she'd loved it.

He'd been patient, encouraging. He hadn't laughed when her feet went off in different directions, or slipped out from under her and she ended up on her bottom. He'd praised her when she managed a few steps on her own. Most important of all he'd stayed by her side, only going off on his own when she gave up and collapsed on one of the rink-side chairs. Watching him she'd thought how lucky she was to have him as her husband.

She looked at him now. He was still there by her side.

"And snow? Is there snow?"

James chuckled.

"Up to the porch, sometimes even higher. You have to shovel it away before you can get out of the house."

"I bet it looks pretty."

"Very. It sparkles, like sequins. Over the Christmas holidays we kids used to spend most of the day out in it, tobogganing, pelting each other with snow balls. Getting red in the face and famished, of course. Which was just as well because the food never stopped coming, turkey, pumpkin pie, marshmallows…"

"I'd like see it some time, your New England snow. When the was is over."

James was still looking at her. He didn't move.

"Then I'll take you. We'll go upstate to where I grew up, spend Christmas in a log cabin in front of a blazing fire, just the three of us. It'll be the best Christmas ever."

It was hard to imagine snow, such cold. It seemed like another world, another life.

"James, I..."

Lily stopped, unsure what she wanted to say. He waited.

"I'm looking forward to it already," she said then.

And to coming back to Italy, she thought. One day. She wouldn't be able to leave if she thought she'd never come back. But he'd know that, of course. He'd know.

THE END